The Lotus and the Grail

The Lotus and the Grail

LEGENDS FROM EAST TO WEST

By Rosemary Harris

Illustrated by
Errol Le Cain

FABER AND FABER
3 Queen Square
London

First published in 1974
by Faber and Faber Limited
3 Queen Square London WC1
Printed in Great Britain by
BAS Printers Limited, Wallop, Hampshire
and W. S. Cowell Limited, Ipswich
All rights reserved

British Library Cataloguing in Publication Data
Harris, Rosemary, 1923-
The lotus and the grail : legends from East to West.
1. Tales
I. Title   II. Le Cain, Errol
398.2   PZ8.1

ISBN 0-571-13536-6

to David Holt

Contents

Foreword

The eighteen stories retold in *The Lotus and the Grail* are based on legends from many different countries. I thought the book should have a theme, and intended to use tales that could be grouped together under one general heading like "The Search"; but this proved limiting, for some places lack this kind of legend, while others possess disappointing versions. For instance—the South Seas fable of a Sun Child who, returning to the Sun, falls into the sea and is devoured by a shark. Although there's no reason why a search should always be successful, his fate—poor Sun Child!—still seems harsh, to say the least. Many of the other stories were so alike that to put several of them side by side was to create an appearance of monotony.

And so the legends in this book now come from different groups, but in all of them something, someone: wholeness; wisdom; blessing; another person who perhaps represents a kind of anima or animus figure; or even the swallowing of someone else's father to make strong magic, is the goal. The finding or bestowing of gold as a reward is a common ingredient in quite a number of them. None are meant to be read as correct folklore versions, but simply as fresh interpretations of old tales. Of course the traditional storyline skeletons are still there, but where bits were missing the narrative has been completed, though I have tried to retain the feeling and contour of the originals.

Legends told down the centuries tend to develop a magnetic power and glamour of their own. A writer bitten by the folklore bug resembles not only a musician looking for a theme, but an archaeologist scratching up old bones: the juggling with bits and pieces becomes as fascinating as a jigsaw. Some stories in this book can be found in many different forms and in different countries. I followed one general rule: to use only those legends that seemed really typical of a country and its culture, and were not brought in by conquerors; all those Spanish-Portuguese tales found in South America were discarded, in favour of an ancient Inca legend.

But there are two borderline cases: a Caribbean story, *The Guardian Snake*, which comes from the Dominican Republic in Hispaniola; and *The Small Red Ox*, from Iceland. Since the Caribbean was so overrun, and the inhabitants almost entirely supplanted by its conquerors, a mixture of racial elements here seemed inevitable. And Icelanders—or at least enthusiasts for the Sagas—might frown on the inclusion of what they would term a "lying saga", an obvious migrant from Europe. Yet tales like *The Small Red Ox* were in fact brought home by the much-travelled Icelanders themselves—who were the tourists of the Middle Ages—and then absorbed into their own culture.

And finally a note about the last story in this book: the well-known Breton fairytale of *Peronik*, here re-told as *The Castle of Ker Glas*. Some controversy has always surrounded this one: is it an early Grail legend—or a nineteenth-century invention? The argument has never been resolved. But I think that *Peronik is* genuine—for one thing, it contains episodes that match some in early Scandinavian tales: they too possess symbols like the black-gowned woman who invites the hero across the ford. These sinister intruders represented the Black Death which ravaged Europe—especially Sweden—in the Middle Ages (it was fairly typical of that time for people to look upon the Plague as feminine!), and the presence of such a figure in *Peronik* does seem to suggest an early date of origin.

And *Peronik* is also included here because it is a perfect

example of esoteric beliefs masquerading in fairytale and adventure form. It is a marvellous story, able to bear any number of re-tellings. And so the book ends with what has been called the first legend of the Grail—and begins with the legend of an Eastern Prince who, seeking the Lotus of Enlightenment, found that it transformed his life. . . .

Irani and the Cuckoos

There lived a king in India, near high Tibet, who had an only son, child of a devout and lovely mother. Though she wore jewelled ornaments and brilliant saris the Ranee's thoughts were upon greater things, and she raised her son to be devout as she herself: *his* one desire was to be a Buddhist monk. However, the Rajah was dismayed—he had much wealth, and power, to leave behind him when he died. He thought the young Irani far too serious, and decided he must have a playmate: Jalawarla, son of a proud Minister who was immersed in the *maya* of all worldly things, and more given to burning passions than to burning incense. When Jalawarla first arrived he captivated everyone. He was gay and agile as the young monkeys that swung from tree to tree around the Palace gardens. His slanting black eyes gleamed with subtle mischief, and he brought smiles to every face—except those of the Ranee and her gentle son.

"My mother—Maṇi, thou jewel!" said Irani, anxiously fingering the gold and silver that hung tinkling from her wrists. "What are your thoughts of Jalawarla? Do you like him?"

"Indeed, I love him, little son." But there was a crease between the Ranee's eyebrows, and her large eyes were pensive.

"Through *and* through?"

"Which of us *knows* anyone through and through! Unless we've reached those god-like heights from where we can look back on all past lives, we cannot know what lies hidden in our depths—or other people's."

"Perhaps you would warn me not to be too sure about myself, beloved Maṇi!"

"Perhaps. . . ! Perhaps I would merely caution you: play with Jalawarla, love him as a brother; but do not trust him altogether."

"Oh, Maṇi—I'm glad I didn't have these thoughts alone!" Once more he touched her bracelets, to hear them jingle. "Do you know, we're to go riding now, and try out the new horses that my father gave us? And we shall shoot with bows."

His mother laughed, and kissed him. "Ah," she mocked, "I see you're less steadfast than I thought—you forgo the lotus crown! And the saffron robe and begging bowl that you had set your heart on! It will be the jewelled turban of your father's court instead, and silks and—" her face clouded —"dancing girls."

"Never that! I'll marry somebody like you—if I must marry. For you know, Maṇi, the Rajah forbids me the religious life. Though it may be in my karma."

She saw that he looked downcast, teased him a little, then let him go. He was off like light, to try the new horses with his friend.

Jalawarla, the born spellbinder, soon made himself quite indispensable. He even tried to draw Irani into occult practices—though the worldly Minister's son was no mystic, he liked that power the strange pathways bring. After some while, "Do you know, Prince, my brother," he whispered as though awestruck, "what our august teacher the Brahman tells me? Sometimes he goes at night to the fearsome burning-ground, and enters any corpse he chooses, makes it move and speak, and lives in it as long as he desires. Instead of acting as a Rajah's servant he can strut and fight, make love to any girl, or drink wine till dawn!"

"*I* would be a monk!" said Irani, laughing. "But no, Jalawarla, it's impossible—what happens to his body?"

"Oh—he hides it somewhere, till he needs it. What deep games he plays with everyone!"

12

Irani and the Cuckoos

The Prince shuddered. "I wouldn't care to enter a dead body in the burning-ground."

"Wouldn't care? Wouldn't dare! I shall beg him to teach *me*—and I dare you, Prince, to do the same."

Irani gave a second, longer shudder. But a Rajah's son must be braver than his companions, or he's unworthy of his father's throne. "Very well: if *I* command him, he will teach us. But"—and he shuddered a third time—"what happens if you meet with accident, or—or death, when you're in someone else's form?"

"It would be dangerous," admitted Jalawarla. "We must certainly be careful! But we're not bound to stay as people— we could be strong tigers if you can find us dead ones, from a hunt. Or—or anything we choose."

So the two boys acquired the strangest of the Brahman's arts, and went everywhere about the Rajah's lands and cities. Some years passed, and by the time the beloved Ranee died her son had learned much of how the wealthy and poor, the struggling and happy, the wicked and the good, behaved. His journeys with Jalawarla had opened his eyes to many things, and sometimes made him sad. The wheel of effort, gain, and suffering seemed endless.

One day Jalawarla said, "Do you know what everyone says now? His Highness has decided to arrange your marriage."

Irani quailed. He knew about the usual marriages of kings. Now and then they brought true love and happiness, but more often were miserable ties to the treadmill that he still longed to renounce. He looked so horrified that even careless, merry, gossiping Jalawarla tried to comfort him.

"I tell you what we'll do, my Prince! They *say* that Princess Sundrun has been chosen—the daughter of our neighbour king. Now: at the first chance we'll change ourselves into whatever or whoever may come near her, and you'll learn much about the girl you'll marry."

Irani still looked mournful, but agreed. Next time the royal entourage was near the frontier, the two of them slipped across to seek the right means for their plan. Jalawarla failed: he found the body of a slave who had served Sundrun's father, but the Palace women shrieked when they saw him coming, and he ran off. However, Prince Irani found a dead bird lying on the ground, transformed himself, and in its shape flew to the Princess's window. Inside the women's quarters sat Sundrun, surrounded by her ladies. She wore a diamond stud in her left nostril, and her silky hair flowed almost to her feet. Once she gazed straight in his direction; and sighed, so that her elderly companion asked, "What troubles you, rich treasure of my heart?"

Sundrun sighed more heavily. "His Highness my father is quite adamant. I must marry, whether I will or no."

"That's almost every woman's fate!"

"But all women don't marry into glittering courts, with heartless princes who care only for their goods and nothing for their people, or True Doctrine. Suppose this Prince is warlike—even a worshipper of Kali?"

"Courage!" The old woman began to speak of how such trials could be overcome. But Irani had heard enough, and flew joyfully away, lighter of heart than he had been for a long while.

So Princess Sundrun and Prince Irani were married—and were very happy. Sundrun wasn't only lovely and devout: she was clever, and her gentle sympathy heartened her young husband, who was much isolated at court in his devotion to the Buddha. Often he held Sundrun's hands and, gazing in her eyes, would say she was the twin of his own soul. Such devotion touched some people, but others laughed at him and thought him stupidly enthralled. There were more beauties in the Palace—the traditional royal concubines. One of these laughed not at all: she was too jealous.

If Sundrun hadn't come, she thought sullenly, she herself might have lain night after night wrapped in the Prince's

arms. She began to hate the Princess with the powerful
loathing of a woman who feels her own life starved because
of someone else.

"What right has she to keep the Heir entirely to herself?"
she demanded passionately of Jalawarla. "Is that her sweet
compassion? Or is it greed? Jalawarla, my little friend, help
me . . ."

"Help you?" Jalawarla gently ran his finger up her downy
arm. "What am *I* to do, my opal?" Usually, a commoner
like him would have had no chance to be alone with her,
but because he was the Prince's intimate, almost his brother,
he came and went as freely as he chose.

Gaya looked sideways at him. "When one loves, is it the
other's True Self or body one desires?"

"Would you join with Sundrun in debate?" mocked
Jalawarla. "Our Prince would say it is the Self—but if that's
so, why shouldn't he spend nights in company of Baba
Yadanur, the dung-smeared holy woman at the gates?"

Gaya's laugh was shrill as any peacock's scream. "Not our
sweet Prince! It's Sundrun's body that he loves, as I love
his! Jalawarla, my little friend, *help* me!"

Jalawarla shook his head, and smiled lopsidedly. "He's been
my companion for so long! Ask someone else's help." Then
he looked up, and she was crying. Her huge brown eyes
pearled with tears, and the tip of her small nose quivered
like a hare's. She was lovely as Sundrun, he thought, and
more desirable: for she was plumper, and he liked women
soft as cushions. He looked round him, then whispered
coaxingly, "Come, forget him! Would I not do instead?"

The brown eyes hardened, as she lowered her lids. She
said softly, hiding her ambition, "That would be—unchaste.
If you were in his place, I could be yours." She raised her
eyes again, innocently, "Is it not sad, Jalawarla, that things
are as they are?"

"Yes—and so they stay!" responded Jalawarla shortly.
All the same, he looked back when he walked away.

Afterwards it seemed to Jalawarla that he was always in Gaya's company, whether he chose or no. When he went into the gardens, she was there. When he and Irani relaxed on the terrace after hunting, and the peacocks spread their gaudy tails and shrieked and strutted, and jasmine scented the whole coming night, it was Gaya who served him heady drinks, or sherbet and little scented cakes. Often, when no one looked, he would feel her plump hand touch his neck, and hear her whisper in his ear, "Ah, Jalawarla! I'm dying of this love—if only your essence were in the Prince's form! Take his place for me, Jalawarla. Jalawarla—" she would lean forward so that her musk-scented hair fell across his cheek, "take his place?"

At first Jalawarla tried not to listen, but it wasn't long before he grew equally obsessed by jealousy, and Gaya's longings became his. He watched Irani and Sundrun, and thought scornfully: What a fool he is, to bemuse himself with words! Gaya's right—the changing forms of *maya* are the only things that count. And he brooded: All these rich possessions, sensations, luscious women, for a man who doesn't even notice them! Then he would feverishly go hunting, to escape. But, when he returned, Gaya was always waiting for him, to murmur, "O Prince's friend! Was there good sport today? Think of the greater sport you could have here. Help me, Jalawarla, for I die of this desire—O Jalawarla, take his place!"

One day he flung angrily away from her, afraid to listen any more. At that moment Irani called, "Remount, Jalawarla! We're going to the gardens of Ardesha. I would see his new azaleas—flame-coloured as a symbol of the sun."

The Prince's company rode out toward the city walls. In the gardens Irani walked alone with his companion, telling the others not to trouble them. They reached a flowing river which reflected the hot blue of midday sky. Jalawarla was silent, looked down sullenly, and barely listened while the Prince spoke enraptured of the scene's wild beauty, the colours, scents, and thick-massed trees on the far bank.

When Jalawarla did look up, it was to say, "Prince, my companion! Shall we explore those woods together?"

"You know the Rajah's lands stop here. Those woods are strange—It almost seems that they belong to no one—" Irani looked round him pensively, captivated by thought of escaping from his courtiers, and murmured, "*If we could find a boat—*"

Jalawarla looked down again, touched the Prince's arm, and pointed. "See there—a little tragedy. Someone has slain two moon cuckoos."

Small draggled corpses lay beside the path. The feathers were ruffled, the throats still jewelled with shining blue. There was no sound but the wind in the trees and azalea bushes. The place was eerie, and beautiful. It was easy to imagine Krishna might appear, either playing with the Gopis, bathing in streams of water, or in the form of a glorious and dark-blue lotus, swarmed on by multitudes of bees.

Irani smiled his delightful smile, and looked at his friend— who looked away. "Jalawarla, what are you tempting me to do? Sundrun has often begged me to give up these tricks— it's the one request of hers that I've not granted, for it gives me freedom from our stifling grandeur. But she fears the Brahman's art, as I once did."

"What have women's fears to do with men? In this, I understand you better than she does. Dear Prince, you were in bird form when your heart first turned toward Sundrun— what harm could come to you in a short flight?" He bent to pick up one of the small corpses. It hung cold and heavy from his hand, with throat-feathers ruffled by the wind.

"Poor bird—" said Irani slowly—"which will never see its mate again . . ."

"Ah, come," said Jalawarla briskly. "We'll hide our bodies deep in these bushes, then our friends won't stumble on them in dismay!"

Where the azaleas flamed by the path there was a sudden emptiness, and lack of movement, while Irani and Jalawarla laid down their bodies at the twining snaky blackness of the roots. Then there was a fluttering, and rustle of flight, as dull beaks and eyes and plump, soft, bird forms came to life. The Prince's household looked up as two moon cuckoos flew above them, striped and handsome birds with bright blue throats.

Irani and Jalawarla could see far off the Rajah's Palace—so far that it looked like a small model, carved in ivory, and gay with coloured pennants. While Sundrun, looking from a fretted gallery toward the distant gardens of Ardesha, saw two minute black specks rise in the air and fly toward the woods. Involuntarily she raised a hand to her throat, and cried out as though someone had struck her. But when her women came running in alarm, she could give no reason for her cry.

The land beyond the river rose to join the foothills of the mountains. The trees and shrubs were exquisite; clear air, sweet soil, and sunlight made them thrive. Irani, flying just ahead of Jalawarla, gave his wild cuckoo's call, he was so pleased by all he saw. They flew from space to space, around huge tree trunks, then higher up where sunlight could caress their mottled feathers. The slate-blue bars upon their wings were like the bars of shadow on the ground.

"It's all Illusion to *want* anything," called Irani to his friend, "but if it weren't, I might like to be a bird—though only with Sundrun at my side!" Jalawarla made no reply.

At first they flew close together, then farther and farther apart. Irani was so happy flying to and fro and calling, "Jalawarla! See this strange fruit? . . . How the birds sing . . . I seem to understand them for the first time . . . Their simple needs and sorrows—" that he never heard the distant shouts of his own household. But his friend did: once the Prince was far enough ahead, Jalawarla turned on his strong wings, and flew towards the river. He crossed it, flying very low, and swooped to the azaleas, while his feathered breast

19

palpitated with his haste and suspense. Down he dropped by Irani's discarded body. His triumphant last cuckoo call was cut short as his bird form sank into corpse stillness, and by its side Irani's body came to life.

For a moment the false Prince looked around him, breathing fast. He feared to see the other cuckoo, calling its reproach—but nothing stirred. He parted the azaleas, and peered out. No one! Then he picked up his own abandoned body. He trembled as he looked into its empty eyes, but with one determined muscular heave he cast it from the river bank, and watched it borne away on rapid currents and gradually drawn under out of sight.

Sundrun was still seated in the gallery. Beside her stood a young lama monk from high Tibet, who turned his prayer wheel as he spoke of the Buddha's life. She heard the clatter of her husband's household returning to the Palace; then, as the monk ceased speaking, she realised the fine young men were silent too. Only the clanging hoofbeats, the neighing of half-wild stallions, told of the return. She leaned from the pierced window, and felt again that stab of terror at her throat.

Yet looking down she saw her fears were groundless, for Irani was riding past below. But then Gaya, beside her, suddenly exclaimed, "Where's Jalawarla?" And they both saw his empty-saddled horse led by a servant, and that Irani wept.

"Gaya—the Prince has lost his friend in some catastrophe!" mourned Sundrun. "See how he weeps!"

"Jalawarla—dead?" questioned Gaya in a little voice; and dug her nails into her henna-ed palms.

Deep in the woods one blue-jewel-throated cuckoo flew on heavy wings, calling in puzzlement. No other cuckoo answered, and the sound drew further and further away from Ardesha's gardens and the riverside, as Irani searched for his companion, and began to fear him either lost or slain.

Days passed, and Sundrun grew most sad. After her husband told her how Jalawarla had fallen in the river and been drawn down by its fast current, he turned silent for some days. Then, to Sundrun's amazement, he began to scoff at her concern, and brusquely ended all religious mourning ceremonies.

"Jalawarla is no more!" he told her roughly, when she spoke of it. "Chants and prayers will neither call to him nor bring him back. They're Illusion, Sundrun—as is friendship, too! I forbid you to pray more with Buddhist monks, for a man wants love and laughter from his wife—not a face the colour of a saffron robe."

"Irani—his death has strangely altered you! Where are your devotions now? Your priests and monks are sorrowful. It's hard to lose a friend, but even so—"

"And harder still to have you speak of him all day! Look round you, my Sundrun: here's heat and colour, scents and flowers, flutes! Can cold prayer comfort Jalawarla for their loss? I tire of these sad Buddhist doctrines—there's more life in the harsh worship of destructive Kali."

Sundrun looked her amazement, and resisted when he tried to take her hand; she wondered if he was unbalanced. But Jalawarla laughed at her, and said, "Come now to Krishna's temple—that may warm your love for me. The union of Sakti with Samvara is hotter than your liking for your husband!"

With words like these, and praises of erotic Tantric sects, Jalawarla wounded her. She turned even more to Buddhism, and mourned not only Jalawarla, but her husband who had changed completely with his death. At last she thought, It's as though he had come back as someone else—as the worst side of *Jalawarla* . . . And she wept, but kept her strange suspicions to herself, as Jalawarla began to look at her with poisoned glances, and then avoided her.

"So!" said Gaya, drawing up her mauve and silver sari to cover a triumphant face; she had met Jalawarla in the hot temple courts where baboons gambolled with innocent obscenity near the carved gods and lovers on the walls. "So— it *is* my little Jalawarla after all, behind Irani's eyes."

"What's that you called me?" Jalawarla smiled, and pulled her down to lie beside him on a patch of baking ground. "Be careful what you say to other people!"

"They wouldn't listen . . ." Gaya let fall the fold of bright material, and turned her face to his. "They all believe you the true Prince—who has reached earth at last, and leaves the problem of eternity until he faces it. Though our clever, pale Princess may guess at something different!"

It was very quiet, except for the baboons. Jalawarla drew her close, and soon they were as caressingly entwined as the lovers in the ancient carvings on the reddish, silent walls.

When Jalawarla had disappeared in his moon-cuckoo form, Irani had flown and flown, calling for him, until he was exhausted; then he had settled on a branch and looked about him. Far off, through trees, he could see distant mountains turn to glory with the setting sun. Where *was* Jalawarla?

Suddenly, where darkness should have swathed the tree-trunks, there was light. The man-bird, swaying on his bough, blinked his thin-lidded eyes and cocked his head. There was a stillness, as though earth waited, listening, and then a sound as though silk curtains were undrawn: from the heavens came deities and Bodhisattvas, awe-inspiring with the tremendous vibrations of their joy. Kettledrums throbbed, and flutes. Where the dark woods were light, the light turned into form, and the form was seated Buddha absorbed in meditation, his eyes downcast. His whole Presence breathed compassion towards deluded life. The treetops bent in homage and the earth opened to let free Muchalinda, who twined himself at Buddha's feet, and spread his great hood to protect the Blessed One if it should rain. There was a distant sound as though a million prayer wheels turned to the chant of OM maṇi padme HUM.

And then, as suddenly as the vision had appeared, the sun sank, earth and heavens closed. Muchalinda, gods and Bodhisattvas vanished. In the dimness Irani could only see a slight, pale form sitting crosslegged on the ground and contemplating *him*.

"Jalawarla has betrayed you, my devoted Prince. He returned to Sundrun in your body, while his own lies on the riverbed. Alas—his charm made you forget the danger you first saw in him."

At the Buddha's words Irani felt pain in his heart as though someone struck it with an arrow.

"But you know the Truth, Irani, my disciple: the wheel turns only as past thought and action set it turning. You will grieve, and your wife too as she lives with Jalawarla—but she also knows the unreality of human life. Devoted child, though you lose your two companions, I myself will be your friend in these first days of your despair."

The pale form seemed to shrink and dim, and change. From the place where Buddha had appeared there flew up a moon cuckoo, whose jewelled blue throat pulsated and gave out streams of light. Then Irani bowed his head, and did startled homage to the Blessed One. Afterwards, the two of them preached daily to the flocks of migrant birds, which flew on joyful wings from North, South, East and West to join them. And at last, after Irani's first bitterness was healed, the Buddha gently showed him that it was now his destiny to remain here in the woods, preach to the birds, and wait for a Great Lama to come from high Tibet and complete his true Enlightenment.

One day, Irani woke at dawn to find the second moon cuckoo had gone. The other birds rose and circled in the air as an old man approached, whose saffron robe was worn and tattered from his harsh existence. When the Great Lama reached the clearing he sat himself crosslegged upon the ground, and stared at the lone cuckoo.

"Ah, my young Prince in humble shape! It's given to few men to change their form already in this life. How close your Highness reaches to a state where all is just a shadow of one Truth! Lord Buddha sends me to you—" There, in the wood carpeted with birds and strewn with feathers, the Great Lama spoke of all Irani's long-past lives, his good and evil deeds that had brought him good and evil recompense. He spoke of Dogma, and Right Action, and drove his points home with many stories drawn from long experience. His eloquent discourse flowed for days and nights, until Irani's feathered form grew small and thin from the severe strain of concentration.

At last the ancient Lama's face, which had expressed only solemnity and wisdom, creased itself into a smile. He ceased to speak. The silence was full of benevolence, and awe. Irani broke it by begging still to be enlightened on one point: why Jalawarla had felt he must betray him.

"In your last existence, Prince, Jalawarla was your neighbour king, and hostile: you fought many acts of war against each other. When he was tempted to betrayal your dual past actions overcame the later growth of love, which was not deep-rooted. Now, let us meditate a little—"

When the sun rose again—

"It's in my power to return you to your wife—in your true form—if that is your desire?" said the Great Lama.

Irani shifted on his branch. He felt the scaly hardness of his claws, and longed to resume human shape. He asked a question that he hadn't dared to think about before: "Does my dear Sundrun—does she *guess* he has usurped my place?"

"She has guessed! And sadly keeps herself apart—which isn't hard, since Jalawarla, far from enlightenment at present, prefers plump concubines."

Irani felt an uprush of joy, but he said steadfastly, "If I should return—what comes to Jalawarla?"

The Lama's face became inscrutable. He shook his head. It was his only answer, but enough.

"And if I—don't return?"

24

Irani and the Cuckoos

The Great Lama's eyes turned upward and inward, as though he saw a vision just above or in his head. At last he roused himself, and sighed. "He will live a long while in his evil ways, my Prince, which will bring him at the last to retribution and much suffering. Then, in his age, the Princess Sundrun may convert him, so perhaps in his next life—" He left the phrase unfinished.

Irani stayed silent for a while, his small claws clenched upon the swaying bough; then he murmured, "The Lord Buddha has laid on me no charge—but in all the words you speak, Great Lama, I seem to hear his voice when he preached beside me to the birds. I always knew that teaching others was my destiny; only the love of Sundrun drew me from it. I shall stay where the Compassionate One set me his own example—if, benign Great Lama, you'll accept from me one charge?"

"Gladly I will."

"Go to my wife, my father, and my friends, and tell them what became of me and how I live among the birds; and tell them not to punish Jalawarla, for it was our destiny. Tell Sundrun, too, I'll come to her each year, and preach in her own gardens."

The Great Lama bowed his head above his folded hands. After a short meditation of three days he went quietly to the river, where his sixth sense told him he would find a boat. Irani stretched the muscles in his strong, barred wings, and felt the cramping smallness of this plumage he would wear till his next death.

Each year, in Sundrun's private gardens, the whole court—except for Jalawarla and his concubines—would meet together. When the assemblage was complete, the sky would darken and grow heavy with a rustle of soft wings and small swooping bodies pouring down like rain. Each flower head would bend under the invasion; each bush and tree was hidden by the thronging wings. At last, once the sky was clear again, Irani's joyous calling could be heard as he came flying to the central tree, a mulberry, where he perched in solitary splendour, and preached while his blue throat throbbed with the eloquence of passion.

Later, when his audience had walked or flown away, he would linger for a while on Sundrun's shoulder, and feel her hand caress his feathers, and see her loving smile. The two of them, silent in understanding of each other, would watch the sky gradually empty itself of wings.

White Orchid, Red Mountain

All day long White Orchid worked in the house of her much-loved husband, young Li Ching. At first, after her wedding, she would move lightly on tiny bound feet from room to room, a song on her lips, a smile on her entrancing face. She sang. She prepared rice with delicacies, and served it in porcelain bowls of green and white. She was never still, and never lazy; yet her husband's stepmother would shuffle behind her, breathe angrily down the back of her neck and mutter, "Ah—misbegotten child! Why son marry such silly, thoughtless wretch? Old Mother taste rice: ugh! —cold, flavourless! . . . Now too hot; now sticky. Aie— daughter soon learn duties to husband and family." White Orchid, whose food was as perfect as her looks, would be dragged by the high collar of her blue robe into the next room, and beaten till she lay sobbing on the floor.

It was the year of the Dragon, and from the first day to the last Li Ching's stepmother grew more angry and beat harder. He was powerless to intervene, or the neighbours would have risen up and cast him out: in that society it was the custom for sons' wives to be subject to their mothers-in-law, and beaten too—though none beat so often and ferociously as Li Ching's stepmother in that Dragon year.

The sages have said, "All banquets end, but love between some husbands and their wives is everlasting." Li Ching felt sick with misery to see White Orchid lose her looks as she grew thinner and thinner, and the peach colour faded from her lips and cheeks, and her small backside was permanently red from such harsh beatings. One day he came back from the fields to find her crouched on the floor of their own room, sobbing in despair.

"Li Ching," she murmured as he kissed her neck, trying to comfort her, "Stepmother too much! White Orchid too much beaten by she-devil! Perhaps poor Orchid run away, for if she stay with Li Ching, she die." She sobbed again, and wrung her hands. Li Ching looked at them in horror; the knuckles stood out sharp as chickenbones.

"White Orchid—white flower, *we* go soon," he said tenderly. "Not work drive stepmother to cruelty—but jealousy. Only honourable dead father able control tigress! Li Ching now spurn her before faces of all ancestors: today, we go. Better disgrace with White Orchid, than terror of wife's death."

Is it not said that fresh horses fly faster than the wind? At midnight Li Ching and White Orchid crept to the stables, and mounted two of the least valuable horses—scrawny beasts which yet had strength to go, and to keep going, as they cantered up many roads and through a hundred villages. But the runaways found nowhere to settle down; they left the highway for a mountain path which seemed to draw White Orchid with a strong attraction.

There the scrawny horses flew yet faster; their hooves thudded on rocky soil, and the slopes rose high. Cranes flew above, beating ahead of them as though to guide the way. Kestrels hovered. White Orchid laughed joyously for the first time in many days. Her long black hair had come loose from its careful braiding, and streamed behind her in the wind. Li Ching's impassive, slightly melancholy face broke into smiles as they called to one another. It is well said that "when two people understand each other in their inmost hearts, their words are sweet and strong, like the fragrance of orchids."

They rode always north-west, and at night beneath the stars. When dawn came they found themselves high on a mountain's empty slopes. Often, in such a place, there would have been a small shrine poised upon a ledge; here, there was little but a sense of emptiness. The horses stirred uneasily, raised their heads, and whickered. All the same it was very beautiful, the grass studded with bright flowers as though most careful artists had placed them there. When she heard birdsong all about them, White Orchid sighed.

"White Orchid unhappy?" murmured Li Ching, dismounting, and coming to lift her down.

She slid into his arms. He could feel her thinness.

"No, no . . . yet hear, Li Ching: is Spring—now birds nest all around. White Orchid sigh only because runaways so homeless."

He held her close, and smiled. "Still many groves of trees where runaways sleep in peace. Is no stepmother, no cruel big stick!"

Then White Orchid smiled too, and clung to him. "Wherever Li Ching live, *my* home."

Later, they rode on. The mountain, with its misty gulfs and towered peaks, was like a picture on some fine silk scroll. Still the tired runaways rode on, into the next day. When the sun rose they reached a place even greener than the other slopes: a cup-shaped glade, with its own bubbling spring.

"How strange!" exclaimed White Orchid. "See—surface pink—no, red: water hold all colours of pure cherry-apple blossom!" She blinked. Did she see things that weren't there, after her long, exhausting ride?

But Li Ching answered, "Yes! Water such colour not seen before." He gazed about him and murmured in astonishment, "Look, White Orchid—no blossom, no red. tree nearby. Perhaps not right that runaways stay here?"

But already White Orchid had dismounted, and was cupping her hands together to drink from the stream. "Water so very good!" She laughed up at him. "See Orchid drink and drink. Smell what fragrance everywhere! Look— red flowers everywhere in grass."

"Not flowers," said Li Ching uneasily, "but grass itself

29

all red—and in shade, is crimson!" He tried to pull his horse's head up, but the beast was stubbornly cropping the red grass, as was White Orchid's mare.

"Li Ching look so funny with mouth wide open! This strange place indeed. Ahhh! This water sweet with special flavour—" She sipped from her hands, then plunged her face into the stream to drink and drink from the deeply-coloured water, which held a glow of maple red beneath the hurrying, tumbling crystal of its surface. "Li Ching, look!" She stood and stretched, raising her arms high above her head. "White Orchid now strong and well! And warm—Red water quite warm, is sun-warm syrup! Drink too, Li Ching?"

But he only stared. He saw his wife as she had been when he first married her: arms and face rounded, lips and cheeks bright with rose and peach.

"Something now wrong, husband?" she faltered; then noticed her own hands, and how their work-worn thinness had been replaced by unlined flesh. And the horses cropping the red grass were quite plump-muscled as though fed lushly every day! Li Ching alone still had haggard looks, after the strain of their escape; yet he felt no urge to drink, only desire to leave the hollow place. White Orchid caught his uneasiness and gave a shiver. She mounted hurriedly, and with one accord they smacked their horses into a fast trot.

Now the hard mountain ways might have been easy village paths, the gulleys no more than ditches dug by children at their games—for the strange red grass seemed to have lent the horses amazing strength and fleetness. White Orchid and Li Ching rode all day, and other days, and nights. Instinctively they wished to put much ground between themselves and that odd mountain. One evening, when they looked back, it appeared to be no more than a blue molehill, almost lost on the horizon.

Li Ching sighed his relief; he was very tired. "See!" he exclaimed thankfully, "Fresh village! Small place where cottages stand close together, all lamps friendly in bright

30

welcome. Something at last say 'runaways find peace with happiness.' Come, White Orchid—knock upon first door."

The peremptory sound was answered by an old woman, whose wizened face was wrinkled like a ripe almond's surface. Her hair was still black, but scanty, oiled, and stretched into a small bun at the nape of her neck. Her blue country garments were faded, though neat and clean, and she bore the look of wisdom and charity that long life with its inevitable suffering brings to a truly good human being. On that dark evening she seemed unafraid of strangers. "Life bring young ones to Old Woman's door?" She peered at the two shabby wanderers. "Newcomers to humble village no brigands; or so Old Woman guess!"

"No—no brigands," stammered White Orchid, drooping like a cut flower as she spoke. "Homeless, homeless—with only trees for shelter, ground for sleep." Li Ching said nothing, but looked pleadingly at Old Woman, and put an arm around his wife.

The Old Woman bowed in greeting over her joined hands. "Enter, most welcome!" She smiled a happy smile. "Long, Old Woman live alone, since she widowed." She showed them to her West room; she herself would move to one that faced the East. Li Ching recalled that, for the sages, East signified the Spring, and West—the Autumn. He wondered uneasily if Old Woman's action could be seen as some omen for their future lives.

Yet how happy they all were in that small house! Old Woman cherished them just like a mother. Her meals were cooked with love—not eaten with hatred as they would have been in Li Ching's home.

But over rice on that first evening White Orchid spoke of their adventures, and when she praised the red water's entrancing flavour Old Woman bent her head and wept. "Aie-ee, poor children! What wreckage children bring for new life! How children's innocence cursed already—for when Autumn come, wife soon torn away . . ."

Li Ching's hand sought for White Orchid's. The fears he had suffered on that mountain crept over him again. White Orchid looked aghast. Her other hand stole to her cheek.

Old Woman was still weeping. "That place Red Mountain spring—thick with syrup-juice which seep from perfect maple's roots; ordinary, harmless maple . . . But in Autumn, when leaves turn colour—then tree take on proper shape: of devil! With devil-face crimson as maple leaf! Red eyes shine like stars of scarlet fire! Nothing evade devil-eyes—yes, look this way, that way, through mountain rocks and houses, through any distance! Big knotty feet-roots untwine from hollow on Red Mountain as devil climb to summit, where turn, turn ugly head. He searching . . . searching for young beauty who unwisely swallow magic maple water—" Old Woman raised her head, looked long at White Orchid, and moaned almost inaudibly, "New Daughter not escape! Maple Devil snare lovely Orchid for all time—before Red Mountain white with snow, Devil once more maple tree with White Orchid as maple bride." She sobbed aloud.

They had been terrified; but—acting as though nothing troubled them—had comforted her fears. They had declared that no devil in this world or the next could part them from each other. They had accepted an invitation to be Old Woman's family, and continued living happily together. Li Ching worked his new mother's fields, while White Orchid prepared food that was never scorned. The happiest summer they had ever known went by, till the wheat was harvested, the millet plumped up fat and golden-green, and the grapes grew a bloom as velvet-soft as any baby's skin. But on the far-off mountains the maples' leaves slowly turned colour too.

Now Old Woman lay awake at night. Her hands were like birds' claws, and jerked, plucking at the coverlets. Or her fingers counted out the days of Autumn's slow though certain passage.

"If Winter only come!" she kept saying, "If Winter only come, then my White Orchid safe! Then perhaps other girl cruel devil's bride . . ."

"Is Old Woman's age make her imagine things," said Li Ching thankfully to White Orchid, as the days went by and shortened towards Autumn's end. The two of them had finished work that evening, and were just cutting fodder for the horses.

"Look—full moon!" exclaimed White Orchid, holding a bunch of grasses to her, and thinking they smelt as fragrant as those by the red spring. "Such very different moon tonight! Round white face stare straight at Li Ching's wife!"

"O sensible bright moon!"

Old Woman had just placed rice in her best bowls of porcelain. She shuffled across the room, out into the courtyard, and also looked upward at the moon. Something dark fluttered between her and it. A bat? She was glad, for bats are symbols of all happiness. But no bats flew that night: what came twisting, turning, from the sky was one large red maple leaf, dancing a dance of triumph all alone. It swirled and grew, and drew the air after it into a wicked whirlwind, coloured like crimson fire: then from its centre blossomed a red devil.

Devil he might be, but he was grand as any mandarin— and all red from head to foot. His robes and cap, his beard and willow-sweeping moustaches, his fine eyes, and his sleeves. One of these he flapped contemptuously in Old Woman's face. She wailed heartbrokenly, a long wail of "Aieeeeee!" and fell helpless to the ground.

In the stables Li Ching and White Orchid heard her, dropped their grass bundles, and came hurrying to the courtyard.

Maple Devil threw back his head, and laughed. "Ah, graceful, pure White Orchid, soon Red Maple Flower! Here she come forward just like eager new wife, what happy

33

augury! What delicate maple tree she make upon my mountain!"

As he spoke, he flapped his other sleeve. The maple leaf at his feet folded itself, expanded; changed to a bridal sedan chair, all draped and decorated in red. "Get in, get in, Flower of Beauty—Poor husband lose pleasure of Honey Presence since White Orchid love water from red spring! Come—no waiting—" His sleeves shot out till their long edges touched her, and she felt herself helplessly drawn inside the sinister red chair, which rumbled off into the sky with no visible bearers to support it. Maple Devil followed behind it, using his sleeves as wings.

Old Woman howled and screamed, and bit her knuckles in despair. Li Ching's misery and horror were tremendous, but he only cried out between his teeth, "Old Mother not weep like that! Adopted son soon fetch New Daughter back!"

"Child, child," moaned Old Woman. "Why not understand? New Daughter gone for ever—no one find Maple Devil brides again. Husbands who seek Maple Devil, not return!" She sobbed and sobbed quite hopelessly. Li Ching carried her inside the house.

The moon was halfway up the sky when he left home. Old Woman had tried to stop him; but when she saw how his face set, and how he meant to go, she offered him her best and longest knife as a weapon—it had a curved blade, needle-sharp. Li Ching rode the faster of his two horses. The red grass seemed to have lent it magic powers of endurance; even so, its pace, compared with Maple Devil's flight, was unquestionably slow. All through the night the drumming roll of hoof-beats sounded as they galloped toward the distant hills.

When Li Ching thought they had reached their goal he pulled up, and began searching for the spring. Dawn had come already, and the sky was red, but nowhere could he see a hollow with red water and red grass. Tears poured down his face. "Horse, Maple Devil fly so far! Mountains so deceptive—" He gazed about him. "That peak—or that peak far in distance? Come—" He kicked his mount's flanks. "Li Ching seek over all mountains in all China till he find young wife's prison—"

There was no slope, no precipice, no gulley that was too dangerous for Li Ching and his mount to cover in their mad search for the missing girl.

Maple Devil had White Orchid hidden deep inside the highest mountain. She hardly recognised his refuge for a cave. Its interior was exquisitely arranged; and Maple Devil, a connoisseur of Chinese art who prided himself on his good taste, had modelled it on a highborn scholar's room. Here was a T'ang horse, there a small bronze Ting once used in the service of the Yellow Emperor, and on the walls hung scrolls of silk decorated by the finest artists of the day. He himself was very expert with a brush, and—in some ways—sensitive.

"If Lady find redness not to her taste," he said gravely, "then Maple Devil take pallor of spring maple leaf." So his fearful colour faded to the yellow-ivory of an ascetic scholar's face; his features grew gentle, like a poet's; and soon there stood before White Orchid the very picture of a highborn scholar, wistful and attractive—except for a red glow lurking behind his eyes, like the glow of a banked fire.

"Lady approve silk coverings on bed? Quilt of plum pattern please her?" asked Maple Devil, smoothing the bed hangings with a fine, long hand.

White Orchid made no reply.

"Must not bore Lady, before even Lady married!" Maple Devil smirked, turned South, flicked the sleeve of his severe black robe, and showed her the Hall of Light with its Skyward House or Spirit Tower. It smelt fragrantly, and was inlaid with white quartz, green jasper, and rock crystal scrollwork.

White Orchid, Red Mountain

White Orchid wept.

So he turned North-east, flapped his sleeve, and showed her the Dragon King's Castle of Bright Splendour, where dragon princes slept. Some were in reptile form; others were waking, dressed as men in high hats and brilliant robes. One of them looked up, and smiled, and held out a cushion which bore rhinoceros horn and a blue cloud box containing pearls.

White Orchid screamed.

"Ts'ah, ts'ah, t'sin," clucked Maple Devil, and tried to soothe her with a sound of strings, flutes and bells; but White Orchid would not be soothed: she merely buried her face in her small hands and wouldn't speak.

Then Maple Devil flew into a passion; his face worked till it turned red again, which ill accorded with his scholar's robes.

"Lady act like loving maple tree, not silly weeping willow!" he declared passionately.

"Oh, have pity, Maple Devil!" White Orchid's huge eyes looked up at him piteously. "Orchid only love Li Ching."

"Lady still think to see husband on Red Mountain?" Maple Devil smirked again. "*If* husband enter cave, *then* husband take Lady back." He bent double in unkind mirth; but, as he straightened again, his fire-star eyes saw through walls and mountains, and saw Li Ching's approach.

"Ho-hhhhhhhhhhhhhhhh-ah!" howled Maple Devil; and flowered into his crimson form. His belt was stripey black and red. He tore it from his waist, and flapped it high above his head. Immediately it turned into a handsome black and crimson tiger, which shot like a thunderbolt from the cave's mouth, and disappeared.

Li Ching was pleased with his progress. He had caught sight of a giant peak, which was surely the Red Mountain?

"Steady, Horse!" he muttered, as the beast stumbled on the steep path. Then he looked up—and gaped. What were

37

these two glowing red lights, rushing towards him so fast that he'd no time to rein in his frightened mount? They were the eyes of a gigantic tiger, which stopped in front of him, and opened its huge jaws, and waited. Horse and Li Ching— no time to escape, both screaming—rushed into the open trap and fell down the enormous tiger's throat. There was an awful smell inside, and a seething and a rumbling which were the tiger's gastric juices on the boil. The contents of his stomach were red hot and liquid and most unpleasant. But Li Ching bore the agony and, keeping his mouth closed, dived with his arms above his head and Old Woman's knife clasped in his right hand. He slit the stomach wall as though it were part of a paper tiger.

There was a bigger rumble than before as Li Ching and his horse flew through the gap. They sped on up the mountain; looking back, Li Ching could see no dead tiger anywhere, but only a harmless black and crimson belt lying on the path.

"Husband now warm, safe, and dead inside tiger!" murmured Maple Devil as he fingered White Orchid's neck. He had changed himself into the image of a young man in love: only a deep red glow within his eyes betrayed him. He stroked her black hair, and kissed her ears. She cried and cried, but otherwise ignored him. He ground his teeth in a most unlover-like fashion, glared straight at the wall, and through it saw Li Ching and his horse galloping near and nearer. Maple Devil's jaw dropped open, showing his crimson gums and purple wisdom teeth.

He made a sound of demon anger. He tore one of his treasured landscapes from the cave wall, and waved his sleeve at it. Quick as a flash the artist's cruel, steep, intimidating mountain, higher than five towers, slid out of the cave, and set itself between Li Ching and his goal. This time the horse refused the obstacle: his hooves slithered on the rock face and could get no hold. Then Li Ching tried, on foot. Oh, how the breath laboured in his lungs—how his hands bled, as he crawled painfully upward from handhold to tiny ledge! How his heart sank when, halfway to success, he slipped and slid all the way down again. But Li Ching was greathearted—he made two, three, four, five, *six* attempts on that harsh mountain; and, after falling six times, breathed deep, spat on his hands, and ran at it again.

It had vanished! Li Ching found himself, to his amazement, in a cup-shaped glade. Nearby a silk scroll, wet with his own sweat and tears, hung upon a tree. He stood there awe-struck, panting; then looked up. Seeming quite close, towering above the rise of the next slope, a huge red mountain peak jutted into the sky. Li Ching set his jaw grimly, remounted his patient horse, and rode towards the peak.

Maple Devil stared through the cave wall and saw him coming. His fire-star eyes revolved with anger in his head. "All honourable devils keep promises!" he swore. "But this husband too much!" He turned to White Orchid and elegantly waved his sleeves above her head. She became a dumb, living statue. He looked round for inspiration, and waved his sleeves over two cushions, which stood up, shuffled over to White Orchid, and gradually flowered into duplicates of her delicate, frozen form.

"Now let interfering husband choose true wife, if he feel able to!" cried Maple Devil furiously, and flew away.

When Li Ching pushed aside the hangings of the cave mouth, and entered it, he almost froze as well—with shock. Dear, beloved White Orchid—no! dear, beloved Triple Orchid! *Three* Orchids, and not one of them who smiled a greeting, or ran to kiss him with delight. Six great eyes stared at him, three pairs of lips stayed mute. When he could speak himself, he said sorrowfully, "Precious Orchid, say something for Li Ching! Perhaps arrival after many dangers not very welcome. Perhaps Maple Devil better lover?"

39

Still three White Orchids watched him with sad eyes and silent lips. The real Orchid felt torn in many pieces by her terrible, fruitless desire to answer him. She longed to take him in her arms. She was in agony, but she could move no muscle, nor do anything but weep. A small rivulet crept from each large, expressive eye, and down her cheeks.

Then Li Ching felt joy. He knew which was his true White Orchid. He ran to her, and took her in his arms. Still she didn't move. And how she weighed: like stone carved from the great Red Mountain! He struggled to pick her up, and just managed to carry her unresponsive, rigid body from the cave, though even his strong arms couldn't lift her to the horse's saddle. "Come, Horse—way home so very long! Now, lead . . ."

Soon his shoulders ached and ached. White Orchid seemed heavier than any statue. He only knew she was alive by her continual weeping; but he guessed her suffering, which was truly bitter. Li Ching suffered too. He would sooner have died beneath Maple Devil's spells than have her endure such misery. He trudged on and on, gently stroking her cheek with one caressing finger till at last her tears stopped flowing. Her huge eyes peered up at him pleadingly. She wanted to explain that he must put her down and leave her, for she couldn't bear to be his death—how *could* he carry her back home, even if they escaped Maple Devil's wrath? But Li Ching misunderstood her look of fear, and murmured lovingly, "White Orchid now very safe! For Li Ching stay faithful always . . . even though she still as stone."

He stumbled on through a small maple grove till something fell lightly against his face. It was a maple leaf, and others followed, swirling into a miniature whirlpool before them both. Li Ching stared in horror when Maple Devil blossomed from the flurry. White Orchid was almost dropped as his right hand sought for Old Woman's knife. He was about to lunge when—

"Young lovers very brave!" Maple Devil's voice was

40

husky with feeling, and he wept red tears. "Always, Devil's feelings stony as poor White Orchid now. Tiger-cruel, merciless. Yet constant love beyond all price, which cause Devil's first defeat. Husband: go with wife! Tell other pretty ladies safe as well—for Maple Devil never seem so cruel again."

As he finished speaking, he changed before their eyes. The grove of maple trees, his former brides, swayed towards him in a sudden breeze. He too became a maple: the largest and strongest on the mountain, his leaves blazing with fiery red and orange. Crimson drops dripped, dripped from their jagged edges, but soon turned to crystal clarity, like rain. As Li Ching stood there, savouring sudden deliverance, his mouth agape, the mountain breeze grew fiercer and swayed the branches; water showered from the leaves on to White Orchid's upturned face. She grew warm and light in Li Ching's arms, peach colour came into her cheeks, and she cried out with tears and laughter, "Most virtuous, kindly Maple Devil—no, Maple Spirit! Li Ching—take disenchanted young wife home . . ."

Three days later the sun was rising as Old Woman pottered out into the courtyard, looking, always looking, for her adopted children, though in her heart she knew them dead. She murmured sadly, "Old . . . old. All loving gone forever!"

Then she glanced up. The horse was just turning into the yard, White Orchid on his back clasped in Li Ching's arms. Old Woman's face wrinkled into a smiling mask of sheer delight and astonishment. She bowed her head above her clasped hands in thankfulness. "Ah, great Kwan-Yin!"

That night they all three burned tapers to the Goddess of Compassion. And, in time to come, much, much incense was burned in that far province, too: for no girl who rashly drank the maple syrup-water was ever harmed again. Maple Devil, surrounded by his grove of smaller maple trees, was made happy by these earlier, transfigured wives.

Sankichi's Gift

To be a renowned wrestler is a true achievement; don't all men know that those who are accomplished in the art of Sumo bring blessings to their parents and their villages, and abundant crops of rice? This is so because Sumo is of the gods, having its origins in divine ritual. A strong male child, whose muscles bulge and whose heart is of high courage equal to the courage of the samurai, and who shows talent for fine wrestling, is bound to be a favourite with his father.

A long, long while ago there was born in Gojonome-machi a boy who grew to be a wrestler of such brilliance that the local people said admiringly, "He'll be the greatest wrestler in Japan!" Yet, since his family was poor, his father sent him unwillingly to serve with a great lord, a Daimyo, whose house was in the neighbourhood.

There it was all day long, "Daihachi, do this", and "Daihachi, do that", till the boy's courage and purpose almost broke, and he saw himself no more as fortune's favoured one, but as slave to a capricious lord. He turned silent, and stood apart from everyone. Even music of the koto or the flute, sounding from paper-screened rooms on summer evenings, or the high laughter of pretty maidservants, or the fierce beauty of swordplay when the young lords met to try their skill against each other, couldn't draw him from his melancholy.

The only happiness he still enjoyed was when he had permission to attend some local festival. Then, his round face one large beam of pleasure, he would wash himself from head to foot, oil his hair, and present himself as candidate in

those matches held to honour gods and the great Emperor.
As he rocked from foot to foot in the ritual opening and
strange frog-like postures of his art, Daihachi would feel
himself reborn, once more rewarded by the Kami who
possessed him; *and* know himself different from other men—
as different as the Daimyo or the Emperor himself.

Always, he won his matches; though afterwards his pride
would shatter when he went home to the servants' quarters
to hear the young lords calling, "Where's our boaster?
Daihachi, our fine wrestler, bring us wine!—A stool, too—
Daihachi, you lazy scoundrel, hurry up!" "Ah!" the
Daimyo's son would sneer to all his friends. "Here's a fellow
grown too full of some bold Kami to keep his thoughts upon
his work!" and he would fling the dregs from his jade wine cup
into his servant's face, or drop the cup itself and berate him
for having caused the accident that broke it. As Daihachi
crawled to and fro upon the floor to pick up shards, and the
young lords sat by to mock him, he felt hatred in his heart.
One day he turned on them, unable to contain himself, and
cried out, "I've that within me to make me famous, even
among you all!" But this only made them double up with
laughter, and the young lord spat his beanshoots on the
floor, and commanded Daihachi to lick them up as though
he were a dog.

"Fat boy—he needs more work!"

"Yes indeed—he's far too rough for indoor labour!"

"Let him sweat a little in the paddy—"

"My honoured father will find some proper work for
you, impudence," added the young heir in tones of menace.
"Work to oil those muscles you're so proud of! Let your
Kami help you then, Daihachi—you'll need *all* his strength."

Next day the Daimyo sent for Daihachi, and eyed him up
and down as though he were a horse.

"My honoured lord has sent for me?" asked the boy
calmly, though his heart knocked against his ribs. Japan was
a ferocious country in those days; insolent servants could
expect no mercy. There were many punishments, and the

crueller lords used them with pleasure. Fortunately Daihachi's lord wasn't one of them—*his* great fault was meanness.

"Yes, he'll do—" he murmured to himself, and aloud, "My son tells me you're exceptionally strong, and believe yourself born to be a wrestler?"

Daihachi didn't know what else to say but "Yes, lord!" His heart and thoughts swelled with longing. Many great lords might have sent him to be trained, to fight matches till glory was reflected on them and their province. But Daihachi knew his Daimyo's meanness and that he cared little for glory; even his own son's swordplay meant nothing to him.

"At this season we owe our land tax to our powerful overlord of Akita—this year it's one whole cart of rice. Usually I must send at least three men to draw it, but my excellent son recommends that you should go alone, thus leaving others free to do more work. You can find the way safely to Akita?"

Daihachi felt the Kami swell so strong and angrily within him that he could have found his way anywhere and then run on and away without a pause. He was a servant, not a labourer! To draw this cart like a beast of burden wasn't only punishment, but a deliberate insult to lower him in the eyes of all his fellows. He almost said so, just in time recalled the old man's power to kill or torture him, and muttered in a tone that hardly disguised his feelings, "Lord, I can find my way—if I *can* draw this rice cart!"

His Daimyo answered sharply, "Tomorrow, then. And certainly you'll draw it safely there, for if you fail you shall be stripped and beaten till you howl to sweet Kannon—and that will teach you not to boast of divine strength! If you succeed, we'll find you further work. Strong horses must be broken to the plough." He eyed Daihachi's plumply muscled arms with fresh approval. The servant bowed, raging, from his presence, conscious that the young lord's jealousy had caught him in a silk snare either way.

Next day he set out, straining and heaving at the heavy

cart of rice. His fellow servants stood round him as he left, laughing openly. Little boys ran alongside, whooping and calling to one another, "Come and see Daihachi pull a cart! Better than an ox is our Daihachi! What a famous wrestler he could be, if he weren't bound in service to the lord!" Daihachi's humiliation knew no bounds.

The cart seemed to get heavier and heavier, and the road to Akita steeper and steeper. It ran between river gorges, and up toward the mountains. Daihachi sweated and strained. The cart slipped back a little farther each time he paused to rest. He saw the dark pines rise upon each side of him, and heard the sound of running water. He passed a goryo shrine, and hoped that the embittered spirit for whose appeasement it had once been raised was now controlled by higher powers. He wondered if his Kami, the tutelary deity whom the young lord had dared to mock, had left him to this servile work. But Kami or no Kami, thought Daihachi dismally as he tugged his load, I do hope that I shan't meet with a kappa or a tengu in these mountains. . . . Those demons were very terrible!

Ahead of him now, beyond a long winding path and the bridge that crossed a river gorge, he could see the lord of Akita's splendid castle, with its flaring gold and crimson eaves stark and proud in silhouette against the sky. For a moment he paused, moaning aloud, to clutch at the cart shafts. His efforts on that steep path had almost made him faint. The sweat poured down his face and muscled shoulders.

Just then he heard a little voice chant to itself in malicious tones of pure enjoyment, "Weak, weak, weak! What a weak, weak, weakling fellow is this weak one, who so weakly cannot pull a cart!" And there walking, or rather skipping, along the path beside the road, was a slender, bold-eyed child, his face alight with mischievous intention to torment.

Daihachi felt even angrier than when his lord had told him of the task. His usually good-tempered face, round and fat

45

like many wrestlers', creased into as furious an expression as it could assume. He cried out, "Just put your hands to this load, wretched one! Try for yourself to move this cart, and see if *I* am weak, you demon child! One who mocks hardworking men may live to find himself beset."

The child came nearer. He was beautifully made, and his dark eyes danced. They weren't unfriendly, in spite of Daihachi's harsh-sounding words.

"*Yes*," his voice was now melodious as birds calling in the pines, or the song of piney-smelling wind, "I'll move your cart—see me pull it by myself. With one little finger only, I could pull ten such carts: and with no effort! Come—make room!" And he placed himself between the shafts like a draught beast, put his little fingers under them, and walked ahead uphill, dragging the cart as lightly and gaily as though it were made of paper and quite empty.

After a short while he stopped, and looked sideways beneath his lashes. He began to laugh and laugh. But Daihachi guessed this was no laughing matter—this child was *too* unusual! With deep respect, and some fear also, he asked, "Who are you?" The words stuttered on his tongue.

"*My* name?" asked the boy indifferently, moving from between the shafts, "Never ask it! But you, Daihachi—yes, I do know yours—listen: you're proud, and smart under humiliation, for you know yourself to be superior, a man of strength watched over by a Kami—*you've* not yet been beaten in the contests at the festivals! But, my Daihachi, don't be self-satisfied: so far, even your strength's nothing to what it could be—" Then, drawing himself up while the lineaments of his face radiated pride and graciousness as though lit from other worlds, the boy added, "If you want to be truly great in strength, and aid the Kami with your fullest powers, then you must come first to *me*. To me, Daihachi, secretly, by night. Only on Mount Taihei will you find my home."

Daihachi turned yet paler than his terrible exertions had already made him. He knew now who stood there and spoke

46

to him with mixed sternness and tenderness: renowned
Sankichi, most famous and awe-inspiring of the deities!
Afraid to look again, he flung himself at the god's feet in
self-abasement. Sankichi vanished. There was left only a
sound of joyous, bubbling laughter borne on the pine-
scented wind, and something like a swift breeze rippled the
face of the deep river before it blew itself away behind the
woods. The trembling Daihachi slowly raised himself
again, and began to pull the cart uphill.

The castle of Akita seemed to be in turmoil. People were
running to and fro like startled geese. The old Daimyo's
land tax, and the peasant who carted it, were roughly
shouldered on one side as a company of samurai rode past.
Their armour, wrought in shape and colour to make an
enemy afraid, might have scared any foe to death. But
Daihachi, still marvelling at his encounter with the deity,
felt that no samurai could even make him cringe. Among
these warriors rode powerful Akita's lord, carried in a litter—
its curtains drawn aside. The agitated flutter of his fan was
more expressive than the angry looks of his followers, as he
leaned forward and cried to their commander: "He does
this to make us all lose face! Now Yokho is so ill, how can I
find a wrestler strong enough and skilled enough to fight
the lord of Iso's wrestler on the feast of compassionate
Kannon? Why else has he issued this challenge now, except
that he has heard of Yokho's state?" Then the litter was
borne past, and the young commander's answer lost to
Daihachi's ears.

"Who is this lord of Iso?" he inquired.

"Ah—" replied a good-natured young steward, who stood
nearby, "only my lord's great enemy! And this *is* a challenge,
as all Akita knows. And well my lord of Iso knows of our
true Sumo champion's strange illness, or he wouldn't be so
bold! Now—come with me: I'll let you have some proof of
having brought your own Daimyo's land tax. Then get you
home to him—for if he's a tempestuous, fiery lord, he'll
stripe your back for having loitered here!"

Sankichi's Gift

Daihachi followed. Afterwards, he begged some small provisions, which were kindly granted him. But, instead of going home, he dodged the crowd, grasped his cart again, and pushed it unobtrusively into a deserted stall where he hoped no one would steal or notice it. Then, hardly daring to consider the consequences of his action, and his Daimyo's wrath, he set his face resolutely toward Mount Taihei.

The path led up and up, winding through endless groves of mountain shrubs, some bright with flowers. The day grew darker, and its dwindling light lent everything an eerie, brooding strangeness that made Daihachi conscious of his solitude and what he looked on now as his small strength. The scent of flowers was very strong, as though something drew added sweetness from the earth. His spirit was awe-struck. A sense of threat, a sense of holiness—these lower flanks of mountain held them both. He looked upward to where the lovely peak of Mount Taihei rose clear above the pines, its pale tip reaching toward skies of deep, unearthly blue. All was very still.

To many woodcutters these secret, lonely woods held tabu: they used special language when they came here, so that no casually-used word should cause offence. Kappa and tengu, those mischievous—often lethal!—spirits of the landscape, could well haunt this place. Daihachi shivered, stoutly reminded himself of his own guardian Kami, and strode on upwards, determined not to fear.

At last he saw the carved roofs of the shrine, with its lacquered vermilion and gilded eaves spread outward like protecting hands beneath the darkening sky. The many lanterns, which worshippers had given to the shrine as votive offerings, were already lit. A gilded cockerel spread his wings upon one roof beam, and a phoenix on another. Both were sacred to that Heaven Shining Great August Deity: the Sun. Daihachi felt even smaller than he had before, for all his bulging muscles. What worthy offering could *he* bring to Sankichi? A receptive heart?

Sankichi's Gift

He entered the shrine's enclosure, and put some rice—from the small store that Akita's steward had allowed him—in a carved jade bowl placed ready for the purpose. He took a stick of incense, lit it from a lantern, and let the fragrant smoke curl heavenward as he cried aloud, "Great Sankichi! I am here—"

No one answered him. There was no boyish laughter, no sudden terrible appearance of the god—in a celestial form or any other. There was only a deepened and accepting silence. Daihachi remained reverently bowed to the ground, but the only signs of life were the glowing pulsing flames of the great lanterns overhead. At this mountain height the air was bitterly cold. The floor seemed to grow colder and colder beneath his knees as he worshipped there. All night he tried to hold constantly in mind the remembrance of Sankichi's promise. But at last dawn came, painting the mountain's summit with fire colours, and still no god had moved or spoken.

For seven days and nights Daihachi lived about the shrine: worshipping, wandering in its precincts, watching its guardian come to light the lanterns. He lived off palmfuls of rice, and icy water from the nearby stream. Dreadful doubts started to assail him: had he been deluded by exhaustion, and imagined that Sankichi had once drawn his cart? He had risked everything to come here, and began to wish he hadn't—for he seemed likely to receive as payment the lash, torture and the young lords' scorn. He must have been unfortunate enough to meet a demon who had dared to use Sankichi's name!

Then he would burn more incense, and pray, "O heavenly one, beloved Sankichi, fulfil the promise that you made to your unworthy servant on Akita's path!" But all he heard was the stream bubbling and singing to itself nearby. The shrine's vermilion eaves dripped moisture. The Heaven Shining Great August Deity sank low behind Mount Taihei on the evening of the seventh day.

It was now even colder up here than it had been at first.

49

The peak shimmered in the dusk as though someone had outlined it with frost. Daihachi hugged himself, and stamped his feet. He couldn't get warm. His round, cheerful face was gaunt with tiredness. As daylight waned, the sadness of betrayal waxed in him.

Tomorrow I'll return home for my punishment . . .

The thought was bitter as the thought of death.

For the last time he went to stand before Sankichi's shrine. He bowed his forehead to his hands. The corner of his eye caught a movement, then the flutter of a skirt. He started, and turned to find another worshipper beside him: a young woman. Her face glimmered pale in the strange evening light. She looked thin, and almost exhausted. To her breast she clutched a bundle, wrapped in dirty cloth. Something inside it stirred, then gave out wails as piercing as the cold. The woman, murmuring, pulled back the cloth. Two slanting eyes peered up hungrily towards Daihachi. The baby wailed again.

His mother jogged him desperately in her thin arms, then kneeled, holding him against her. She bowed herself near to the ground as possible. While she worshipped, the child made little moping sounds, and two small, surprisingly energetic fists fought with the cloth. Daihachi gazed in some perplexity. He pitied the pathetic travellers, wondering why such a frail young woman should have braved the mountain paths on this bitter night. Perhaps she urgently wanted a blessing for the child—perhaps it didn't thrive. It would thrive less if it caught cold!

At last the young woman rose clumsily to her feet, and smiled at him with a timid air. She would have been beautiful, if she weren't so hungry looking. When she spoke her voice was low and clear: "Fellow worshipper of great Sankichi, may I ask a favour of you?"

"If you need food, I've none to give," replied Daihachi; awkwardness made his voice sound rough. "My last grains of rice have gone."

"Yes, I'm hungry—though not for food! I ask only for a

kindness." She held out the baby. "Nurse him for me, while I enter the shrine to pray and offer incense to the god?"

"Willingly I'll hold him—but you trust strangers readily! How do you know I'm not some wicked robber who'll vanish with your child?"

She smiled. "By your face! I was watching you for some time, from the woods. A man so devoted to Sankichi wouldn't do me wrong—"

"Alas, the god has failed me!" said Daihachi, with a bitter laugh. "I've lost everything by coming here. May *you* have better fortune at the shrine, and answer to your prayers. Come, baby—" He held out his arms.

She gave him the bundle, crooning over it, and arranging folds of cloth to keep the baby warm. It ceased crying, and its eyes looked wonderingly into Daihachi's face. "There!" he said, rocking it a little. He was accustomed to nurse the children of the Daimyo's household, and had a way with them. "There, little one! Quietly, till your mother comes again—" The baby's face crumpled into what might have been a responsive smile. It seemed placid enough at the exchange. Not had cause yet to distrust the world, thought Daihachi grimly.

The young woman smiled her thanks, and slipped into the shrine. He stood there a long while, holding the child close, and feeling its warmth against his chest. At first the baby made sucking noises, and then closed his eyes and fell asleep. Daihachi shifted from one foot to the other. His situation was mildly ridiculous, to say the least. He shut *his* eyes, and thought about Sankichi. He prayed, although now it seemed so hopeless. Gradually the moon rose high above Mount Taihei and—as always happened here at night—the flower scents grew very strong. Still the young woman stayed within the shrine.

Daihachi opened his eyes; his thoughts had begun to wander. He was amazed to see how far the moon had risen already—time must have passed quicker than he thought. That young woman was a fervent worshipper! He hoped *she* didn't mean to pray for seven days and seven nights . . .

He shifted the baby from his left arm to his right. Soon he moved it back again, for it seemed to weigh heavier and heavier.

Ah! That young demon who deceived me on the road knew too much of me! A wrestler who can't even hold a child for any length of time without wanting to drop it is unfit to speak of Sumo! But truly, *this* child weighs like a stone . . . it must be sleep that makes him feel so heavy: he's relaxed. But could that make such a difference?

Once more he moved the child from left to right; and glanced hopefully toward the shrine. Would she never come?

Light from the great lanterns flared in a sudden icy wind. Daihachi began to feel quite desperate. It was hard to keep his mind on his own problems. His arms tingled to the shoulders, and one of them had cramp. The sleeping babe seemed to weigh more and more. Should he enter the shrine to find the mother, or would that wake the child? When at last he made up his mind, and crept inside, no one was there, though he heard slight movement in an outer court.

Poor girl, perhaps her husband's left her! Perhaps she's desperate to pray all night . . . Yes, that's why she hides from me. Well, I mustn't blunder in, I must be patient; after all, it doesn't really hurt me!

He called softly, "I'll hold him till you're ready, though at dawn I have to go . . ." and went back outside, where he resumed his position as before. Once the child opened his eyes and moped a little, making soft, gurgling, hungry sounds. He didn't cry, and eventually went to sleep again. Daihachi, cradling him in both arms, tried a gentle rocking movement, but beneath the baby's weight his arms were forced low as his own waist, and sweat poured down his face even though the night seemed colder still. How his wrists ached! Cautiously he lowered one knee to the ground, and balanced his burden on the other: *that* was better . . .

But soon the baby felt even heavier upon his knee, which ached worse than his wrists. Daihachi flexed his tremendous muscles and tried to forget his cramp. He transferred the child to the other knee. Quite soon that was worse! Was there no way to hold him that was comfortable? He was amazed. Within the heavy folds of cloth this baby must be far larger than it seemed—it weighed more and more, like some great stone.

My knees will break! thought Daihachi desperately. Sankichi, great deity, have you eaten that young worshipper? Does she still pray—or has she abandoned us? He was sweating now not just from effort, but from fear. Was he to be landed with this child, as well as with his own bad situation? His muscles strained, his mind grew blank with effort; pain in his arms and legs mounted alarmingly. Sweat rolled off his forehead in such large drops that they fell upon the child like dew. All the time it lay there so peacefully, its eyes shut and its button nose blue with cold. The sight held pathos, though Daihachi was unaware of it— he was only conscious of grinding his teeth, and that his eyes were surely starting from his head, the bones in his legs about to break.

He thought, I can't ... can't ... *can't* support this. Yet ... must. Promised ... Ahhh—we're both falling—

He felt his knees start to give way. Pain of sustained effort swamped him. Blood throbbed against his eardrums. The child's extraordinary, unimaginable weight was overwhelming him ... Daihachi gave a strangled cry.

There was sudden movement from the direction of the shrine. The flutter of a sleeve. The young woman came running, breathless and apologetic. "Kindly one! I've kept you waiting long ... Does he sleep?" Anxiously she held out her arms, and took the child as though it weighed no more than paper. She stood there smiling at Daihachi, who was bowed, gasping, to the ground.

She stood like a slender willow twig which didn't even bend. The exhausted, stupefied Daihachi stared up at her. She shone with light—it grew and grew and grew, just as the baby's weight had grown and grown. Mother and child

D

were bathed in strange streamers of radiance. From the centre of this light, which was both awesome and magnetic, he heard a clear voice saying, "You who thought Sankichi had deserted you! Know that you've seen me here, the most high deity and protecting spirit of these regions. Yes—I'm Sankichi Daimyojin! All night, Daihachi, you've bravely endured this test of keeping the child safe. You suffered much until your own strength foundered—but I've told you once already that it was as nothing to what you could possess. You've deserved fulfilment of my promise: from this night on, know your strength limitless!"

Daihachi could barely speak. He threw himself down in adoration, murmuring broken words of thanks, and sorrow for his unbelief. At last he dared to raise his head. On the air was sketched a faint glow of the former radiance. It faded. Mother and child had gone.

When dawn came he went down the sacred mountain. The air was pure, ice-cold, and the sun's flaming disk touched the tip of Mount Taihei to a cap of fire. The pines' dark needles shone with depths of green. To Daihachi's eyes the budding shrubs and flowers, and the birds, looked joyous as he felt. Strength flowed through him—he felt strong enough to shake the Mount itself. Once he looked back over his shoulder and saw his own footprints were carved deep into the soil behind him. It was as though a great hammer in each foot had almost pierced the rock.

"Ahhh—" growled the old Daimyo, grinding his teeth when messengers brought him news of how his runaway servant had wrestled for Akito's lord, and thrown the lord of Iso's wrestler, and won himself renown. "*That* villain! Send to my feudal overlord, and ask him to return my servant, as is lawful. I'll have Daihachi beaten till he begs to die." But, while his messengers were still upon the road, he realised what men might think and say of a Daimyo who wouldn't honour Sumo; and when Daihachi stood unhappily before him, welcomed him with a cunning smile.

"What rare flowers lie hidden in the shadow of a pine—my son!"

Daihachi could only blink sheepishly, and wonder what was coming next.

The mean old lord rubbed his hands together, within the long sleeves of his robe. "But we always said it here. *We* knew it—service, then glory! Unshackle him!" When Daihachi stood there free, he added, "We ourselves will be your patron, and spend rice for you to go to Edo, where you'll win favour for us all from gods and men."

And so it happened: even the precious Son of Heaven honoured the poor boy who became great in Sumo—the greatest wrestler in Japan. The mean Daimyo learned to enjoy reflected glory, and basked in it like an old frog basking slimily in the hot sun. But the young lord felt shamed, and killed himself with his own sword. The whole village rejoiced when Daihachi ended as his rich patron's heir.

Sun and Moon are Different People

꙰

Ki lived on Kiwai; it was the centre of the world. When the initiation ceremonies rocked the ceremonial house he was filled with awe and wonder that someone like himself had come from the race of the crocodile father. He would look round him at the bush, the swamps, the beach, and think: yes, Ki is here; that is what it's all about—a place for Ki. Yet there was plenty of reason still to be uneasy. It was not even very safe to be Ki, in case someone came in a canoe and took your head for the building of a new ceremonial house elsewhere. Then there were spirits in two-headed snakes or lizards. Ki often felt safer after the *Horiomu*, annual ghost pantomime, had taken place. It meant that the ghosts knew where they were, just as Ki often felt he knew where he was —till something unsettled him again.

Ki sighed. If only he could have been the great hero Marunogere. What a great one! He who had taught men how to build themselves ceremonial houses, and had instituted the *moguru*: the life-giving ceremony which could make men noted fighters. Suddenly Ki felt small and insecure. *He* was no great fighter: no great anything! He had only just survived the initiation trials without disgrace. When he had embraced a young girl, she had laughed. The memory of her laugh could still make Ki sweat all down his spine.

He was remembering, when Kardabo came down to the beach and stood staring out to sea, hands on hips. Ki pretended not to see him. During initiation Kardabo's weight had crushed the *Kaiaimunu*—a monster formed of wickerwork—without help from a contemptuous adult hand. Later, no girl had laughed at him when the long house rocked to tribal love-making. So Ki pretended not to see Kardabo now; he too stared out at the horizon.

Kardabo turned his head. The piece of slit bone in his flaring nostrils seemed to point jeeringly at Ki.

"One man does not quarrel!" said Kardabo softly. "It is two men who quarrel."

"Why should two men quarrel?" asked Ki; staring at the horizon. He felt Ki's place in the world start to shrink.

Kardabo shrugged. His white teeth showed in the moonlight. "Spirits quarrel. Ancestors quarrel. Tribes quarrel. Women quarrel!" He picked his teeth with a sliver of bamboo. Then his head turned towards Ki again, who felt the sweat trickle down his spine, and his place in the world grow smaller still. "Kambini is worth a quarrel," added Kardabo, looking—he, too—towards the horizon.

Kambini! So that was it. Ki's place shrank till it was no more than the beach he sat on. Kambini was the young girl who had laughed at him; the girl his mother's brother had intended for Ki's wife.

"I do not want to quarrel with anyone!" said Ki, and knew he had put himself hopelessly in the wrong.

"Not about Kambini?"

"No." He had no place in the world now. Not even the damp beach he sat on.

Kardabo was silent for a time. His shadow looked black and menacing, his outline arrogant. He laughed. He said, "I will give her yams, and fruit. She will bring me pigs. We will eat coconuts and cucumbers. Our children shall wear the crescent ornament of pearl."

That Kardabo should talk of Kambini and his children, when she was almost Ki's! At last Ki's anger rose enough to make his world-place seem possible again.

"I do not quarrel but—Kambini is mine."

"You will not quarrel for her? And she laughed! So— what will you quarrel for, Ki? Tell me, are sun and moon

57

one person—or two people? I say they are one, as Kardabo and Kambini shall be!"

"They are two!" said Ki, but breathless. "Two! As Kardabo and Kambini are."

"One! Everyone knows—except stupid clumsy Ki!—that sun and moon are the same person."

Ki got up, agitatedly. He forgot his fear. He said, "My mother's brother, and my father, have always said sun and moon are two separate persons! Look—there is the moon, now. He is one person: Ganumi, the moon. How is he the sun as well?"

Kardabo's bone-piece quivered. He said, "I do not argue. I fight." He turned and fell on Ki, without warning, panting with rage, dark muscular arms bulging with his hate. Ki was much smaller, and less strong, but he could move his feet very fast, and when he did overcome his fear he fought like a male wallaby fighting another for a mate. All the same, Kardabo's weight told, and he trounced Ki up and down the beach till he tripped on a turtle shell and crumpled on his face. Then Kardabo hit him, and kicked him, and picked up a sharp stone and made a cut right down his shoulder; and then, with one furious last kick, walked off saying, "Sun and moon *is* one person! This is what I now teach Kambini . . . Gardener! Not fit to fight or fish! Go and put sago milk on your face, and sit with women . . ." His taunts could still be heard as he disappeared towards the village.

Ki lay there, very miserable. Hurt and hating. He thought of his friends receiving Kardabo in the village. How they would laugh! Secretly they would be for the great fighter, for he who made an impression. After a time he sat up. There were tears on his face, but no one to see them. He looked at his canoe, drawn up safely on the beach. He had carved its prow himself—Marunogere should be the protector spirit of the canoe. He had thought much of Marunogere as he carved it, and though it had little form *he* knew it for Marunogere his particular hero and his friend. He went down to the canoe, and pushed it into the water.

Sun and Moon are Different People

Marunogere—I am going! Going to the moon's own land. I will learn the truth . . . I will prove to Kardabo that moon and sun are two people.

He paddled and paddled. Sometimes he stopped paddling and played his drum, while the canoe rocked on the waves. He saw a great shark's fin here and there, and coral islands. He ate yams and sago and once or twice caught a young turtle. Still he paddled on. A long, long while it took Ki from Kiwai to find the moon's own land. Then at last he drifted in towards sandy beaches as white as picked bone, lit by a subdued white light much paler and weaker than the sun's light. The tide was low, and the sea motionless—so near the moon it seemed at peace. A good place, thought Ki. Why didn't crocodile father make his children in a place so calm? Still, here at last Ki was, and now he would see Ganumi on his own lands. He sat in his canoe, and waited.

Presently, in the far distance, he saw a very small luminous form coming towards him. By now Ki had been at sea so long that the moon had grown to his full age, and died, and been reborn again. So here was Ganumi, very small and young, and without much light.

Ki and Ganumi looked at one another.

"Who are you?" asked the little boy.

"I am Ki; I have come to put a question to Ganumi."

The boy smiled, and a ray of light shot from his teeth and made a path across the waves. Not a large path, for he was not yet grown. "I'm Ganumi! I'm so pleased to see a stranger in my lands after all this time! I am always chasing the sun around the sky, but I've never caught up yet. Come —land! I will show you all my home."

But Ki looked sideways at him. He was *very* small. Much, much smaller than Ki when he had endured those humiliations in the ceremonial house. Ki didn't know where he had landed, but he told himself: This cannot be Ganumi.

He stretched out flat in his canoe, so that only his head showed above its side, and said in an affronted voice, "I do not come to jest, only to find truth. If Ganumi the moon asks me ashore, I shall come, but not till then. Is it even sure this is his home?"

The small boy danced up and down on the beach, and cold light streamed in rays around him. He bent slightly sideways as he danced, almost a crescent shape. "Ki, Ki! Can't you see that I'm Ganumi? I am, I am, I am the moon."

Ki snorted, and pictured himself arrogant and aloof like Kardabo. The bit of bone in his nose quivered as Kardabo's had quivered on the beach at Kiwai. "How is this? Is a child large enough to light the sky?"

Then Ganumi turned very sadly and went back up the beach. Ki ate a yam, and went to sleep.

Some days later, towards evening, Ki was still stubbornly sitting in his canoe, when he saw light shining inland. Soon a young man appeared with a broad, luminous smile. His teeth flashed; streams of light spread across the darkening sea, and made paths of silver dance up and down upon the wavecrests.

"Ah!" said Ki disdainfully, seeing himself as bold and arrogant Kardabo, "You've come to tell me you're Ganumi? Well, *I* know what Ganumi looks like, I've studied him night after night when he's full, and when he's old in the heavens. Everyone knows that the farthest part of our dark sky is nothing but a thatched roof, which anyone can climb. Often I've watched Ganumi—old, old Ganumi—climb there when he wills!" The young man ceased smiling, shook his head sadly, and went back up the beach. Ki caressed the carved form of Marunogere, and murmured, "He thought he could fool *us*!" His thin dark brown chest swelled with pride. He slept.

Several times while Ki sat stubbornly in his canoe, feasting frugally off yams and sago and turtle flesh, he had a visitor. An older man, a middle-aged man, an ageing man. "I am Ganumi!" said each of these to him in turn, but each time Ki shook his head most firmly, and said, "I know Ganumi—he is not like you." Then at last, just as he was growing sick of yam and turtle without even coconut to vary things, he looked up and saw, coming down the pale coral beach of this quiet land, an ancient man with snowy hair; he had an air of pride and leaned heavily on a carved white staff. He gave out little light, but Ki knew him at once, and eagerly stood upright to address him: "Welcome, Ganumi! Welcome, true moon I've waited for so long. How happy I am to see Ganumi the real moon at last!"

The old man coughed. He replied reedily, with some show of crossness, "Eh, ugh, stupid one from far Kiwai! Night after night I have looked down and seen your homeland, where they all bewail you, thinking you eaten by sharks or carried off by a sea ghost. Yet I, *I* kept my own counsel— though I saw you here when I was young, and middle-aged, and elderly. *Now* will you believe me when I say that I'm Ganumi? Will you come ashore?"

"At once," said Ki hurriedly, somewhat ashamed of himself. He was glad Kambini wasn't there to laugh while he humbly followed Ganumi up the beach. It was shadowy, for Ganumi's white hair gave out very little light, and he had lost all his sparkling teeth. He was bent into a thin crescent shape and at first moved with difficulty, then with spryer steps as he took Ki into his own house and proudly indicated first this and then that one of his belongings.

"Don't you have any coloured things?"

Ganumi looked at Ki as though he were mad. "I, the moon? How could I swallow anything but the whitest of white food? Or grow anything but white flowers? Or live in a *coloured* house? I would turn it white at once!" He added, "Come, and let me show you what everything looks like when it is Duo's!" Now Duo is the night; black night.

So Ganumi took Ki to a part of the land where they could see nothing at all. Ki kept stumbling, and couldn't see night's house, which was so black it was invisible. He could smell the flowers but couldn't see them, and smell the food— delicious!—but could find none to eat since it was so dark. "And you can see nothing of Duo himself, even when he's in his house," said Ganumi. "There are times when he's too dark for me to light him—we've almost reached one of those times now." He gave a yawn, and a weak ray of light came from his throat. Ki became afraid, in case he couldn't see to reach his beached canoe again.

But the moon was still stronger than he looked, and leaning ever more crescent-shaped upon his staff, led Ki towards the farthest point of land. There was nothing dark here: it was all gold, and blazing red and orange, tawny in a way to make Ki wonder. He said "Ahhhhh!" and held out his arms, for warmth. Ganumi seemed piqued, and said, "Well—it's not so wonderful as all that, is it? This part is the sun's. Come—let us return to my house, with its more natural light."

Seeing he had offended, Ki followed humbly. They ate white fish with white cucumber, and poured dazzling milk from moon coconuts. "I must go now," said Ganumi. "Wait here for me, Ki. It's time I went up in that sky, for the sun is coming down."

He jumped. He had to jump several times, being old, before he left the ground and sailed up into the sky; yet he managed somehow, and perched uneasily on a low cloud, where he lay sideways, almost on his back. At once the heavens lightened, the seas silvered, and Ganumi on his cloud was reflected in its rippling surface. Ki sat there on the beach all night, looking up at his new friend; and hoped he wouldn't die on this sky journey. Now and then he fingered his nose-bone, and felt great new strength, and self-possession. It was certain now that Kardabo could be wrong! "Ganumi is not the sun! The sun is someone entirely separate . . ." he said aloud.

At daybreak he saw the sun leap off the land so swiftly that the running golden legs went like a wheel and seemed a ball of flame. Some while afterwards Ganumi, looking more bent and tired than before, came limping down the sky and landed, barely silvering the sea at all and causing only slight reflections on the prow of Ki's canoe.

"Come now, Ki! You can be foolish, but your villagers

are sometimes foolish too. Help yourself to these white cucumbers which I will give you, and borrow black yams from the night, and tawny-yellow turtle from the sun. If your friends are so foolish they need proof that sun, moon and night are different beings, take them proof." Ganumi hobbled to a white carved box, and drew out a long white rope.

"Here, Ki—" he was knotting a loop of it round his own waist—"take hold of that end of my rope—So! Now, when you're back in your canoe I'll cross the sky again and draw you home. Your island is a long way off: you came from far to find me—in return I'll take you back. But remember, tug your end once you reach Kiwai, or I shall sail serenely on and take you far beyond the islands—"

"To where the sky is thatched?" asked Ki innocently; but Ganumi only smiled, and kept his own wise counsel on the nature of things above.

As night fell, Ganumi made his tottery leap upward once again. Ki, who had settled himself in readiness behind his Marunogere prow, watched the old moon's painful rising to the evening cloud. He felt a jerk on the rope's end, and held it very fast. The canoe swung sideways to the waves and almost foundered, but righted itself plungingly and, drawn by Ganumi, swept across the sea and underwater coral reefs so fast that white fountains sprang from beneath it, and the wake was cut clean on the sea's night-green and silver surface as though with a great dual-bladed spear.

Ki's hands blistered; now and then he feared to rise straight up out of the canoe. He leaned forward, and took a turn of the rope right round Marunogere, and so, fast bound to the great culture hero he admired, came safely home.

It was almost daylight when he saw the line of surf breaking on Kiwai's beach, and Ganumi was ready to totter feebly down the sky. Ki looked up, and there were two birds of paradise flying overhead, with their long tail-feathers flitter-fluttering like bits of seaweed in a strong offshore current. His canoe grounded gently, and as it did

63

so he gave a shout, and a tremendous tug on his rope's end.

Then he raised his eyes shorewards. It was black with his own people! His friends were there, and Kardabo, and Kambini—who stood well apart from one another. All were staring at Ki in awestruck silence, and then upward at Ganumi; their eyes followed the long white snakiness of the rope which held Ki's canoe to the old crescent moon.

Ki pretended indifference to the sensation he was causing, and paid his people no attention whatsoever. As though absent-mindedly he grunted a few words of a hunting song to himself while he took out the strange-coloured food from his canoe. He felt almost as though he and his shadow had grown in size while he was away: as though Ki's place in the world was now larger, and secure.

Kambini was waiting for him as he stepped ashore. Her long hair was wet with spray. She held up her hands and exclaimed, "Ki! White—white food!"

"That's what Ganumi eats," said Ki carelessly, placing the white cucumbers in her hands. "And this—this black yam I hold belongs to night itself. But the gold and tawny food—*that* is of the sun." He looked round him almost insolently, and the slant of his nose-bone was as arrogant as it could be.

"Great fighter!" he said to Kardabo, who stood some paces off—and his intonation was yet more insolent—"Will you take the sun's own food ashore—?" He held out the turtle. "The sun—who is one different person from the moon?" He flung the golden turtle straight and unexpectedly at Kardabo, who had hard work to catch it in time; even so, the shell's edge scored his chest.

Ki kept the black yam in one hand. With the other he untied the white rope from the Marunogere prow—his canoe was already tugging as though it wanted to go on out to sea. "This belongs to my friend, Ganumi! See—now he takes it back into the sky! Kind Ganumi who has brought me home before the *second person* has mounted to the sky!"

"Ahhhhhh!" sighed the villagers, open-mouthed, as they

turned their faces up to watch the rope's end twisting and twining like a fast-vanishing tail of white snake flicking up into the blue, where Ganumi waited to wind it round his waist, and then limp home to his white land.

Ki also watched it go. Afterwards, he took hold of his canoe, gave a great heave, and beached it. All his movements were slow, deliberate; very much those of a man who knows what he is about.

Someone standing farther up the beach began a rhythmic clapping of his palms. Others joined in. Some children picked up shells and banged them eagerly together. Soon all the people were drumming and clapping in a rhythmic language which meant, "Ki—welcome, Ki! Great man, great visitor to the one and only moon Ganumi—welcome to Kiwai."

Ki didn't look at Kambini as he walked up the beach among his swaying, drumming, clapping friends, but as he passed her he took her hand roughly to pull her after him. The crowd scattered then, to let him through. Kardabo stood at the very edge of the pathway, but Ki looked him indifferently in the eyes and walked by, Kambini stumbling after him with her head bent. He walked with her into the forest. They were there all day.

No Ganumi rose that night: he was very tired, resting till he grew small again. By the light of fires and torches the villagers feasted Ki, and danced in his honour. The white moon food, the black night food, and the gold sun food were divided into many little bits and passed round so that everyone could taste a piece. The sound of flutes and gongs grew and grew, while inside the ceremonial house the bullroarers began to groan and rattle as though many spirit monsters fought there. Coconuts were shaken from the palms and banged to the ground, loosened by the vibrations of rocking feet, and the tremendous din.

Ki looked about him, at the men who honoured him; at his father, and his mother's brother, who wore complacent, proprietary smiles. He felt his chest expand. He gazed at the white food, and the golden, and laughed in Kardabo's face. He took a piece of the black yam, the food of the night, and crumbled it into his hand and Kambini's. He felt himself a man. He stood up, and drew her after him into the deep shade of the trees. There he lay down beside her, and his hands gently explored her face. Her full lips quivered.

"It is not moon and sun who are one person, Kambini! But it is black, black night which makes one person out of two. And I have come back to tell you so."

The Cockleshell

It was during the dancing at a tribal gathering that Tahito
fell in love with Tao-putaputa; but though he was young
and strong and handsome, he was shy. He couldn't tell her
how he felt. So he went home to his own place at Kaiti,
walked with the young warriors, and spoke of fights and
fishing; but he left his heart behind him at Opape.

All day long he thought of Tao. What forest paths and
distance lay between them now! What separate future might
not claim her before they met again! She might even die . . .
Then he would find himself thinking of the god-like Maui:
he who had tried to vanquish death—and failed. O Maui,
why didn't you overcome the dreadful goddess Hìne-nui-
te-po—she who brings death to men? Why did the little
fantail have to laugh and wake her—terrible ogress with
sharkteeth and flashing eyes!—just as you entered her to
steal her heart? Maui, you were great indeed till by your
death you brought disaster on us all.

He couldn't sleep at night for thinking that Hine-nui-te-
po might pounce on Tao-putaputa and extinguish her.
Death is jealous! And he thought more sadly still of the
unlucky Maui's final adventure. Yet some people say that
you were stupid, Maui . . . that you offended the fantail first,
and that is why . . . Had I been you . . .

His thoughts trailed away. He slept uneasily, and dreamed
of dancing opposite to Tao-putaputa. Then the wistful
dream became entangled with another one of legendary
Hine-mokemoke, "the lonely girl", who used to sing eerily
from the bottom of the sea. Hine-mokemoke was a cockle-

shell, and she was caught by a cray fisherman. She had clung to his basket, and had sung so strangely and so sorrowfully that that was how she got her name. People said she was a *tipua*—demon-haunted. He woke, still thinking of the cockleshell.

If only I could sing like Hine-mokemoke! My song would go straight to Tao-putaputa's heart. I never spoke to her— but I could sing to her. I would sing until she came to me.

Then he longed to be Tawhaki—divine Tawhaki, who was said to be a man and yet a god. He longed and longed to be someone more effective than himself.

A flock of kaka flew over his head: gaudy and noisy parrots, bright and quick. He followed listlessly in the direction of their flight, down to the beach.

The cockles that Tahito knew as pipi were lying here and there, half-buried in the sand. He was so lovesick that he pretended one of them might turn out to be another magical Hine-mokemoke. She would teach him to sing.

"Come, Hine—" He scooped a little one out of the sand, and dangled it before his eyes. "Show me! Better still, go yourself to Tao! Take her my message—say I die unless she comes to me."

So he whispered like a madman to the shellfish, holding it close and closer to his face, and finally pressing it against his cheek. Then he waded far out into the surf and cast the living pipi from him. When he turned shoreward again he shook his head wryly at his fantasies. The beach at Opape was very far away!

But the little pipi was filled with love now, and a sense of mission. She didn't stop to sing like Hine-mokemoke, but hurried through the water. No wave was too high, nor any enemy too strong, to deter her. Tahito's passion drove her in the right direction. At last she reached the Bay of Plenty and landed at Opape. Then she trembled in case the wrong person should find her, pick her up, and eat her; and she crept into a patch of sand and half hid herself, and waited.

Tao-putaputa soon came scouring the beach for cockles.

She came with her companions, but wandered off alone—for she was often sad these days, she didn't quite know why. She had felt oddly sad ever since the tribal dancing. As though she missed something, and everything that had been colourful and full of joy was dull and grey. At night she dreamed of Tahito, but by day could put no name to the need that haunted her sleep. She was just confused. As for the man she dreamed of—where had she seen him in the flesh?

Her companions were calling, "Tao-putaputa! Where are you going?" as she walked farther off. She pretended not to hear them, and searched diligently for bigger and bigger pipi. But whenever she tried to pick up larger shells she found a little pipi in the way. She pushed it aside.

"Little pipi are no good," she said aloud. "They do not make a meal. Oh—who would eat, if they were dull and lonely as I am?" She put her hand down to a big fat pipi—and found herself picking up the little one again.

So it went on all the time. She would walk away and bend over a big shell, only to find the little pipi just in front of it. The pipi seemed to move about the beach! It drove her mad.

"Isn't it bad enough to be unhappy, without being pestered by a pipi?" Soon she was really angry. She seized the pipi, meaning to throw it out to sea—*that* might relieve her feelings . . .

No . . . it wouldn't. It wouldn't relieve them nearly enough. She was suffering. Oh—she wanted to make someone else suffer. Someone—she couldn't imagine who. The pipi would do instead.

She declared, between fine pearly teeth, "O pipi, you are no good for anything at all! I will annoy you, as you annoy me. *That* will teach you to get in the way of good stout pipi which could make a meal!"

She scraped together driftwood and dried seaweed, and made a little fire. The pipi watched her in alarm, but staunchly made no effort to retreat.

Tao took hold of the shell almost gently, stroked it, and said involuntarily, "O! If you were only—" and then very

69

E

angrily and suddenly she set it down right by the fire, and said, "Now—see what happens to you, for so tormenting me!"

The poor little pipi felt its shell starting to strain and break apart. Cowering within, it began to make unhappy sounds, and then, as the heat of Tahito's passion met the heat of the fire, it started to sing enchantingly even in the middle of its suffering. It sang of Tahito and all he felt for Tao. While the heat grew and the shell opened wider so the pipi's voice grew stronger, its words more eloquent, and the power of its melodic invention more intense.

Tao-putaputa sank down upon the sand in wonder. As she listened to the song about Tahito and heard his name constantly repeated she knew at last why she felt so dull and sad. Her confusion cleared. And now she could put a name to the face that haunted every dream of hers! For she knew where she had seen Tahito—at the tribal dancing; he had danced opposite her once, and then shyly gone away.

The pipi was singing now of how Tahito had been too shy to come and find her for himself. It sang of how he pined at Titiranga. Tao was seized with remorse for her cruel treatment of the cockleshell. Her happiness to hear of Tahito's longing made her eager to be kind. She doused the fire with sand.

"Cockleshell—my little pipi! You bring me life—and I've tormented you. How faithfully you followed me about the beach, while I didn't understand, and only hurt you in my temper! See—I make amends." She left the shell to cool, and went away to fetch a piece of flax. When she returned she threaded the little pipi on it, and placed it carefully around her neck.

How the other girls laughed to see her new decoration:

"Tao-putaputa loves a cockleshell!" But she paid them no attention. She was aware only that far away in Titiranga a lovelorn Tahito was thinking of her. Quickly, quickly— she told herself—Tao must go to join Tahito. She found herself dreading that his heart would grow cold towards her if he were long snared in hopelessness; then some woman of his own tribe might snare *him*.

All the while, as the shell lay snug in the hollow of her neck, it poured out the sighs and yearning of Tahito. At night Tao couldn't rest, for the shell, nestling closer, was a constant reminder of his need and his despair. And it sang softly even in its sleep.

A day passed, and another night—and then Tao could no longer bear her suspense and her separation from Tahito. The old women of the tribe were calling the unmarried girls to come and help them with a meal they were preparing.

"*I* go to the beaches, for some kuku and more cockles!" she cried out; while no one watched, she ran into the forest.

Her heart beat fast—for it was a long journey, this one that she had undertaken, and an arduous one that women seldom made alone. Deep gorges cut the forest path, her hands and feet were scraped as she climbed through them. But, if she faltered, the pipi hanging at her throat reminded her of Tahito. She stroked the fanshaped shell, and was heartened, and set out again. The sudden cries of kaka overhead would often make her jump, and run behind a tree. That night the ruru's call terrified her—she slept with her hands covering her ears; and when she woke she clutched the pipi, and thought about Tahito. Often she was haunted by a fear of failure.

Perhaps the cockle mocks me because I hurt it! Perhaps, when I reach Titiranga, Tahito will mock me too and turn away, and I shall see some other beauty at his side, with long long hair, and loving eyes, and flowers round her neck! Yes —they'll both mock me, and go into the woods together. Then my tribe and his will cast me off, and I shall wander all alone until I die.

By morning she was very tired, and very hungry. The sun's light, striking through the treetops, hurt her eyes. The light, shining on the river's surface, made her blink. Beyond the river was yet another forest, and farther still mountain peaks reared into the sky.

71

"Courage!" said the pipi, which felt her faltering. And it began to sing again of Tahito and his love.

Tao, who had been about to retrace her steps, was heartened. She raised her great eyes again—and saw, on the bright shimmering surface, the shadow of a man who waited half-hidden on the river's other side. Her heart beat poum-poum-poum with terror. For an instant she stood there, full in the sun's rays. Then she fled behind a tree.

Tahito, who at last had summoned up courage to come in search of Tao-putaputa, also stood aghast. Surely he had seen her where she could never be! His chief fear was realised: Hine-nui-te-po had lain in wait for her and caught her; Tao had died, and he had seen a vision of her lonely spirit, her wairua, on its way to Te Reinga.

O Tao—why did I start out on this journey that could only end in sorrow? Why was I sure that little pipi would win your heart for me?—I have come in hope, only to be faced with final despair—

He too was ready to turn back.

Yet first he stepped forward to hold out his arms supplicatingly toward the forest. "Tao, my beloved! Always you'll be the only woman in my heart! Wait for me at Te Reinga—and I will join you before you can choose between the underworlds or overworlds!"

Across the river Tao-putaputa ran from her hiding-place. Tao, real and alive, the cockle on its flax cord about her neck.

"Tahito! I am no wairua! See—I too set out desirous of our meeting"—and she added shyly, "The pipi was your messenger, its song brought me life . . ."

Then they began to ford the river, and thigh deep in water they met and clung together. Tahito touched Tao's face as though he could barely believe she was alive.

"You are as brave as faithful Hine-moa! I was afraid that Hine-nui-te-po had taken you from me forever. How filled with joy and gladness is my heart."

The Search for Little Water

A young Chief, oiled and painted for war, was running down a forest trail. He had been cut off from a War-party of his own people, but still hoped to rejoin them as they returned home after battle. The forest about him was very still, and it was midday and hot as he loped in and out of shadow. He ran as an Indian does, with delicate, sure, silent steps, and one foot planted before the other in a line straight as an arrow. It was so sultry that the Eight Thunders must have been walking somewhere in the sky country. Many people might have been drowsy from the heat, but the warrior's senses were too alert. As he ran, he noticed everything around him: what was new, and what was old. His young wife was waiting at his lodge, but he didn't think of her. He thought only of the forest; of sight or sound or movement that might betray animal or human life.

The Dew Eagle, flying far overhead, looked downward with piercing sight. He saw bright paint and bobbing scalplock below him as the runner followed the trail. Something about that agile figure was familiar. The giant bird swooped lower.

Ah, it is my friend! he thought. My friend the Hunter. He who is not greedy: who never kills for sport, nor slays the doe with fawn at foot. Yet, when he kills for food, he offers thanks to the Great Spirit, and calls both bird and animal to feast on what he sets aside . . . I am glad my friend is safe returned from battle.

He flew away.

Within the sun-streaked forest other birds, and animals,

73

looked down—or up—as their benefactor ran lightly by. A sleepy bear licked his chops reflectively, and remembered thick, sweet honey the Hunter had left him from the wild bees' nests. All the animals who saw him—skilled though the young Chief was, he did not see them all—remembered his many acts of kindness, and how his prey was always treated fairly in the chase, and none had cause to lament a needless brutality so usual in a harsh way of life.

Now the heat within the forest was even stronger: the sun seemed trapped in the tall trees. The young Chief blinked. He had been running a long while, and sweat trickled down him in gummy streams, mingled with war-paint and the blood of enemies. He ran a little slower, though his senses were just as alert as they had been. There were few birds and no unusual sounds here in the forest. The air was heavy. The Eight Thunders had gathered in the South.

From a bough a tree-cat watched him with the cold, hard glare that lynxes have. A black-and-white striped squirrel peered bright-eyed from a feathery, dark-stemmed pine. A line of huge oaks gave a pleasant, richer shade, and here the runner's feet fell on soft grass and small pale flowers. There was a scent of balsam, sweet-fern, sweet briar. The young Chief's chest heaved from his running; he slowed to a gentler lope. He was many miles now from where the furious clash had taken place, and the war-cries no longer rang so sharply in his mind. For the first time his thoughts strayed to his young wife, waiting for him in her garment of soft doe-skin. Her Corn Soup would be already boiling for the feast.

He glanced about him. The oaks had given way to bluish, short-needled pines. The sun's rays burning through between red stems caused the dusty trail to glow like yellow fog.

He was tired, now; the battle had been harsh, victory hardly won, and the running harder. Just ahead was a place where two trails met: here he hoped to see signs that might tell of his own War-party's return. Its members had last seen him grappling with three enemies, and must surely think him dead. Instead, he had taken two Cherokees' scalps with his sharp hatchet, while the other man had run away.

The hoped-for signs were there: his weary, experienced eyes saw them in the dust, estimated the number of feet. There were more than he expected (some of his companions had been killed). He was heartened, raised his head to look about him, and ran on. But he ran slower still, and as he started up a small, half-moon-shaped ravine, his senses were no longer so alert. No bird rose at his approach—which might have warned him. Who—or what—had scared them first?

At one side of the ravine, hidden by pine stump and boulder, crouched two Cherokees. They had taken the shorter trail and tailed the victorious War-party in dogged silence, determined on revenge. They had assured themselves that the young Chief wasn't with his war leaders; yet they knew him still alive. So they waited, each man with a fresh scalp dangling from his quiver. Each with merciless eyes on the narrow trail.

Now he was before them, their quarry. The War Leader leaped forward, took aim, and yelled his defiant battlecry. The hatchet blow was clumsy, yet seemed as it came no more than a blinding flash of gold ray from a forest-embedded sun. The young Chief gave a startled grunt and fell backwards, clawing with his hands. His war-paint was suddenly a patchwork of startling brightness on the sandy trail. His two enemies leaned over him, laughing, thinking there was no need to use the death-maul to smash out his brains. They scalped him, and then ran, whooping their triumph, back along the way that they had come. Their dead brothers were avenged.

Shadows began to creep among the pines, as the sun sank lower. The red-and-yellow warpaint was dulled to orange.

Blood, seeping from the young Chief's head, appeared almost black under the fierce evening rays.

There was a sound in the deep forest. A throbbing, groaning wail which rose and fell like the howling of a mighty dog, and sobbed away to silence. After a while there was a soft padding on the trail, and the gaunt, grey form of a large timberwolf appeared. He pricked his ears, drew nearer, bent his head towards the fallen warrior, and began to lick at the sinister dark pool by the head. And then—then he sat back on his haunches, pointed his muzzle skywards, and let out howl on howl of true distress: a forest version of the cry used only at the death of a Chief Sachem of the Six Nations. For he had realised whose blood he licked—it was *the* Hunter's! He who was the loved friend of the birds and animals.

So they were summoned to a Council: Bear, Beaver, Lynx, all the forest animals came to make a circle round the young Chief's body; and soon the circle was six deep, so many came. Racoons were there, and foxes; rabbits, too. Animals which preyed upon each other forgot their murderous differences in mighty grief. There were birds too, the pine tops were bent beneath their numbers. None was missing, from Oriole to Dew Eagle, Humming-bird to Heron, Owl to Crow.

"If we could only bring our dear friend back to life!" mourned Wolf, as Bear padded up beside him.

"Stand back, stand back," said Fox fussily, whisking his friends and foes away with his strong brush, "and let Bear try; it is Bear who knew all his habits; it is Bear—"

"It is Bear who knows the habits! It is Bear whose head is eaten in Corn Soup and whose brains are thereby honoured for their goodness," chanted the other animals in chorus. "Let Bear try—was our Hunter friend not of the Clan?"

Bear came forward, moving lightly yet lumpily, with hunched shoulders; his wise head nodded over the young Chief's body. He felt with his paws, and pressed knowingly upon the chest.

He decreed: "I feel a patch of warmth. A *small* patch—" and he glanced round to shake his head gloomily at an otter which had chirped too cheerfully and a squirrel much inclined to chatter. "My friends—quiet. We must try to bring him back to life." (Here *one* bird of prey was heard to speak in favour of ripe warrior, but was stonily ignored.) "Yes—back to life!" said Bear. And he invoked the name of the Great Spirit, while the other animals chanted, "O Holder of the Heavens, is not this fallen Chief a Keeper of the Western Door for that great People of the Long House, your Iroquois?" And the Eight Thunders grumbled in the sky country as though they walked there and thought deeply on the matter.

Bear all this time was warming the Hunter, and holding him; and feeling him to make sure the small warm patch was still there.

"Some powerful Medicine is needed, to bring our friend back to life!" He looked questioningly at the other animals. They didn't shrink, though all guessed what Bear meant: that each must give a bit of his own flesh, from heart or brain ("That is best," said Bear). And when they had given it, and repaired each other's damage as best they could, they mixed it carefully, and prepared it with saxifrage and other things.

Meanwhile, it struck them all that man cannot live without a scalp.

"Who will go and find our friend's?" asked Bear.

It was getting dark. The animals shivered as they thought of approaching the Cherokees' fire to snatch back the Hunter's scalp before the eyes of those fierce warriors, so quick and eager with the bow or hatchet. Fox excused himself; so—though less hurriedly—did Wolf. The little animals feared they mightn't find it, or it might be hung somewhere too high for them to reach. The bigger ones frankly said they would be struck down before they got there.

"A bird must go," said Bear.

"Owl sees well at night."

77

"Crow so often scavenges nearby, they will not notice him."

"Heron is forgetful—he would only stop to fish."

"Humming-bird is small, quick and clever—he could hover wherever that poor scalp is hung."

(Dew Eagle, most honoured bird among the Iroquois, declined the scalp-retrieving mission after Porcupine declared he would be seen.)

"No argument!" said Bear, feeling the spot of warmth, and rubbing with his paw to prevent a cooling. "Humming-bird is suitable: this is no time for corn-eaters, birds of prey or fishers! It is the time of small birds—a quick wing-fanner, who hovers and snatches and is barely seen—" And, as he spoke, Humming-bird bowed himself to Bear's wisdom and flew off through the forest: a bright-winged, long-beaked, jewel-eyed, tiny dart.

While Humming-bird went to seek the scalp, Bear kept on trying to revive the young Chief, his friend, by rubbing the warm spot, and gradually it grew warmer and spread wider. Animals and birds were working on the Medicine; and Dew Eagle, who keeps dew upon his back, prepared to shed it by humping and twitching the big shoulder-muscles of his wings. ("We will bind it together with Dew Eagle's dew," the birds and animals had said.) They were all rubbing and pounding and jumping on the medicine pieces to mix everything together and make it small.

"Sing a Medicine Song," directed Bear. "Sing strength into the Medicine for our friend the Hunter."

So animals and birds moved into a circle and began to chant and sing a Medicine Song, while otters and beavers began drumming on fallen logs as though drumming on the witch-drums at the Council fires of Onondaga.

During this time the spirit of the young Hunter still hovered above the scene. He had expected to set off at once upon a difficult journey—for after death each warrior must cross a turbulent stream spanned by a treetrunk; and on that fragile bridge must fight ferocious dogs barring his entry to the Spirit Land. Now he didn't know if he should go or stay. He grew increasingly conscious of a lot going on: a splendour of song and drumming which came in waves of sound. He looked down on his body, lying scalpless in its war-paint, and saw Bear constantly pressing the warm spot on the chest. Then he would feel as though a black wind were tearing him away, and he heard waters tumbling along, and knew he must clamber on the treetrunk and meet those dogs that were barking first near, then far, then suddenly much farther off—

It was about this time, when the barking of the dogs receded, that Humming-bird had reached the Cherokee settlement. He hovered by a sweet briar, to see what was going on by firelight. There was both sadness among the Cherokee squaws who had lost their men, and rejoicing that some of the enemy had fallen too, among them the young Chief. A group of warriors were cleaning the fresh scalps that were their battle trophies, and stretching them on scalp-loops. Humming-bird hovered and hovered, anxious to fulfil his task yet fearful of mistakes. He sipped at a night flower here and there, and presently worked close enough to recognise the shiny scalplock of his Hunter friend: it was already cleaned and set upon its loop to dry above the smoke-place. He strengthened himself with a last sip of nectar, and then, wings thrumming, darted over to seize the scalp and carry it up into the air before the astonished warriors could loose their arrows at the small, strange thief.

Meanwhile Bear, surrounded by singing, pounding, drumming animals and birds, was still warming the young Hunter as much as possible; and soon directed Wolf to lick where blood was drying on the head. "Lick—lick hard, Wolf! Or scalp and head will never more unite—" So it was kept moist all the while; yet when at last Humming-bird returned in triumph with the scalp it was already rather smoke-dried, and not quite large enough to fit the head. In vain birds and animals tried to replace it; then Dew Eagle said it needed moistening as well.

The scalp was reverently laid upon the ground. And Crow said he ought to vomit on it: for his vomit had special properties which he could vouch for as being almost magical. But after some argument the vomit was rejected in favour of the dew. While it was applied, most of the animals were still singing and singing, and blackbirds fluted, and the logdrums rolled and tumper-tumped like witch-drums making rhythm beneath song.

As the scalp was put back on to his head the young Chief's spirit began to feel its way into his body. The animals crowded closer, and the essence of what they had pounded together from themselves and from the forest was fed to him in little sips. When mixed with Dew Eagle's offering it was a very small amount, and could have been held in one of Squirrel's shells. This is why they chose to call it Little Water.

As he came to himself the young Chief was very conscious of the animals' singing; how strange that he could hear and memorise the words they sang! One bird was telling another that the Great Spirit must have led them to give this Medicine for the healing of men's hurts. He lay there, absorbing the marvellous sounds and words of their special song, and knew that it would never be forgotten. He was alive—and, though still unseeing, he could *feel* the presences around him: Bear, Wolf, Humming-bird, and all the others.

The first dawn light, filtered through pine tops, turned the sandy trail in the ravine to pink. The log-drumming ceased. Some animals were already quietly leaving. He heard the padding of their paws, and called out, "My friends, I thank you! I thank the Great Spirit, and I thank you too. You have brought me life with your song and powerful Medicine. The song I remember; tell me the secret of your Medicine, that others may be healed by it?"

Bear's voice refused: "Young Chief—your wife awaits you; only if you were virgin still could you receive our secret. Go home. Bring some of your people together if one of them is hurt or in sickness; sing our song—you will receive our help. Sing it as you have heard it in the forest."

"Medicine is always needed too?"

"Yes—and one day we will teach whoever hears us singing this Little Water song. Whoever hears must follow us and learn the truth: it will be shown."

While Bear spoke, the other animals had slipped away into the forest. The birds had flown, or settled down to roost. Owl took up station in a feathery pine, clicking his beak: he had only just restrained himself from scalping Mouse.

The young Chief felt paws helping him to rise. His eyes opened. He blinked them rapidly; they felt as though they had been sealed by gummy resin from the pines. He gazed round him in joy and amazement. Bear, who had been supporting him, shambled away behind him with surprising speed; only his dark, stubby tail and thick, strong back legs could be seen as he worked his way between two bushes. On the ground were many signs of paw and claw that the good Hunter could understand. He looked downward. He felt his thighs, touched the crown of his head, gazed at his hands, and drew deep breaths. He raised his eyes again and rejoiced to see the sun's pure disk rise just above a sapling pine as though impaled upon a spear. It was a ray of light and no cruel hatchet that descended. In his heart he spoke thanks to the Great Spirit.

When he reached home his young wife ran to meet him, laughing with pure pleasure and delight to see him there unharmed; his friends had been mourning him, she had despaired of his return. How they feasted the young Chief who had been restored by Little Water Medicine! And in the Corn Soup, on that occasion, there was no Bear's head.

Now, in the Clan of this young Chief there was a youth who was to marry with the girl he loved. They often spoke together of the healing song, and of their tribe's sadness that

81

the Medicine secret—some while after the first cure—was still unknown. It was not yet the time of autumn cold, though the hickory nuts were ripening, and berries turned ruddier each day. The corn was plump and golden on its thick stems within the nests of leaves.

This young couple went down by the river to speak about their future. They picked wild strawberries, and listened to the whippoorwill. The sun was hot but the air frost-tinctured from the Canadas across the great lake, and the girl wore her best doeskin tunic. She had sewn the bead embroidery into emblems of the sky dome, the night sun, and the world turtle: no skilled old woman could have worked so well.

"How lucky you are not of my own Clan—or we couldn't marry," murmured the youth. "How could we have borne it?"

"I would have been as a sister to you all our lives," she replied demurely. "Would it have been well?"

"It would not have been well!" He gazed into her beautiful dark eyes. While they were still looking at each other, they heard a distant sound of singing . . .

She turned her head. "Is it in the village? It is the Little Water Medicine song!"

"It is not in the village . . . It is over there."

"No . . . *There!*"

"From the forest."

"It *is* the song the young Chief taught us . . . It is the animals singing!"

"They sing for us?" he questioned; and then nodded to himself. "Since we have heard, it is for us. You are not afraid to go and seek it?"

"I am not afraid. Let us go!"

They went hand-in-hand, searching for the singers. The song led them farther off, and he said to her, "Now it's not like animals at all. Who—or what—is singing?"

They continued seeking until evening, and she led him eagerly; then he led her. In turn they led each other, though she was always longing to go faster, farther. He was a little doubting, and perhaps he feared for her. He had with him only a light hatchet, and its blade was dulled. Very soon they were in darkness, though always the song rang out ahead of them. They held hands still, and stumbled; and his other hand was on the hatchet, for they had reached a dreadful place—something like a vast, swampy trap, its edges bounded by weird fallen trees whose leafless branches twined upward like stags' horns and almost shut out the sky. Their feet were caught and mired by sticky mud between tall, sighing rushes. He gripped her hand yet harder, and feared more for her.

As they strove to extricate themselves the song broke out again, farther off; and near them came encouraging bird-calls, and the unnerving laughter of a woodpecker as he flew ahead. Then came a rush of wings as Dew Eagle swooped to lead the way.

"Who is walking with us?" whispered the girl.

"No one!"

"Something brushed past me in the dark! I saw witch-lights!" Her hand trembled.

He said, "They were the shining eyes of some big lynx."

"From where did they borrow light?" She shivered.

As they still floundered Owl hooted nearby, hoping to comfort them. But enemies sometimes imitated that cry, and the young man recalled the Cherokees, and cursed himself for bringing the girl into a trap. As though she heard his thoughts she said very softly, "Do not fear for me! I had to come with you—so the Great Spirit has ordered this, I know, and will protect us." This time his hand tightened gratefully on hers. A moment later, following the birdcalls, they stumbled from the tree-surrounded swamp.

"Now things will be easier—"

"But there is a sound of rushing water—perhaps we need not go that way."

Yet the song was inexorable. It came from beyond a wide ravine which contained no shallow stream but a

narrow river hurling itself at intervals down thunderous
cataracts. Here the youth would have stopped, to send her
back, but she was already dragging off her doeskin tunic and
tying it into a bundle. Clutching each other, now struggling
to stand upright, now slipping from stone to stone, then
plunging into a deep pool where they must swim, they
crossed the icy river. "Is the tunic wet?" he asked as they
reached the other side; and he spoke so anxiously that she
laughed, and answered, "Very little! Though the bundle
almost fell off my head while we were swimming." She
dressed herself again; the doeskin, its fringes dripping wet,
did run water as icy as the river.

"Hark—the wolf-call!"

She shuddered, as they listened to a panther roaring in
reply. After the panther's deep-throated speaking came
the harsh, authoritative grumbling of a bear.

"Bear! It was Bear who held our young Chief—"

"It is Bear who leads us."

"The way is steep, now—Can we climb?"

"We must—the whippoorwill is telling us to come."

A flash of light seemed to streak above their heads, and
then to circle them; birdcalls came again.

Her doeskin garment was dry by the time they had
clambered up that pitiless, steep mountainside. Their hands
and feet were bleeding, scraped by the knife-sharp edges of
the rocks and sliding stones.

They reached the summit. All at once their hands could
have touched the night clouds that went drifting by. The
Seven Dancers were clear above them in a patch of sky. Was
it from the top of this high mountain that the song had
issued? They heard it all about them still, and around them
felt the presence of the guiding animals. Dew Eagle swooped
again, seeming the shadow of a cloud.

"There!" cried the young woman, pointing. "Look
there!"

Like a lone feather in a chief's braided scalplock one huge
cornstalk crowned the top ledge of the mountain peak. It

84

was the cornstalk that was singing! All the animal presences were silent.

Light streaked above them once more, as something quick and winged circled their heads. A voice spoke gently, telling the young couple to make an offering: there they would find sacred tobacco close at hand. Once they had lit it, smoke rose acceptably skyward in a thin spiral and formed into a miniature cloud.

As the youth bent to sever the cornplant at its root they both gave a gasp of horror: for at the first cut the stalk yielded a flow of human blood which burst out of the root in scarlet streams. It was like the cutting of a limb.

But—"Look! It is already healed!" The young man spoke in wondering tones. It was true: the wound had instantly grown clean and dry.

"And listen!" murmured the young woman.

They heard Bear's voice upraised, and Dew Eagle. Panther and Lynx joined in, and Beaver, Squirrel, Wolf and Doe—each forest beast in turn told something of what was in the Medicine or how to make it; and how the ritual song must be sung and the Medicine given when the rite of healing was employed.

Then the young man and woman stood there on the mountain while dawn came. Under the care and in the name of the Great Spirit they thanked the animal presences who went quietly, solemnly away from them down the mountainside—on that bright morning when the secret of Little Water Medicine was first given to that people of the Long House who are also the Keepers of the Western Door.

F

The Guardian Snake

There was a girl. She was beautiful. Her skin was the colour
of pale coffee when cream is well stirred into it. Her eyes—
ah, those eyes! There is no describing them, though their
effect can be described: the young men followed her like
dogs. They brought gifts of fruit and finery. They went to
set Obi for her, to make her theirs. It was said there was no
Obeahman in all Jamaica who hadn't obeahed her good and
plenty. Poor sad young men: the influences devoured each
other, and the girl went free.

Her father was very proud of her, that girl. When they
walked together people gasped; *his* fathers had been Princes
of Dahomey, till they were slaves. He was black, wide-
lipped, a man like a bronze statue. Deep in himself he felt the
arrogance of princes and the miseries of slaves. But the girl—
whatever conflicts bedevilled her unconscious, she seemed
unaffected by them. She laughed and danced, drank rum
from calabashes, and sang for joy.

One day, she lay alone on a white beach, dazzled by the
sun. She could see blue mountains in the distance. She could
hear children play. She thought of the young men, and
stretched her body, and laughed. Oh, she was pleased to be
herself, in that hot sun! Hot, hot—it was so hot that she sat
drinking from a coconut and wished the drink was iced.
Then, suddenly, she was afraid. There were men she didn't
like—and she knew they all set Obi for her. What is to
become of me? she thought. Ah—God send an answer soon!
For she was devout.

There was a little movement in the sand; not much. No—
it wasn't much, but she lowered the nutshell and looked

closely. A green snake lay there, of a kind unknown to her. She sat very still, looking. Where had he come from? There was driftwood near him—had he floated ashore from some other island? Such things could happen. She knew of Martinique and how the terrible javelin snake, *fer de lance*, had come there.

The snake lay like a limp green ribbon. Was he dying— was he sick? The girl was afraid, and yet her kind heart suffered. Poor little snake, she thought. Dying, in the hot sun. Surely you will not fear me, if I give you milk. Surely you will only bite me if you fear? Very cautiously she edged forward and placed the nutshell so that it was touching the snake's mouth. He reared up slightly, green as emerald; less limp than she had thought. Yet she sat, saying softly, "Snake, drink, snake . . ." and the small green head lowered to the shell. He drank. His gold eyes watched her all the time. Then, suddenly, he rippled over the sand and up her arm, and gently pressed her neck with his mouth. Bump, bump. It is how a snake shows affection. Now she was no more afraid, though her heart had gone bump, bump too at his first rippling touch. She laughed. She stroked his long green tail. "Ah!" she said. "Little snake!" She sat playing with him in the sun.

When she left, she first ran into the sea, to cool herself deep in seawater. Afterwards she raised her hands to shake away the drops. They fell glinting, shining, on to the beach; and how she stared—gold coins dropped from her fingers! She bent to the water, straightened, shook her hands again. More coins dropped. She looked back up the beach to where the green snake lay coiled in the sand and watched her. His gold eyes were full of mirth. She picked up the coins and went towards him. She said, "It are like that, little snake? Thank you for your gift." She passed him, and went slowly home.

Her father brooded on her strange beauty, and the gold: he considered, "Is she to be nothing?" He turned his eyes North-East, and his thoughts to Hispaniola and the black

Emperor. His white teeth flashed as he spoke sternly to her godmother—his wife was long dead—and commanded, "Guard her! I am speaking to the Emperor for her!" Then he took ship and sailed away. He sailed the warm blue Caribbean, beguiling waters that held sharp cruelties lurking in their depths.

"Girl!" (said her godmother) "Stay indoors. Are shocking how you sway by men. Do *my* girl so?"

The godmother's daughter was quite pretty, with white teeth, but her eyes were small; she had a mean expression. The godmother was black and buxom. She wrapped her fat and muscular body in bright-coloured clothes; when she walked she was like a big flag always on the move. She had a full, warm laugh that comforted by its sound. She had eyes so small and dark that when they focused and stared suddenly it was as though blackness speared straight from them, like a black beam, the opposite of a sun ray. The sight of that black beam could make a watcher's forehead sweat. When the father sent word that he was sailing home to fetch his daughter for the Emperor, she stared particularly hard.

"Put chicken in the pot, with yams," she told *her* daughter. "See that girl not go out. Empress!" And she laughed; her full, warm, comfortable laugh.

"Are going out, Mamma?" asked her daughter. "Are going to visit Obeahman?"

"Now see," said the godmother. "What is this talk, huh? Obeahman! When friends talk, is that Obeah? Small mouth, less talk, my daughter."

"Steal her shadow! Let her pine! Let the duppies in the silk cotton keep her shadow, Mamma . . . Let the deaths lurking in silk cotton trunk eat it up."

"You are silly girl. What then? Are gold coins dropping from silk cotton tree? Will her father not pay Angelman the Shadow-catcher heap money so she *not* pine? No—now this noble Emperor wait . . . And we go! *We* go, too! Now are there talk with one old friend, tonight; just talk." So she went out, laughing that laugh.

The Guardian Snake

Obeahman sat before his hut. He was staring at the sun. He stared for minutes straight into the solar rays and, though his eyes were wide and blank, they were unharmed. When at last the sun went down surrounded by a blaze of orange, green and purple light, two old friends had well understood each other. In a grotto lit by candle stumps they had worked the matter out. The godmother contentedly took home a little bag containing parrot beak, grave dirt, eggshells, and rum.

"Mamma? Is you, Mamma? Are you set Obi for her?"

"Quiet, stupid girl, what talk is that? Sleep, Empress my daughter," said the godmother, swaying her big muscular body under its many-coloured dress as though she danced to drums, "for black Emperor wishing one pretty bride." She went into the next room, where the lovely girl lay, and tied the little bag around her neck as she lay sleeping. Something moved beneath the bed—a small green head flickered out to watch, then was withdrawn. The girl turned on her side, moaned uneasily, and put her hand up to her neck. Then she slept again.

Next day she said, "What are this thing? I do not like it, take it off." She tugged, but the leather strap was strong, and the godmother had knotted it so tightly, tightly.

"Charm shall make Emperor a loving bridegroom." The fat black woman stroked her godchild's neck lingeringly. "Let it rest there, girl—how else shall his love last, that Emperor? It cost much, ungrateful one! Today, see, we sail—you and I and Eulalie, who are your maid when you married. Come, pack!"

But the lovely girl sat, saying stupidly, "I have bad bad headache—oh, the head I have from the hot sun!" She swayed and suffered. They took her by the arms and led her gently to the ship, which swayed too. The sight was dreadful to her. She begged, "Not today!" But they braced their muscles and pushed her up the gangplank. Eulalie carried her bag. She said, "Are heavy!" She didn't know that the long green snake was curled inside among the clothes.

89

The ship tossed on the water, and the girl moaned. When dawn came, and with it Hispaniola rising with its mountains and savannahs and its mahogany and palm groves from a dark sea, her godmother went to the girl's cabin. "Why you not up, lazy one? When you is married, you not lie sleeping still! Already we are at the quay. Runners from Emperor himself wait to fetch you ashore! Hark, they blow horns of conchshell." The ship was still two miles out; there was no sound but the singing of the sea.

The girl's eyes were wide and blank. "I—I see nothing! I hear nothing but the sea! Godmother—I am blind, I am blind! Take away this thing—it hurts me!" She plucked at her neck.

The big woman leaned down, and with muscular black arms pulled her upright, and held her there. "Child, what you say? Blowing of those conchshells are so loud! Come—I am walking you down the gangplank; Eulalie—take her other arm . . ." Together they marched her up on deck, and there they stood behind her to heave her higher than the rail—no one watched in the dawn light—and throw her out, blind, into the sea. She screamed once, as she felt empty air beneath her feet. Then she went down under the water, and the ship sailed on—though not before something small and green had slithered over its side to find the threshing figure in the deep.

"If that Obeah fellow say true, now gold coins drop from *your* fingers, Eulalie, my Empress! Come to your cabin, girl, and wash there, wash." Yet, when Eulalie washed, only crawling things came from beneath her nails. Now *she* screamed. Even her mother's dark skin took on a livid tinge, but she said fiercely, "Never care! Lawd, girl, you not wash again till you is wed! Here, some special, small gold pieces that I brought. Keep them in your sleeves. You got smile . . . then let drop one little piece . . . They men, even Emperors, are being fools. That so lovely girl! What fish eat her, now?"

The Guardian Snake

No fish ate her. That pale coffee skin went unmarred. The long green snake had reached her in time to twine himself about her waist, where he remained like a lifebelt to hold her above the waves. The savage dwellers in the depths gave them a wide berth. Her great blind eyes stared upward. When a fisherman sailed nearby he saw them looking up—so beautiful, and so pleadingly from out the sea that he never shuddered at the strangeness of it, but only knew that he must rescue her. After he discovered she was blind—and almost dumb with shock—he took her home, dried her, and cared for her. He was of Spanish descent, devoutly Catholic; he owned pictures of the saints, and a silver crucifix.

This was the South-Eastern side of Hispaniola, far from the Emperor at Cap Haitien. No one here had heard of a lovely girl coming from across the sea, whose hands dripped gold and who could wed the Emperor. The fisherman thought her his special miracle. He guarded her secret closely. His young son gently held her hands and washed them for her. Each day they saved the coins and kept them hidden in a big clay pot.

"Girl, in spite of blindness you shall marry, for you have a dowry!" said the kind fisherman. "And I and my son shall never want, praise to the Queen of Heaven!" And he went to Mass.

In his unique palace, so imposing with its portico and many colonnades and staircases all set there surprisingly on the green mountain, the black Emperor was waiting. His nobles strolled together among arches and pleasances and star-apple trees. The Counts of Marmalade and Limonade, the Duc de la Grande Rivière and the Prince of Gonaïves chatted with ladies of the Blood Royal—dusky beauties whose flaunted jewels and silks and satins vied in colour with the Caribbean flowers. Far up above, a good journey still by horse or mule, lay the vast martial Citadel, built to repel the Emperor's enemies if they should come over the shining turquoise sea. Now he waited for no enemy. Hours passed slowly, as he thought of the bronze man from Jamaica who had sailed to fetch a beauty—one whose hands dripped gold. It would be a while before she landed; no need yet to send an escort of ebony courtiers, in plumed hats. No need to hurry them across the dusty plain of the Artibonite with its strange spiked cactuses. Surely—no need . . .?

But already the godmother and Eulalie were shut together in a black, decrepit carriage, driven by a grey-headed negro. It was like some vehicle of death, drawn by a scarecrow horse. Creaking and swaying, it crawled along between cane-fields and savannahs.

The godmother scowled and scolded. "You sulk, my girl—sulk for no meeting, no courtiers, no sweet talk? Go—you act like fool! Is no need for Emperor at once—oh dear no. There are more to do."

"What more to do, Mamma? I am tired." Eulalie started crying, and was slapped for her silly, blubbery expression.

"Tonight—tomorrow night—ah! then you understand, my girl, my Empress, foolish one! Tired, are you? Tired! You are more tired soon, I say. Yet two days we go, perhaps, and long mule ride, and up all night still before us. Sleep, now—for you not sleep much at night soon, I promise you."

The scarecrow horse drew them on, hour by hour.

High in the mountains, somewhere close to Cap Haitien, the *Rada* drums were beating. Pulse, pulse, a talking through the night. The *houmfort* altar was already dressed with signs and symbols and things to eat and drink. The *houmfort* itself was still empty except for the three drummers, and the sacrificial birds and one small goat penned in the ante-chamber. He bleated, and moved restlessly. Outside the temple there was greater restlessness—dark shapes and faces contorted with excitement; there were runnings and pre-parings. The air was brimful of expectation. The old gods of Africa, of *Nan Guinan*, already sensed that they were wanted there. *Papaloi* and *mamaloi* were ready—he in a scarlet turban and embroidered stole, and she in scarlet robe and a head-

dress of black and crimson ostrich feathers. This priest was a
"server with both hands": one versed in all rites. Boum-
boum, boum, boum, pam-pam *boum*, muttered the drums.
The drummers swayed, hit harder, snarled, sweated. This
was not the beginning of the Guinea rite, nor for the
benevolent *vodun* alone. It was the darker Petro—rite of the
blood sacrifice.

People were now walking softly through the antechamber
where the sacrifices waited. The rectangle before the loaded
altar was filling up. Ah—the loud breathing for that pro-
cession's entrance! An initiate carried a sword. The *mamaloi*
revolved in a stately manner, chanting. Beaded banners,
embroidered with Damballa's symbol, were crossed above
the *papaloi's* head. More initiates, white-robed, came in
singing. Eulalie and her mother were among the worshippers, the girl fearful, the woman already rippling to the
drumbeats, her vast haunches moving, her big feet shifting
on the mud floor.

Signs were drawn before the altar in white maize-flour,
and a network of lines and circles by the doorway—now
the room was sealed, no alien or unwanted influences could
enter without entanglement. Already the gods from Africa
were gathering above the thatched roof. Who was there—
Legba? "Papa Legba, *ouvrí barrière pour li—*" sang the
initiates, as the drummers drummed out Papa Legba's
special rhythms, and the *mamaloi* prostrated herself before
the altar and then rose to revolve again. The first birds were
sacrificed, their bodies torn, their blood spilled into bowls
for drinking. Boum, boum, pam-pam-pam *boum—*

On the altar, so many things! Three joined wooden
bowls which contain the soul of an initiate. Pots of oil and
wine, plates filled with offering foods: little sweet cakes,
plantains, cassava, mangoes and coconuts. The silver comb
and backglass of Maîtresse Erzulie, a painted schooner for
Ogoun Agoúe, God of the Sea. There is the serpent staff of
Damballa, the sabre of Ogoun Ferraille, the sacred thunder-
stone of Ogoun Badagris the bloody one. There are cala-

bashes, and dried flowers. Boum-boum, *boum*—boum, boum.

At one side is a little kennel, and inside it a small fire burning near some half-glimpsed objects: a black cross, chains and—shackles? Tongs and two small swords are heating to a red glow in the fire, which is *le feu Marinette*: Marinette, darker goddess of love, the evil one, who is tonight called from *Nan Guinan* . . .

Boum-boum, *boum* boum boum.

Eulalie looked up, her eyes starting from her head. She saw white doves swirled in the air, the scarlet-robed *mamaloi* holding them at arm's length, and raising them: the strong hands gleamed with sweat. The birds had accepted consecrated grain. A white whirling of wings, a white flashing of teeth; a sudden scarlet as bright as that bright robe; a dripping, a drinking, a *boum*-boum boum. Eulalie stared at the altar and saw, among the other clustered objects, the *ouanga* charm prepared for her. She kneeled entranced, frightened, sweating.

Little goat, brought from the sacrificial chamber, your eyes are frightened, for the air smells of death. The birds have tasted offerings, and been killed. Little goat, you are dressed, ready. Your horns are wreathed with ribbons, your hooves smeared with oil. Will you be enough? The godmother is frowning. She had begged for the finest sacrifice to make her Eulalie secure—the hornless goat, *cabrit sans cor'*; but it isn't often that this *papaloi* arranges human sacrifice, and never at short notice. Now he is down on his knees, speaking to the little goat. He has reassured it. The time has come to open the path, and go ahead. But it needn't be afraid: magic protects it.

"Papa Legba, *ouvrí barrière pour li—*"

Now a girl is carried to the central space before the altar. She is drugged, and face to face with the little goat she sits and sings as though possessed. Anointed girl, anointed goat who takes her place in the blood sacrifice! The fervour of her singing grows, filled with poignant longing for *Nan Guinan*.

The gods are near, the seas are nothing to them. Have they not always been present to their children, even in slavery?

Drumming, drumming, singing, singing. The song rises to a pitch of piercing misery . . .

A knife flashes. The painted gods along the *houmfort's* walls seem to move in the flickering light.

The goat's body is flung away, useless. The drugged girl is carried off. Eulalie, kneeling in the dust, is anointed with fresh blood, and given her *ouanga* as the *mamaloi* embraces her.

Sway, sway, in the dancing— The gods hover, ready to pounce. Ah, Bon-Dieu-Bon the remote, who from *Nan Guinan* will descend? Is it Marinette or Ogoun Badagris who comes? The symbol of good Erzulie, a criss-crossed heart pierced like the heart of Our Lady of Sorrows, is to one side of the altar. Oleographs of Saint James the Major and Lord Jesus look on—remote, too? Amazed? Damballa Ouedda, the hooded one, serpent, will you join the frenzy?

Now it has happened. A dark form falls to the ground with a strangled cry. A *vodun*, a *mystère*, is here. Which is it, which? There is a rattling of the *papaloi's* açon, the long-necked gourd twined with snake's vertebrae, as the priest bends to the body.

But the fallen one is up, speaking in strange tongues, moving strangely. He is recognised—it is Ogoun Badagris, the bloody one, who has descended. The people fall back, frightened but gratified. Ogoun Badagris snatches the sword and swirls it. He dances alone. And then suddenly the gods are falling from the skies as thick as leaves. *Nan Guinan* is empty tonight! The drums beat faster, first one god's rhythm, then another's, trying to keep pace with this massive descent as first one negro and then another drops to the ground or staggers under the impact of possession. Erzulie has come! Legba has come! Ah, Bon-Dieu-Bon, look what is happening in that corner—it is Marinette!

Haunches sway, sweat pours, couples join together and dance. Some flee into the dark night outside. All the time the girl Eulalie kneels ecstatic but terrified in the dust, marked with cornmeal and blood, and clutches to her poor frightened heart the *ouanga* that contains the powdered corpses of two humming-birds; and other things. The Emperor is surely hers, even if Obeahman did partly fail.

But, on the other side of the island, people had begun to talk. Where the fisherman still marvelled at his riches, news came about the Emperor, and the girl who was to come from overseas. People talked—and, in a little while, drums spoke from Cap Haitien. They told how the Emperor seemed disappointed in his new bride's looks, though he accepted her into the palace, and was—they said—to marry her.

"Why would so powerful an Emperor marry a girl like that?"

"Why! Emperor is making promise! *And* she are true bride, for now and then her hands drop gold."

So the story reached the fisherman's ears, and he grew frightened. How had *this* girl, whose hands truly dripped gold, come to him, a poor man of Spanish descent, who had never heard of the Emperor's intentions?

Then the long green snake slid from beneath the girl's couch, where he had lain hidden all this time. He wound himself about the fisherman's boy like a long green rope, and spoke: "Fisherman! You are enriched. Shall I kill your son— or will you take his sight and give it to the girl who has enriched you? Choose, simple heart."

The fisherman burst out wailing, for he loved his only son. But the girl turned her enormous eyes towards him so beseechingly, and the snake looked so unyielding, that at last he stopped his wailing and said quietly, "How may I do this thing?"

"Stroke me," said the snake, "and cut the charm from about her neck and touch it to your son's eyes . . . And now you've done this, put your hands upon the girl's eyes. Pray."

"Father—I—*I* am blind!" cried the boy in horror; while, "I—I see again!" exclaimed the girl. The fisherman looked from one to the other, and tears trickled down his face. He mourned with his son, and rejoiced with his adopted daughter.

The snake slowly uncoiled himself, and slid away beneath the couch, only pausing to move his sinuous neck and say, "Dress her in blazing splendour, and take her to the Emperor; but say Mass before you go. And light candles to St. James, and to the Virgin—for what you work against is very old, and very strong."

When the fisherman and his adopted daughter set out together, they looked an unlikely pair—he in his old wide straw hat and shabby clothes, and she in shimmering silk, ribbons fluttering in her hair, jewelled earrings, and a brooch of diamonds formed like a humming-bird. Her eyes were wide and sparkling, her cream-and-coffee skin glowed with recovered health. Soon the old man wrapped her in a coarse sackcloth cape, and tied a kerchief round her head— he feared she might otherwise be stolen.

They rode on mules. The girl who had been sightless cried out often, "Oh, the hibiscus! Green, green sugarcane!" And she even wept to see the colour of the rice and black beans that they ate at midday, as though it was the rarest sight on earth.

With his whole Court the Emperor had been to Mass that morning, and beside him had stood or kneeled the meek yet triumphant Eulalie, dressed in silver which didn't become her. There was a bulge over her bosom, where the *ouanga* lay concealed. Like some monstrous whale the godmother puffed and floundered in their rear, rolling her eyes, beaming, insolent with the insolence of one whose associates can draw gods from overseas. Yet she kneeled too, devoutly, and crossed herself, and stared soulfully through a haze of

97

incense at the Count of Marmalade, who gazed somewhat haughtily back.

Ah Eulalie, little Empress, what would this good Christian priest before you say if he are knowing—Ah, child—ah Marinette!

The courtiers rose, splendid in silks and satins. They had ringing titles and coal-black, noble faces. The Emperor was dressed more simply. When he strode out Eulalie followed him, her eyes downcast, the *ouanga* in her bosom.

"Monseigneur . . . !"

An agitated messenger!

"Altesse?"

"There is a girl . . . This old man . . . forgive me, Majesté!—says . . ."

The courtiers clustered, beelike. What sensation! What scowling of this meek Eulalie's mother, and timid pressing of the bulging silver bosom, where the girl clutched—what?

The Emperor was puzzled; the Court enthralled, agog.

The godmother waddled forward commandingly— though her ebony skin had a livid hue. "They are impostors, Majesté! You not go listen to that bad girl! Lies, she are telling! This are black magic, sorcery—Wanga!"

"Wanga?" said the Emperor, very loud; he was a powerful man, with a powerful voice. "Wanga, Madame? *Who* uses sorcery?" He looked at the lovely girl's enchanting eyes, and *his* eyes lingered on the soft cream-and-coffee skin.

He said, "Take her sackcloth cape—" And she let it fall into a servant's hands, and stood there with bent head, hardly breathing, almost ready to cry with embarrassment for the Court's staring at her, and the things the courtiers whispered—loud enough for her to hear—about her beauty.

They whispered different things about Eulalie.

The godmother was almost beside herself. Her great bulk writhed within its gaudy coverings like something hidden beneath a clinging, flapping flag. She was filled with evil meanness, she felt it as an almost devouring heat while the black beam of her eyes fell on the *ouanga*: surely the dried humming-birds, surely Ogoun Badagris or Marinette, could cure this shocking resurrection of the dead? "Sorceress she must be,"—the Court heard her outraged murmur—"or she has called on Ogoun Agoué, God of the Sea! Sly girl, evil one . . ."

But the Emperor was bellowing in full rich tones, "Why that girl clutch her bosom all this time? Why her fingers drop so little gold? Bring water! Bring water in a crystal basin, all shall see who speaks truth . . ."

The water was flower-scented, warmed. The lovely girl took a step forward. Tears washed the coffee cheeks as she washed her long creamy-coffee hands. The courtiers drew in their breath, "Ouuuuuuuuuaggh!" For tinkle, tinkle, the bottom of the basin was rich in brightness as the coins fell.

Then it was Eulalie's turn. She shrank back, trying to arrange her silver sleeves so that one or two coins at least might fall before she touched the water. But the Count of Marmalade held back her sleeves while the Duc de la Grande Rivière thrust her hands into the water; and on the gold at the bottom of the basin some ugly, slimy things began to creep.

"Ou-*ough*!" The Emperor's features were convulsed with anger and repulsion. "Who cry 'Wanga' now—you, woman?"

Eulalie flung herself upon her knees, and as she bowed weeping over the Emperor's hands the *ouanga* fell out of her bosom for all to see. As for the gods—there was not a stirring of them anywhere: it seems they were appalled. And in the corner of the room, unnoticed, the old fisherman sat weeping for joy into his straw hat, though some part of him still sorrowed for his boy.

The sun was surrounded by purple evening glory; the sea was calm, and on it, far out, floated one small black dot which gradually grew bigger—this was the ship that carried the girl's father. He had come in search of her.

The Guardian Snake

Before the colonnaded palace the Emperor walked by his shy new love. There was no need for her to find a spell for him. She had charm enough already.

High above, near a green summit, cannon fired roundshot in salute, toy puffs of smoke broke from the mountainside. Down in the valley a different, oily smoke crept upward. There, on the Emperor's command, the godmother and her daughter were being despatched by fire to join their ancestors. On the next strong winds their cruel spirits went homing to *Nan Guinan*, still to make trouble where they could.

"There are such colours here, Majesté!" murmured the girl. "See the green grass, how it ripple in the breeze! See how—Ah! My little snake! My healer—helper little snake!"

And she bent to scoop him up, and let him ripple along her arm as he had rippled through the grass. The Emperor looked narrowly at her, and not quite happily. *Wanga*?

But just then the snake began to ripple upward, and as he went he changed his form. Wings shone, and flashed jewel-like flames. His countenance was as burning coal, and his hair as snow, and his feet like gleaming brass. In his hand he held a sword. He was a guardian, and he rested somewhere behind the lovely girl's left shoulder, and floated in the air while his eyes shone with mirth as they had when she received the gift of gold.

The huge black Emperor and his new love fell upon their knees, overcome by sheer astonishment. The guardian angel remained where he was, just looking at them, till he grinned a highly celestial grin, and vanished. Perhaps, if he had stayed much longer, they might have died from the excitement of it.

And soon, over on the other side of the island, far from Cap Haitien and the Emperor's fine palace, the fisherman's son uttered a cry of joy and amazement! A rushing sound of wind had filled the hut, and as his sight returned to him he caught a glimpse of something swift and shining, winged and gracious, hurriedly departing through the roof.

Place of Rainbows

Between the ranges of the towering Cordilleras, which gleam as blindingly as though the Children of the Sun had covered them with gold leaf—just as they covered the tip of that grim red Rock at Titicaca where the Sun once hid—the plateau is very wide and high, the air so rarefied that it seems scarcely breathable. Lake Titicaca ripples on and on, enormous under an equally enormous sky. Down the mountain flanks flow furious torrents, and impassable *quebradas* rend the porphyry and granite. This land of contrasts seems so close to heaven that it was once thought of as a possession of the Sun. Its people were called Children of the Sun, the woolly llamas were his Flocks; gold was the Sun's Tears when he wept.

Some people swear that Manco Ccapac was the Sun's third son; others say that he had several sisters and brothers and his human father was already elderly when he was born. This child's first cries caused the old man to look about him for his staff, to support his footsteps to his wife's room where she lay after giving birth. The staff was a plain one of polished wood—but when he reached for it he found the wood grown colder and heavier than usual: it had turned to gold! Surely, with Manco Ccapac's coming, something wonderful had come into his home? Yet there, in his wife's arms, was an ordinary, brown, weeping baby. Still, the omen of the gold staff made everybody hold the child in awe.

Manco Ccapac's father was powerful in Peru: a hard man who had conquered many tribes. He couldn't, of course, *possess* the land—that was the Sun's prerogative—but he

G

could, and did, exercise control over it. There was no end to what that old man gathered in: the Flocks of the Sun, the Sun's Tears—and the people's tears as well. But in spite of his dominance there were still some unconquered tribes. Peru was an even wilder, fiercer place then than it was later. In the mountain ranges the *quebradas* cut people off from one another, and much of the high country wasn't yet worked as it could be.

Gradually, through the years, the old man's capacities to grasp and plunder waned. He spent his time dozing, and didn't relish his potatoes or maize liquor. He grumbled incessantly: about the coldness of the air, the aching in his bones, the food's tastelessness and the thin fleeces on his flocks. He said his sons and daughters were a poor bunch on the whole, not a patch on him when he was young. Then he would fall silent and steal sidelong, jealous glances at Manco Ccapac, and touch the gold staff as though he suspected it of something. From being a harsh, unmanageable tyrant he became merely a troublesome old man, but his people and children tolerated him now with great good humour: they believed that as men age they are drawn more within the Sun's power and protection, and slowly return to him.

Sometimes Manco Ccapac would walk down to the shores of Titicaca, and look out over the waters that rippled on and on till it seemed they might merge into infinity. He would sigh, and stare at the pile of reddish sandstone Rock— where legend said the Sun had hidden himself during the Flood—and think about his father's frailty and petulance. At Manco Ccapac's age such a state was almost unbelievable. He himself was never tired. Sometimes he felt a surge of exhilaration, a sense of his own strength, and would long to rush into dangers, and seek huge accomplishment. Then his restlessness would turn into a troubled feeling that some destiny awaited him, one he could never search for while the old man hung on and on, reluctant to depart; but still Manco Ccapac stayed dutifully at home.

At long last the old man started to die—on a day when the Sun gilded the distant Cordilleras, and the lake spread serenely like a sheet of light.

Manco Ccapac's favourite sister, Mama Oello Huaca, came to the door of the dwelling and shouted for him. "O Manco Ccapac! Hurry—call the *mohane*! Our father is very sick—"

The *mohane* was the oracle, or priest; he came scurrying to hang his hammock near the fierce old man, who was now gasping for breath and rolling his eyes from side to side as though he saw enemies surrounding him, and when the exhortations and magic rites began, merely gasped the harder. It was soon clear that the priest, lolling in his hammock, was unable to control this sickness, and at that point Manco Ccapac and his favourite sister fell upon him, correctly and ritually shook him from his hammock, and drove him angrily away.

"Fling those large stones after him!" yelled Manco Ccapac, flexing his muscles, and himself aiding the inefficient priest's departure by hurling heavy bits of wood.

All this time the old man's breath gasped and rattled in his throat; he was very near the end, but Manco Ccapac knew he mustn't let his father die unaided.

"Close his eyes for him!" he commanded; and then wrapped his father tight as a swaddled child in llama fleeces, seized his nostrils between thumb and finger, and filially achieved his suffocation. Afterwards, the whole family joined in sealing doors and windows, cracks and crannies, with all the dirty things that they could find. Mama Oello spread dung liberally upon the threshold.

"Does it stink enough?" she asked anxiously. "Will it prevent his prowling spirit making a return?" And Manco Ccapac, wrinkling his handsome nostrils in disgust, muttered with conviction, "Not even our dead father's spirit would come near the place again, unless it had to." Then, during several days, they wailed and mourned for him.

Very soon after these solemnities, the six brothers and

103

sisters of Manco Ccapac decided he must succeed their
father to the leadership; although the youngest son, he held
a special place by virtue of the omen at his birth. Their
people were summoned for a celebration, and came flocking
with their families and woolly llamas, each bearing heavy
packs of produce: maize, flowers and *chicha* for the sacrifices,
and coca too. What an assemblage there was at the red Rock
of Titicaca, the *paccarisca*—the Sun's holy hiding place! They
called on the maize-mother spirit, and the potato-mother,
chanting "Saramama! Acsumama!" They burned some
llamas, and paraded round them, chanting and pulling off
the fleece; and the first priestesses of Peru wore gold copies
of the sunflower upon their breasts.

Then Manco Ccapac spoke: "My people! You know this
is almost the time of Aymuray Quilla—the harvest moon.
You've brought many offerings to the house of my dead
father, and we thank you. After harvest, bring everything
you can—for I and Mama Oello, and my other sisters and
brothers, must now go travelling, to learn what we may have
to conquer still, and what it could cost us in our people's
wealth."

He spoke at a good time: his people were happy and
relaxed on maize liquor and coca; and with a great shout
they stoically promised him almost all they had, before it
could be taken.

During the period when all this was being gathered in,
Manco Ccapac's sisters were busily preparing fresh garments
for their brothers, and splendidly embroidering their caps
and cloaks. New arms were being made as well—shining
javelins, and tomahawks. When everything was ready,
Mama Oello, urged on by the others, took their dead
father's staff and placed it between Manco Ccapac's hands.

"Behold, my brother—your *tapac-yauri*! Sceptre of the
kings! Be more cunning than the monkey or the fox,
stronger and fiercer than jaguar or bear, and noble of spirit
like the condor. May you see your enemies in the darkness,
as an owl does! May you rule over us with the wisdom of

Thonapa, whose wisdom was truly greater than the serpent's."

Then she handed him the two gold cups that their father had always sworn were once Thonapa's: that hero who had come from heaven and preached to the people from the Rock of Titicaca—and she said: "Do not, our brother, we beg you, disappear from us as Thonapa did, when he reached the sea!"

Tears sprang from Manco Ccapac's eyes—tears which shone as though they were Tears of the Sun. "How could I leave you, Mama Oello? But I must seek what I must seek. The staff turned gold when I was born—and now you give it to me as a sceptre. But it's the Sun alone who shall choose if his energy and life will pour into me so that I shall reign!"

Then the six brothers and sisters gave a tremendous shout of, "Brother, we will never leave you! Let us go together."

They travelled across the plateau towards the mountains, where peak upon peak rose jaggedly into the sky, and glittered in crowns of ice. Up there the snows had never melted, even beneath the fierceness of an equatorial Sun. There were cold colours in the crevasses and on slabs of porphyry and granite. It was a long while before the travellers toiled up to a high ledge. Here they slept, huddled beneath llama fleeces; and in the morning they woke and saw ahead of them an even higher peak—and the Sun rising behind it, so that he seemed to leap into the sky straight from the cone itself. They watched him openmouthed.

Manco Ccapac—even stronger and more muscular than his older brothers—hurried to begin the final climb, not noticing how quickly the others fell behind him. At last he hauled himself on to a ledge so near the summit that he felt almost as airborne as a condor. Infinitely far below him now were the mossy slopes and short yellow grasses at this gigantic mountain's base. The air was even thinner here, and brutally cold. He hugged himself tightly in his woollen cape, and stared into the blue. After a while the dazzle seemed like millions of minute silver arrows, shot straight into his eyes. Then suddenly the sky was full of colour. Rainbows appeared, seven of them, hooped across space in fantastic arcs of colour. One hung above his head like an enormous circle suspended from the Sun.

Manco Ccapac was filled with a sense of dedication and good fortune. Impulsively, as his brothers and sisters came toiling up towards him, his happiness burst from him in a song of joy; the strong tenor notes rose and rebounded from peak to peak, echoing till it sounded as though many singers answered him while some sang in unison. When he fell silent the echoes continued on and on, and at last fell to a distant murmur like people whispering to one another. Manco Ccapac turned toward his brethren. His face was irradiated; the five stared at him in awe.

Five?

One brother was missing. But he had been so zealous a companion on the arduous climbs of that long journey! Manco Ccapac stared his bewilderment.

"He's the most skilled climber of us all! Surely no harm has come to him—he hides to tease us—" He glanced downward and scanned the mountain: there was no sign of the missing youth, and no cheerful voice hailed them from below.

"But he must be here with us when we make an offering to the Sun in this place which is surely another *paccarisca*! Which of you will fetch him for me?"

His younger sister said that she would go; she put her arms round Manco Ccapac, and kissed him warmly. He noticed that her dark cheeks had grown even more sunburned during the climb. Her bronze-coloured hair had escaped from her little woollen cap, and fell on to her shoulders in long braids.

They watched her as she went smiling down the mountainside, leaping from rock to rock and singing to herself some words of Manco Ccapac's song. They waited, sitting in a silent group. They waited and waited—and as the time of her absence lengthened, and the Sun moved across the sky, Manco Ccapac began to feel a rising darkness in his spirit, and a sense of urgency.

"I did wrong to send her"—his voice was rough with anxiety—"although she's trained to endurance like the rest of us. It seems that some strange accident must have engulfed them both! We'll go down ourselves. Let us spread out across the mountainside to find them."

He was filled with foreboding as he leaped or climbed from ledge to rock, or skirted a wide crevasse. His shadow bobbed beside him like a distorted companion: its blue shape flickered across ice and snow; now elongated, now squat and misshapen as a dwarf. Still high above the snowline he looked round him desperately. What had become of his loved younger sister—and his devoted brother? Still a long way below rolled the immense plateau, with the far glitter of Lake Titicaca. Nowhere was any sign of human life.

Again he scanned the mountain. Quite close to where he stood reared up an enormous stone. There was something ominous about it—even Manco Ccapac trembled. As he approached it cautiously he found himself aware of an inhuman presence, remote and sad. Was this some *huaca*—a sacred object to his people? Then, in this lonely place, its power must be terrible indeed! It was said that men and spirits who had been disobedient to the true Creative Power were turned to stone, and their influences darkly permeated those *huacas* where they were eternally confined. But Manco Ccapac was naturally stouthearted, and today was further strengthened by the vision of the rainbows—and, in the slaty shadows of the rock, he had glimpsed two stricken forms.

"Brother! Dearest sister—" he called softly, and hurried toward them and that ominous, looming shape.

"Dear Manco Ccapac!" His sister's voice was a weak and sorrowful thread of sound. "You've come too late—this *huaca* holds us. Keep away! Now you can't help us, it will only draw and hold you too."

"By the Sun's might, I think that *he* will free you!" said Manco Ccapac between his teeth; and still walked on.

"Oh, keep away!" she begged him, weeping. "Our brother was lying nearly dead—I ran to him, and was quickly overcome by a fierce, invisible presence. It holds us strongly, and we shan't escape."

The young man's head was cradled in his sister's lap. His eyes rolled upward—he was plainly dying. The *huaca* was powerful indeed—as she spoke the girl's head bowed, and she began to fail. She had looked so young and joyful as she ran down the mountainside; now she might have been an old woman with crooked shoulders. Sweat poured off her forehead. Her braids had come unfastened, and her hair hung in a dishevelled state over her shoulders. She fell, gasping, across her dying brother.

"Do—not—come—too—close!" were her last words. Then she was silent, her white face as blue-shadowed as the crevasses far above.

Rage rose in Manco Ccapac. To see his sister and brother lost to him by such a cruel enchantment! His trembling left him, and he strode right to the grim stone and struck it violently, using the golden staff. It rang and vibrated in his hand, but neither bent nor broke. The dying man gasped and moaned. Above, there was a sound of wings, as a large condor swooped low as though to watch.

A voice spoke. It came from the stone's heart—a rolling, grinding, grey sort of voice, with granite in it.

"First and greatest of the Children of the Sun! Even my power fails before you."

"Then release my sister and my brother," cried Manco Ccapac, raising the staff to strike again.

"They can never be released. Their sins have brought them here. Their sins will bind them. *They* have fated

108

themselves to stay bound with me in this low, dark state, unillumined in spirit by the Sun."

"How is it possible? They were such innocents—" murmured Manco Ccapac, a sob in his voice. "How could I leave them here to such sorrowful loneliness and a dreadful future?"

"You have no choice—you are as bound to your condition as they to theirs! As soon as the *tapac-yauri* touched my side I knew myself incapable to hold you here. But these—these whom you call 'innocents', had disobeyed the true Creative Power! I cannot touch you—nor can *you* reach *them*—" The stone sighed, as though it yearned emptily and hungrily to engulf Manco Ccapac as well as the disobedient pair already in its grip. "Now go—first of the Incas! Have you not seen and understood the rainbow sign?"

Although himself invulnerable to the dark spirit in the stone, Manco Ccapac stood shivering with horror. He was in pain for this dying pair whom he had dearly loved. If only the gold staff in his hand could help him to release them!— but against the Life-Giver's decree it could have no strength. He looked up, for pity, to the Sun which blazed high above the peaks. The light was pitiless.

He leaned to kiss his brother and sister—now both unconscious in the stone's shade, the girl's hand resting on her brother's shoulder.

Then Manco Ccapac very sorrowfully, and slowly, walked away.

Some little distance up the mountain he found Mama Oello and the other three huddled in an anxious group. Since they had seen and found nobody they had feared his death as well. Tears rolled down his cheeks as he told them briefly what had happened. Then he commanded them to go farther down the mountain and wait for him near the plateau. And then, all alone, he climbed back towards the summit.

Once more on the high ledge, he looked about him. It seemed a long while since he had sung his song of praise and joy. The immense mountain ranges stretched away on either hand, row upon row of silent peaks capped with continual, glittering snows. Manco Ccapac screwed up his eyes against the intensity of light. Down below there were dark shadows, mysteries—but he: he had escaped them! He had come into the light, and the Life-Giver had laid a duty on him—to lead his people in the pathways of the Sun, whatever black punishment his own brother and sister must endure. He must try to expunge his sorrow from his mind.

He was standing where, that morning, he had seen the rainbows, and he thought of them as delicate, exquisite creatures of the Sun, benign and healing, and imagined a place of worship for them. Perhaps, at that moment, he even visualised the dazzling Temple of *Coricancha*: the Place of Gold, that the Incas would build at Cuzco—where the face of the Sun with his gold rays would appear on one huge disk of gold within his temple, while a silver disk would bear the features of the second deity, the Moon. The stars should have a chapel there—thunder and lightning should have another; and the rainbow a third. Yes—the rainbow should never be forgotten either by him or by his people.

Then the first of the Incas, Manco Ccapac, clambered down the mountainside towards the plateau, and with his four young followers went to take up his task.

The Ten-Year Child

🔥

Dada Segbo, King of the Gods—his storyteller, whom they call an Ahanjito, tells this tale of the King's youngest wife's first son: yes, it is in the time of Dada Segbo that this happened, some while but not long after Mawu-Lisa had made the world.

She was with child, this woman, and she expected and expected and expected him. After four years she was tired of it, and five: it was too much. Six, seven, eight, nine years she waited, round as a melon, and with the child kicking and Dada Segbo more and more amazed. She was by this time amazed herself, and no one could tell her what to do: it is a long time to expect a child, nine years. Some people said, ask Mawu—that is, female half of the Creator. Others said, no wait! Hevioso the Thundergod will give an answer. The wife went into the forest and complained aloud. Her complaining could be heard far off, like the sound of Kpanuhwele, white turtledove, when *she* complains.

In the tenth year the King's wife said, "Bother this child!" She took a large axe and went chopping with it. All noon she was chopping in the forest. Hevioso growled once in the distance, but came no nearer. It was not his season. Wututu sang lightly on a bough; he liked the sun. The young wife, by this time not so young, didn't sing. She frowned and chopped. On the last stroke the axe slipped and cut her leg, a long clean cut right down the thigh. Then the child's head popped out from that clean cut. He looked severe. He said, "It has been long, my mother!" He came out quiet but firm, and brought with him a good gun. He sat quieter as his mother washed him while she was bereft of speech.

"My mother," he said then, "do you understand what I am?"

"I understand, child," she said, looking at him fearfully. "You are *tohosu*. You are not as others. You speak when you are born—that shows me. And you are strangely born, child."

"Good," he said, "I am glad you know it."

"I have reason to know! It was long, and I grew tired."

"I was making my gun in there," he said; and looked at it lovingly. "It is a good gun. Call our family, my mother, for I wish to speak."

She looked at him, but she did not refuse. She sent word to Dada Segbo, and to the family. They came together on the day the child named, and sat in steamy heat to hear his voice. They were afraid, but would not show it. A long way off, beneath the earth where he supports it, Aido-Hwedo, rainbow-coloured serpent, stirred a little, and far north there was a minor earthquake. Even Wututu was quiet, and Kpanuhwele's plaintive calling ceased.

The child looked round him with authority. His family wouldn't meet his eyes. They stood in silence. Only Dada Segbo sat, wearing his round beaded hat, and beaded boots with beaded wututus on them. He held his flywhisk in his hand. By his side stood the King's Remembrancer, his Ahanjito.

"Good," said the King to his Remembrancer. "The child will speak: remember it." Ah, but he was a proud father!— ten years, it is a time. But the people were afraid.

The child asked them if they knew his name, and they looked sideways at each other, brown eyes gleaming. They shuffled. They would not answer.

One said boldly, "You are *tohosu*. We know that. How can we know your name?"

The child looked at him in scorn. He said, "Why should you know it? It is enough you know how I was born! Call me He-who-came-from-his-mother's-thigh. Call me that! Is it enough?"

They said it was enough.

"Good," said the child. He came close and looked up at his father. They smiled in each other's eyes. The child held out his gun, and the King touched it with his hand. "Child, what will you do?"

"Because I am *tohosu* I will neither dig the land, my father, nor live as other men!"

"You came with a gun!" said Dada Segbo, and his eyes misted with the pleasure of it. "A Hunter! See," he told the family, looking round at them and marking the child's shoulder with the flywhisk, "he is a Hunter."

The child looked about him proudly, and rubbed his small fingers on the gun. "Yes—that is what I wish to say to you: I will hunt and hunt and hunt and hunt! I will kill many, many beasts. You may buy them of my mother in the marketplace!"

He looked round him, and saw the people shaking, and he laughed. He saw his father didn't shake, and he was pleased. Dada Segbo, King of the Gods, is strong: little surprises him. Even his son didn't surprise him—much.

"My mother!" said the child. She came close and stretched out a hand, and he took it, and pressed her fingers and thumbs one by one into her palm. "Yes, it was a long time!" he said, full of laughter. "But it was worth it, my mother? For I came out well prepared." And he proudly touched his gun.

His mother shook her head at him, but she too was pleased. She told the family, "There, you have heard him!" She raised his right hand for him, and made him gently salute his family, although the King's other wives and children looked on with eyes sharp as knives and cold as leopards' eyes.

"Good," said the King. "Now hunt!" And he rose, stately in his robes and beads; his brown strength, and his firm belly, which was an object of much pride for his wives, it proved his riches. All were proud of Dada Segbo, but still in eye and thought they were sharp as drawn knives when they considered his new son—the *tohosu*, he of abnormal birth.

Well: that child was a strong Hunter. There are still Hunter stories told of him. Few boys the day after they are born can kill an antelope: it is unusual, that. Even though the child, the *tohosu*, knew his powers, he was filled with wild joy when he brought down graceful antelope as she leaped, terrified, across open ground. He slung her weight around his baby shoulders, with her long legs hanging down each side, silver grey-brown flanks still warm. He sang a little, like Wututu, as he went to find his mother. She was in the market, but without much to sell: cocks, cooked pork, some cakes of cereal.

"Good!" she said. "There are not many bring their mothers antelope to sell so soon after their birth. Clever one!"

"It is how I am." He squatted behind her, reached out, and drew lines in the dust.

"Do not put your Fa for all to see!" she said quickly.

"That is not my Fa. I know my own Destiny." Nevertheless, he dusted out the lines.

"Good!" she said. "Yet do not put it there for all to see! For there are some twins coming!" And she shuddered.

"I do not fear twins!" said the child. "I fear no one." Then he looked up, and the twins were small yet strong. People backed away from them, not eager for their custom: afraid. People are cautious about twins. Like *tohosu* they have special powers. These twins had theirs from the forest. Twins and *tohosu* child's mother looked at each other.

One twin then stroked the dead antelope, and the sad stiff legs hanging down. He said, "Ho, he, antelope! How many cowries, Dada Segbo's youngest wife?"

She said, "The antelope? Ah, her? Three cowries."

"Two," they said, moving close up while other people

114

moved away. The mother turned to look behind her where the child was hidden, but he looked sideways at the dust where his Destiny was covered.

"Two cowries, then; all right."

"Now one cowrie! We have one cowrie; what we have, we give," said the other twin. He leaned against her, and where he leaned there was sharp pain like a spearthrust. All the same she said heatedly, "One cowrie is not enough for sweet-flesh antelope!"

The twins smiled and smiled as though they would eat melons. People went behind their stalls.

"Bush people do as we say," said the first twin gently. "Antelope is bush person. Ho, antelope, run, run, run!" And antelope ran, flashing and bucking towards the bush, with wide-open dead eyes, twins after her and no price paid at all.

"It doesn't matter!" said the child, standing behind his mother and dusting down his knees. "Those twins, they are powerful! But the bush is full of game." He picked up his gun where it leaned against a tree. "I know my Fa."

"You must still clear the path!" said his mother sharply. (Meaning "Fa may be set, but you must work the manner out yourself; those twins were sent by Destiny.")

"Peace, mother. Have I not thought it out for ten years? Tomorrow you shall have deer and buffalo to sell."

So she did, but the same thing happened when the twins came again, wide-smiled and greedy. The land rocked slightly and with menace as they came. It is not sure if Aido-Hwedo liked them, and they offered little. When the *tohosu*'s mother wouldn't sell, the animals ran off into the bush just like the antelope, wide dead eyes, tails flicking. "It doesn't matter, my mother," said the indomitable Hunter-baby, and he went away, trailing his gun. Next day he brought her antelopes and deer and buffalo, all dead. He brought them to her hut near Dada Segbo's, and piled them in one great heap.

"Now!" he called to his mother. "Tell the King's other

wives to bring the animals. But you, mother, today must carry me. Carry me upside down, as though I am not big enough to walk."

She did so, and they reached the market. No one looked much at the King's wife with her upsidedown baby on her back. At the stall she put him inside her calabash; it was what he asked for, and—"It is a good calabash," he remarked as he went in. "It is like your belly was, my mother."

"Enough!" she said. "Ten years!"

What filled the calabash was silent when the lid was closed, but it rocked a little, like a reply; and when the earth rocked underneath it, it was tenderly, as though someone rocked a baby. All the dead beasts, silver-grey flanks cold, were rocked as well. When the twins approached, the rocking changed: fierce with menace.

"Do the twins come?" asked the calabash.

"They come," said the mother.

This time those twins didn't even bargain. "One half cowrie for your animals, Dada Segbo's youngest wife."

Inside the calabash there was a spitting noise. Sptt, sptt, small but clear.

The twins kicked it. "What is in the calabash? Snake?"

"It is fierce," said the mother. "Do not annoy it! I will not sell."

"Two days we prove ourselves, and yet you will not sell? Run, run, run," said the twins to the heap of animals: which sorted itself, rose, and ran with dead eyes, and tails flicking.

"Here is our half cowrie," said the twins, polite but grinning with wide mouths, dancing eyes. So proud they were. But the youngest wife of Dada Segbo was haughty too. She said, "I do not want your half cowrie!" She said, "Will you see what is in the calabash now?"—for it rocked with impatience, and there was a scratching noise within.

"We will see," they said, nostrils flaring; but they started back.

Then the child's mother opened up the calabash, and the

child came out, stalwart Hunter-baby. Ah, but he was grown! Four days old, a strong child. He looked at the twins with his big brown eyes, and they looked back, shaken though not showing it. Then one said, "You do not keep babies in calabashes, youngest wife of Dada Segbo."

She said, "You think he is a baby? Find out for yourself. He is large. Try him for what he says and does."

They said, "Well—we are surprised to see you! Will you shake hands?" But they eyed each other sideways, and the whites of their eyes showed. They knew there was a *tohosu* here. They had power from the forest, and it told them.

So the three shook hands.

"You sent me messages?" asked the child. His voice—it was polite!

"No, no," they said hurriedly, "we sent no messages."

"No message to me, a Hunter, how you bargain with my mother these three days?"

They said, "We did not think of you." Eyeing him.

"No," said the child, "I see you did not—but I thank you for your messages!" And he shook hands again, while his mother watched, smiling. Ten years, she thought. Well, let him prove himself. She thought of Dada Segbo in his beaded wututu boots, and her heart was soft as honey.

"So, you are sending back my animals," said the child, soft and sweet. "I hear their hooves like the rains drumming on long grasses."

The twins eyed each other resentfully.

"My mother wishes to sell these animals!"

The twins looked downward. Aido-Hwedo did not stir. It seems he was listening.

"After my mother sells these animals, *then* we can talk . . ." said the child loudly. He stood with his legs wide, wide, and his baby muscles swelled up like beanpods. He shook hands a third time, and their arms went all pins and needles to the shoulder. Then these twins shook their heads at one another, and there was a sound of small hooves, large hooves, drumming on long grass. Soon there were soft grey dead flanks, long sleek legs, hides, closed eyes; one large heap of all these dead animals.

"To sell, my mother?" asked the child, very meek and quiet, as though she commanded him.

So, she sold. Very fast she made a large profit for great Dada Segbo, and her heart was light and sweet as honeycomb. Youngest wife I am, but how I sell! And what a child this one I gave him, here—

Still, twins are twins; and the people hid behind their stalls—those who did not buy. Kpanuhwele and Wututu watched from nearby, they did not sing. Hevioso brooded, ready to break the trees and thresh the rivers.

Wututu said to Kpanuhwele, "The child is terrible! He has a leopard's heart. He has the heart of a bokonon." Now a bokonon is a diviner.

Kpanuhwele murmured. She shook her feathers, and said, "Those twins! Are *they* not of the forest?"

All this the twins thought, too; their hearts were tangled, rooted and grounded in that dark nature. Men are very careful in the forest, they do not treat it lightly. So it is with twins—and why people prudently go behind their stalls.

The first twin bent. He picked three straws from the dust, and held them toward the child. He said, "You see these?"

They saw.

He wove the three straws together in a thread. He waved it in the wind that came with sounds of voices. The forest spirits came from the trees—no one saw them—and wove a strong mat of creepers in the air. It was there weaving and undulating above their heads. It grew quite large, stopped growing, and floated, curling at the edges. There was a calling throughout all the forest while this happened. But no one heard it, although the leopards shrank silent on the boughs, and monkeys clutched each other and their young.

"Come up on our mat, *tohosu* child," said the first twin politely.

They went up. The child's muscles swelled like beanpods

119

H

as he climbed the air. They sat, all three facing; like friends, like enemies.

"Let us drink here," suggested the second twin politely. "Will your mother come?"

"I think she will not," said the child, eyeing them. "But I will drink." He crossed his beanpod legs, and waited till the three tall green bottles were there before them.

Twins and child drank together. It was beautiful! Sheer wine of the forest. So much stolen sap. So many trees never to grow tall—but no matter: that sap was used, which is everything.

"What now?" asked the child politely. "That is *all*?"

"It is not all!" said the second twin. He stood on the mat, opened his mouth wide, and shut his eyes. His white teeth pointed together and just met. He sucked and sucked at the air, and a howling current of coldness came and formed into a huge needle between his teeth. He took it out, and stuck it point downwards in the mat. It grew up, perhaps three feet.

"We will sit on it," said the second twin. "You first," he said politely to the child.

The child said even more politely, "It will be comfortable up there." He went and sat on the point, but his muscles still swelled like beanpods. Perhaps it was not so comfortable as he made out.

"Now you," he said, smiling.

So they joined him, and asked, "Would you eat with us?"

He said, "Delighted. Send for food." (All the time people, and his mother, were watching from the ground; their mouths were open. Some got stuck that way, for it is indiscreet to see too much of what is wonderful.)

When the food came—borne by the spirits of black leopards—it was very, very good: fried pork, fried fish, and acasa. The three ate and ate, patted their bellies, ate again, enjoyed themselves, but watched each other with eyes like slits.

"Yes, you are of the forest!" said the child admiringly, when they had eaten. "And it was a good meal. Now let us smoke." He drew a big pipe out of his beanpod right leg muscles, and the cloud of smoke he blew from it was so fat and thick and wide that it formed a big blue-grey curly smoke-mat above the twins' mat, and cast deep shade.

"Will you come up on my mat?" asked the child. "It will be warm, up there."

They said, "Delighted." Perhaps it was the shade lent a cold look to their faces.

Now they all three left the needle and went up on the mat, and had a sleep. Afterwards, the first twin raised one hand and waved it, and caused six calabashes to appear. As each opened, it disclosed a village. Women carried pots on their heads, men practised with spears, children ate cakes and played.

"Good," said the child; but he yawned.

The second twin raised a foot, and a file of warriors flew past, with raised weapons, preceded by bokonon in grass skirts and tall beaded headdresses. There were drum-beats in the air, and a sense of threat.

"Ha!" said the child. "Is that *all*?" He raised his face and smiled skyward. The sky cracked open, clean as on a hinge. They saw Lisa, the male half of Mawu-Lisa looking down on them, surprised: he is like the moon. They saw Sogbo, who is Hevioso, weighing a lightning charge in his right hand. They saw Metonofi, ruler of the dead. They saw Fa, master of Destiny and of Legba, heavenly trickster. They saw Tetelidja who cares for Vulture, and Ku—who is Death— just waking beside Loko of the trees, who leaned out of the hinged sky and shook his fist at them.

"Is it enough?" asked the child innocently, as he closed the sky again.

"Truly!" said the twins; and their melon smiles were grim, their teeth glinted with their fury.

"It has been a pleasant meeting," said the child. "Now it is done, and my mother has made much wealth."

"No good meeting is ever done," said the twins.

"So?" asked the child.

"So!" they replied. "Come and visit us in five days' time."

"In the forest?" asked the child thoughtfully.

"So! In our forest," said the twins. "Yes—*there*."

Four days that *tohosu* child was very thoughtful. Perhaps he considered Fa. On the fifth day he started out to meet the twins. He walked and walked and walked, while the bush quivered in the heat. His thoughts were very wide, always they embraced much. He walked up and down where the land curved and humped itself. (It curves and humps because Aido-Hwedo, when he first walked the earth with Mawu, moved like that, up and down, winding himself along; and he has left his pattern on the earth.) So this child walked, but he did not really know the way. He was like the butterfly Adjambla-gudo, which dances careless in the sun.

When the child reached a crossroad, he stood and wondered: which way, those twins? There is a time to add and a time to divide. Now, this child divided. He lay on the ground, and he thought and he thought, and in a short time his head and shoulders parted from his loins and legs. Head went one way, feet went other way. He looked up from the crossroads where he lay and saw his head and shoulders on one pathway, and his obedient legs walking in an opposite direction. Good! he said. He waited.

Soon, an old man was coming by the path where that child lay, and the child said, "Ho, grandfather!"

The old man said, "Eyes and tongue should not see or speak what is secret! Yet things happen."

"What things?" asked the child intently; though he sounded careless, and the old man was reassured. He crunched seeds from the palm of his hand, spat one out, and said, "Someone has left his feet where people from my village fetch water up the watertrail. Those feet walking! Then a head and shoulders walk alone on the deep forest

122

path. That head!" The old man shivered, but the *tohosu* gave a radiant smile. "Thank you, grandfather!" He waited till the old man had gone trembling out of sight.

Then he called; he called soundlessly. He called his head, he called his feet. When he was all joined up again he walked and walked till he reached the deep forest; and the twins, who came to meet him. "How do you like our house?" they said.

"It is good," said the child, looking round him at the deep green forest and Adjambla-gudo dancing in the sun. The house was mud and creeper upon logs. It was all silent round that house, except for monkeys' chatter and Wututu.

"If you like our house, stay with us! We will give a house. You shall have a house like ours, and you shall rest. You shall have food!" The twins smiled and smiled, and the child as well. It was all smiles, bright, like sun on the surface of deep forest which hides many things.

"I would like some Hunter's stew," said the child hungrily. "Stew with chicken, and pork and antelope—"

"All right," they said, looking at each other. "Go now into that second hut. We will bring you what we have prepared."

The child went into the second hut—how cool and green! He felt saliva gather in his mouth. He thought of those twins, and his mouth almost stretched into a smile. Almost.

When they brought the stew it smelt delicious, better than any stew made for Dada Segbo by his wives.

The child sniffed and sniffed before he ate—it smelt so good. The sniffing was nearly a meal in itself. Also, before he ate, he told the poison, "Leave my food! I do not want you there." The poison came out pink and bubbling, and spluttered away across the floor. When it had all gone the child ate with appetite, and rubbed his little stomach to help digestion. Then, as he was sleepy, he pulled out his great pipe from the beanpod muscle of his right calf, and gazed into the bowl of smoke where he saw Aido-Hwedo, who said, "I will watch you while you sleep." So the child slept and the ground rocked all about his hut, and the twins stayed in their own: for when Aido-Hwedo really rocks he can bring earthquakes.

The next day they brought more stew, and this time the poison came out blue and singing. It was stronger than the first, which was why it sang. Still, out it had to come, and it turned dark and sticky in the corner of the room, like treacle. After he had eaten and before he slept the child said courteously to Aido-Hwedo, "Do not worry, great long one! I myself this time will be on guard." Then he fell into a true, deep sleep. And the twins came at last with knives.

One said, "How will we divide him?" and the other, "I cut hands, you cut feet."

So they chopped and chopped: head off, limbs off, other bits off. They cut up his trunk too, and put every piece of him into their big cooking pot. They danced, they sang:

> "*Ho, the* tohosu!
> *The* tohosu, tohosu *child!*
> *The child*
> *He is in the pot—*"

They sang and chanted till sundown, and cooked and cooked, and stirred the pot all day, while their old father watched them at the work. As the sun went they swore, "Bother this child! He is still raw!" They were mystified. They said, "What has happened? Have we not worked?"

The old father was hungry, and very angry too. He commanded, "Fetch wood from the forest—go! Cook up this child!" He said, "Here I have waited all this day to eat Dada Segbo's son, and you have sworn to eat him, and you cannot even cook him for us!" But he was angry!

So the twins went off to fetch more wood. High above the forest they heard a strange noise, but didn't understand that it was Mawu-Lisa laughing at them and at Ku. It woke Ku, who was just as angry as that old father. He looked down and saw him dozing by the pot. He saw the child's head bob to the stew's surface, and his eyes open and fix themselves on

the old man. Then, as the child climbed from the stewpot,
Ku went down to join him, and together the child and Ku
began their work.

"Thank you, Ku!" said the child at last, and he took off
the old man's skin to wrap it round himself. Then he nodded
by the pot while Ku went back skyward to laugh with
Mawu-Lisa. In a short time the child took up the twins'
great knife to divide their father, and he tenderly put the
pieces inside the pot where they would stew to best advantage. So, when the twins came back with armfuls of dry
wood, the *tohosu* child was sitting there in darkness and their
father's skin, ready to direct them what to do.

That child—how well he taught them! Soon the saliva
started from their mouths, and they laughed, dipping their
hands into the stew as they said, "Ah good! It is very, very
good! It is the best, most succulent stew we ever ate, not
even antelope makes a stew like this! Each day we must
catch and eat another *tohosu*!" They gave the other one
sitting there so quiet a lion's share—that is, the head. Was he
not aged and their father? And besides, it is the ritual.

After they had all rubbed their stomachs, and belched a
bit, the child shook off the wrinkled skin and stood up to
say, "I thank you for your father! That old one, he cooked
well. I have taken him inside me now, and feel very good and
strong. Thank you, thank you." He stretched his beanpod
muscles and ran while they sat gaping there.

Quick, they were up and running too—like twin antelopes
after that child, yet he was far ahead. Soon he reached a
huge, sluggish river, rolling brown and crocodilish between
his country and their own. He thought, "I should have gone
that other way—" He looked round, but the twins were not
yet coming; when they did there was just one large grey
stone laid there invitingly beside the path.

The first twin picked it up. He said, "Ah, if I could get
my hands on that *tohosu* now—I would kill him! If that boy
were only in this stone's path—" he threw it hard across the
river—"it would surely kill him!"

But the stone skipped up and down on landing and killed no one, for it turned back into the child, who shook off cramp, and shouted at the twins across that huge, brown crocodilish river, "I am all warm inside with the strong wisdom of your good father! I ate what made you, yet you help me across a river!" He said, "It is good to have good friends!" And he ran laughing on the long track through the bush to his own place.

He found his family. He found his mother. He found his father's Ahanjito waiting to learn from him this new story. And he found a feast of celebration, for Dada Segbo put his arms around his son, and the youngest wife became the King's favourite—ah, but they were proud of their *tohosu*, although the people feared him! Dada Segbo thought the child would always come back safe from every journey, and from every hunt—even Kpanuhwele and Wututu thought so. It seems that they were right.

Bata

It was a year of plenty—the black earth of Kemi had produced a precious crop; the watering of Anpu's lands through
new irrigation channels had been more successful than he had
dared to dream. He looked complacently at his ripening
grain, and wondered if he could cheat the tax-gatherers a
little, and decided regretfully that he could not. Still, the
future looked—

What was that . . .? A sudden disturbance had shaken the
tall reeds of the papyrus beds by the river path. There was a
thunder of wings as ducks, geese and flamingos took off into
the sky. Anpu watched them, openmouthed. His hand went
to his amulet—the lovely blue scarab, carved in lapis, a
symbol of his prosperity—that lay against his chest. By Hapi,
what had happened by the Nile?

Running footsteps, and a sound of hysterical sobbing . . .

The reed stems clashed together as Anpu's wife, plump
Nekhset, clutching at her linen skirts, her green fillet
crooked on her head, came stumbling to his side. She was
moaning. Her mouth quivered, and her bulging eyes stared
like a frightened hare's.

Anpu stared too. He had seldom seen Nekhset in disorder;
she was small, neat and useful: a good wife. A good wife, or
so Anpu thought, was one you didn't have to notice.

"Nekhset!" he said severely. "Wife—you are standing on
some corn. You are not yourself."

"Be thankful I am here to stand!" she fluted shrilly,
clutching at his arm. "Husband, I've held my tongue till
now—yet I must speak! Twice I've suspected him—twice

127

told myself not to worry you, good, kind, trusting brother to him that you are! But when he tries to push me in the river—! Look—See here—and this—"

She revolved before him like a spindle. Her small, plump backside was covered with mud. The linen was torn and draggled. Her elbows were badly scratched, and when she turned to face Anpu he could see bruises on her forearms, and a large one, already turning mottled, on her cheek.

"Wife?" he said uncertainly. "You—I see, but—*Bata*? He and I were ever closer than—You're mistaken! It was some— traveller—some—"

"Some traitor! Bata, Bata, *Bata*. Do I not know your brother's face when I look on it? Have I not seen it each day since I was married?"

"But Bata is as gentle and happy as—He is good, beloved of the gods! Why would my brother wish to harm you?"

His eyes roved over her dishevelled state. Sometimes people did rave if the Sun God had afflicted them. Then there was nothing for it but a dark room, and cold cloths on the brow, and a priest of Ptah to drive home the healing power with his hands. But the Sun didn't bruise, scratch, nor cover anyone with mud!

"You were mistaken—it was someone else," he repeated feebly.

"It was *no* one else! I was face to face with him, and he laughed and said, 'You think to get an heir for Anpu, don't you? But this farm shall be mine, mine, *mine*!' And then he tried to push me in the river. When I fought to clamber from the reeds he would have pushed me back again, but someone came—Once it was food, which poisoned me; once, a cord was stretched across the cowhouse door! This time it was Bata, face to face. Husband—" she put her hand more timidly upon his arm. "Will you stand by, and let him kill your wife and unborn children?"

Anpu stood there with folded arms, considering her face. Tearmarks stained the round, childish cheeks. The bruise stood out, yellow-green.

"No, wife," he said at last. "No, little Nekhset. For all the love that was between him and me, for all the memories I have of him, I will not. Before the Sun God's nightly journey through the underworld Bata shall die—yes, he shall go to *his* horizon. Stay in your room. When Bata returns from work this evening, I will deal with him."

The cattle lowed, and moved restlessly. Bata walked among them, carrying a flywhisk. He used it with vigour to dispel a mass of flies which troubled his favourite cow, Lotusbud. It was the hottest day he could remember; so he had removed his linen kilt, and went naked.

"Mother Nut have you in her care, my gentle one," he murmured caressingly, as the flies rose in a black cloud from the silky flanks; Lotusbud watched him approvingly. "Once I've seen your milk frothing in the pail, I shall look forward to my foaming beer with more pleasure than I can remember!" He stretched his brown arms above his head, laughed, and began herding the cattle homeward. Then his brow darkened, as he thought of Nekhset with disgust.

The cattle were black shapes against Re's evening splendour. Each horned head was sharp-outlined as its owner advanced with quickened pace towards her stall. Anpu waited behind the door. He held a stout spear in his hand, and tried to quiet his breathing—nothing must warn Bata! Murderer of my unborn children . . . he thought, steeling himself; and wished that the very idea of a sharp point entering his brother's heart didn't make him feel so queasy. His spine ran with chilly sweat as he peered out from his hiding place.

Bata approached, whistling cheerfully. The spear slipped in Anpu's hand. He clutched it, raised it—

The entrance was blocked by another lumbering black shape, as Lotusbud appeared. Suddenly she hesitated, and gazed accusingly straight into Anpu's eyes. Tufts of hair on her fine, pricked ears quivered. She spoke—or perhaps a god spoke through her: "Run, Bata—run! Anpu waits to kill you with a spear!"

The angry Anpu emerged, pushed her aside, and waved his weapon clumsily. Then naked Bata ran; ran as he'd never run before, his brother puffing after him. The spear's tip was levelled only a short distance behind Bata's buttocks. *I wish I had my linen kilt on!* . . . *This is undignified*, was his inconsequent thought. And he ran and ran, all the time expecting a nasty jab, or death. But Anpu didn't throw. He was unaccustomed to spears, and ran holding his awkwardly before him. He was powerful, tall and slightly fat. In a very dignified way he puffed along, and the small gap between the brothers lessened.

"Anpu!" gasped Bata over his shoulder, as he floundered into marshy ground. "Great Osiris save you—are you mad?"

"You tried to kill Nekhset!" bellowed Anpu. "W-wanted the f-farm for yourself! Just wait—"

"*Anpu!*" Bata almost fell over, and recovered. He raised a desperate face towards the Sun. "Re! True Giver of Life! Help me, I'm innocent—Show this madman . . ."

The great god Re was low in the West, sailing his barque smoothly through the sky. He heard Bata's voice calling in the marshes. He looked down, and smiled.

Between Bata and Anpu the marsh stretched itself out to become a wide, glossy lake. Light moved in turquoise ripples across its surface.

Anpu slithered to a halt, bewildered. He stepped into the water, and hurriedly withdrew. The innocent-looking turquoise lake contained a wealth of crocodiles. He squinted upward nervously at the Sun. He called out, "Bata!"

"Anpu! See how Re tells you I am innocent? Nekhset has lied."

Anpu pondered. "But *why* did Nekhset lie?" he yelled back at last.

"She hates me."

"Hates you? *Why*—why?"

Bata blushed. He blushed all over, till his brown body

looked like a plum.

"She w—she wanted me to love her. When I wouldn't— she—she started screeching. I slapped her face—and she fell backward in the reedbed . . ." His words carried across the water with an appalling ring of truth. The crocodiles turned their sinister heads from side to side as though Truth might fall into their hungry mouths. The water rippled turquoise around their snouts. Overhead, Re's barque sailed serenely on.

"I—see." Anpu lowered his spear. He stood silent. Then he shouted, "Forgive me, Bata. She—she was too convincing. Come home after sunset."

His anger grew in him as he walked away. It grew and grew—as though he had turned black inside. Blackness seemed to rise in his throat, as solid as something he could choke on. His pulsebeat hammered in his ears. Still muddy, trailing his spear, he made straight for Nekhset's room. She was dressed in clean linen, crooning to herself; plump and smiling, smelling freshly of arbeeta scent. Her soft little hands were patting green malachite into her eyelids.

She glanced up, and saw Anpu in the doorway. He looked grim with his hands clenched upon the spear. She stared at them and a small sly smile crept round her mouth. "Is Bata dead, my husband? Do the dogs drink his blood for what he tried to do?"

Anput raised the spear. "The dogs shall have their meal," he answered thickly, "and tomorrow *your* heart shall weigh unevenly upon the Scales . . . cruel, faithless, lying Nekhset! Amun be praised I have no children by you—" And then he killed her.

Bata did return later to the farm; but he was no longer happy there. It was as though everything was tainted by Nekhset's deceit and death. Night after night he sat late with Anpu, talking of farm matters; then one or other of them would fall silent—and the other look away.

One day Bata said, "Anpu, dear brother, I must go! Perhaps, somewhere far off like the Valley of the Acacia, I'll find peace again."

"Don't leave me here alone!" pleaded Anpu. "How shall I manage? The days are long—at night I think only of . . . of Nekhset."

Bata was adamant. "You'll take another wife some time. But the gods will only bless me elsewhere. I know this with strange certainty."

"Shall we never meet again? Send me word, Bata—my heart will be heavy without you."

"No—I'll send no word, it's better so. I shall live like an outcast. But listen, Anpu: for its safety, I shall keep my soul in the highest flower of an acacia tree! And if, one day when you are drinking after midday, the beer boils in your pot, and you call for wine and it's sour, you shall know that I am dead. And then come seeking me."

So Bata put his garments and belongings into two chests, and strapped them on two donkeys; and he went away.

But it was very lonely in the distant valley. At first he didn't mind, for he was far too busy building himself a dwelling place: a small fort of sun-dried mud bricks, which had one square turret. Only when it was finished did he grow truly conscious of his loneliness. He gazed up at the acacia where his Ka rested in safety, and sighed out, "How I wish that some truly beautiful woman—! But never, never would I take a wife like Nekhset!"

The Sun God Re, riding across the sky, looked down and saw Bata, lonely in that very lonely valley. He noted the tall tree, and the soul nestling by itself in the topmost flower. He spoke to the other gods: "Bata must have a wife."

Then Neith and Thoth, Mut and Amun agreed: "We will send him one! We will make her more lovely than any woman in all Kemi."

"She shall be graceful as the oryx."

"Her eyes shall need neither kohl nor malachite to en-
hance them."

"Her beauty shall be so apparent that all men, seeing her,
will fall in love," said the dark god Set.

Thoth, in his wisdom, questioned this last attribute, but it
was too late: the woman whom the gods had made by their
creative thought was already lying—dressed in transparent
linen—beneath the acacia tree, and laughing at Bata's
astonishment. At first he was timid before such beauty, and
then bolder—and at last took her in his arms. They went
into his fort together; where she comforted him extremely,
in every way.

At first they lived in poverty. But Bata's corn flourished,
and he snared hares, and wildfowl, and planted melons and
lettuces. When the cold time approached, he would go
hunting; and then he said very seriously, "Sitamun, you're
too lovely to be left alone. I'm afraid someone will come
and carry you away."

"Never, my husband! I wouldn't go." She smiled
caressingly; and he shivered, halfway between misery and
happiness.

"But if force were used . . . When I'm hunting, you must
promise me to stay indoors?"

"I will do all you ask," she answered dulcetly; yet
privately she thought him foolish. It would be sad to sit
alone in the dark fort, and hide her beauty even from the
light.

As soon as Bata had disappeared beyond the valley she
combed out her long black hair and went walking by the
shore. Then the sea itself fell in love with Bata's wife. The
waves rose in a green swell, and fingers of foam crept
higher and higher up the land.

"Hold her for me!" cried the sea angrily to the acacia
while Sitamun ran up and down, laughing provocatively as
the foam fingers just failed to pull her back. But the acacia

answered, "I'm too stiff to bend so far—and she taunts me, that wicked one, standing out of reach." It struggled to and fro in the wind that had sprung up, and eventually became so angry with Sitamun that it made a desperate effort and managed to tangle her hair about one bough.

She shrieked, and tugged.

The acacia howled with laughter in the wind, and tugged as well. Sitamun was sorry for her wilfulness; she was in pain. She pulled and pulled in the opposite direction—till a long lock of her jetty hair came out. The tree waved it like a flag of blackness, and then dropped it in the sea.

("*Now* something will surely happen!" said the dark god Set.

"Nothing will happen, if everyone is wise—" decreed Thoth; but he sounded as though—from his experience—this was unlikely.)

A long, long way south, in the noble capital of Thebes, Pharaoh's washerwomen were dipping his linen garments in the Nile's sacred waters. Strange fragrance rose from the river as it flowed. The scent grew strong and stronger, till all the linen was steeped in it. The washerwomen stared at each other in amazement: why was the Nile itself suddenly scented with acacia blossom?

Two days later, as his attendants dressed him for the morning rituals, Pharaoh asked his priests, "What unguent has been used today? Something strives sweetly with the Oil of Lotus."

Amun's High Priest went to consult his god, and returned to say, "O Sovereign, my lord, Beloved of Amun! A daughter of the gods sends this sweetness to the Lord of Diadems and wearer of the Double Crown. She lives on earth, in the Valley of the Acacia. A lock of her hair was found floating in the Nile, and all the river and the Sovereign's linen were scented by it."

"She lives on *earth*?" Pharaoh was agitated. He raised the

linen to his face, and breathed in the acacia scent. "Surely the gods themselves mean her to be Great Royal Wife!" And he commanded his army to search till they had found her.

("It will be awkward if she happens to be a wife already," murmured one young priest of Amun to another, as they left the royal apartments.

"Awkward? For *Pharaoh*?" responded the other, looking at him strangely. "Either Re himself shone on you with unusual strength yesterday—or you are mad!")

Bata was making an arrow, when he heard eager shouting. He grabbed his bow, which lay close at hand. He saw his wife come running towards him, her long black hair streaming behind her. Five excited, shouting soldiers panted in her wake. One had almost reached her . . .

Bata didn't hesitate. He had always been an expert marksman, able to bring down the fastest quarry. One after another arrows twanged from his bow; so quickly did he re-arm, and so quickly did the singing flight fall, that four men lay dead before the fifth truly realised his danger. *He* feinted, stepped sideways, and took aim.

But Bata leaped for the acacia's shelter, and from there poured forth such flights of arrows that the sky seemed to be hissing with them; yet he must stay hidden, and so his aim was bad; he could only wing the soldier in his right arm. The man fled, leaving dead comrades scattered on the ground like slain, thieving birds. Sitamun flung herself into her husband's arms, and wept: he held her accusingly away from him.

"Did you hear what they were shouting as they came? They were Pharaoh's men."

She hid her face.

"They said, 'There she is! There's that beauty we are searching for!' Sitamun—you've not obeyed me: someone, somehow, has seen you walking on the shore alone!" He frowned. "And one man escaped me. We shall see more

trouble now—" He gazed upward at the topmost acacia
flower, and was glad his soul lived there in safety.

He had guessed correctly: Pharaoh's men came again, in
strength. This time Bata, returning from hunting, stood
sorrowful on a little hill and saw a litter, royally accompanied, grow small and smaller till it disappeared into the
distance. Isolation closed around him like an icy cloak. He
had glimpsed his wife's face, and she was smiling: it pleased
her to be carried off to Pharaoh. Bata thought bitterly of
women.

He would have been more bitter still, if he had known
what she would say—

"O Sovereign, my lord," she murmured sweetly in
Pharaoh's ear, as she lay clasped in his embrace, "thy
servant is uneasy; while her husband lives she can't forget
that she is nothing but a disloyal wife . . ."

"Count him as dead," recommended Pharaoh, stroking
her hair. "More soldiers shall be sent. And quickly."

"O Sovereign, my lord, Beloved of Amun! It's not Bata's
body they must trap, it is—" and she whispered of the
acacia, where Bata's soul rested in the topmost flower.

Then Pharaoh sent for a Captain of Captains, and told
him to take his men to the Valley of the Acacia, and with
them a woodcutter to cut down the tree.

Meanwhile, Anpu was very lonely on his farm. When the
reeds rustled by the river they seemed like people talking.
It was as though they spoke of happier days when his
dwelling wasn't filled with silence. He even thought of
plump, treacherous Nekhset with desire. One evening he
went into the room where he had killed her in his rage.
Near her copper mirror lay her ivory palette. He remembered how she used to sit grinding malachite for her eyelids,
and chatting in her shrill, woman's voice. He touched the

137

J

ivory with one finger, felt remorse for his ferocity, and quickly left the room. If he could at least see Bata again! The rustling reeds, the lowing cattle, the monosyllabic speech of labourers—that was all.

Anpu began drinking heavily. Then, one midday, his beer frothed and foamed so heartily that he could barely drink it. He shouted for wine instead, but it tasted sour on his palate, and was undrinkable. He recalled his brother's words. Bata must be dead.

"No!" cried Anpu aloud to the heavy silence. "No—he is *not* dead! I will *not* let him rest—Somehow, somewhere, I must bring Bata back to life."

Next day he took a horse, and rode away to the far-distant Valley of the Acacia. A small mud-brick fort stood in the centre, but the valley seemed empty of life. The fort was deserted, ochre-coloured beneath a noonday sun. The sea sighed, foam reached yearning fingers towards the shore. Leaves rustled in the wind. Otherwise, there was silence.

Then Anpu saw Bata, lying apparently asleep by the stump of an acacia. He seized him by the shoulder, and shook him: the brown, slanting eyes stared sightless at the sky.

There were no signs of violence; only—the tree had lately been cut down. Anpu could see that, for the wood was raw, like a fresh wound. He prowled round the stump miserably, thinking, This tree was Bata's guardian—he said that he would keep his soul in an acacia flower. But the more he thought about it, the more puzzling Bata's death became. How had he made another enemy? Who else but some angry woman like Nekhset would have wished to kill him?

Tenderly Anpu placed his own amulet above his brother's heart, and folded his hands upon it. "Ah—Bata! Who could have suspected that your Ka was safe hidden in an acacia flower? Who were your cruel enemies—where shall I find them?" He wrapped his cloak about his brother's body, and then began to search the Valley of the Acacia from end to end. He found many footprints in the black soil, here and there. He found spent arrows, lying on the ground. Inside the fort itself he discovered a woman's garments, and a small palette such as Nekhset used.

"For the second time someone has betrayed you, brother! But I—I, by whose wife your early life was destroyed, shall recover your vanished Ka; *then* you shall speak and tell me who the traitor is . . ."

He searched and searched diligently throughout the whole district, looking for a tree that had been cut down. Occasionally he met someone who spoke of seeing soldiers drag the leafy shape away. But he found no trace of it. After nearly three moons he returned to the valley, to stand despondently by the still form beneath his cloak. He stared up into the blue sky, and thought of Nut. "Great goddess! Of your mercy, help me to restore my brother to this world! Help me find his soul . . ."

The sky looked very empty and unresponsive. Sighing, Anpu looked downward. On the ground lay something small and fragile, delicately shaped. It was the seedpod of an acacia. All about him was a rustling sound, as though invisible leaves spoke in a discourse with the sea. The waves themselves sounded as though they were whispering offshore. The whole valley held a sense of expectation as Anpu carefully carried the seedpod into the fort. When he emerged he was holding a cup, to fetch water from the spring. He placed the seedpod in the cup, and bent his head to watch.

At first he could only see his own reflection; then he saw the water level sinking. The acacia pod was thirsty— it was drinking! It drank so fast that soon there was little water left; it drank faster than plantlife *could* drink: for it was Bata's life that drank; yes, his Ka thirsted, and swallowed from the cup.

Now, beneath the cloak, there was a shivering of limbs, as though life was returning underneath it. The cloak itself fell suddenly away. And the form grew and grew in shape and splendour: red and white spotted hide, flashing eyes,

139

curved horns. Bata had come to life again in the form of a bull!

Anpu dropped the alabaster cup. It shattered on the ground.

The bull spoke soothingly, "Anpu, dear brother, it is I, Bata! The gods have lent me this form at present—come, we go to Thebes."

"To—to Thebes?" stammered Anpu, trying to collect his wits—for it's not every day a dead relative becomes a bull.

"To Thebes, and to Pharaoh. He stole my wife from me—but the Beloved of Amun can scarcely be blamed for *that*: she was fairer than any woman in the land, for she was made by gods, and I loved her most dearly. In my heart I no longer blame her—if the gods gave her loveliness, they also made her nature. Yet she too, like Nekhset, has tried to kill me—some part of Set speaks through her. Yes, Anpu—come with me to Thebes!"

They left the Valley of the Acacia together; and Anpu let loose his horse, and rode on Bata's back.

When Bata in his new form reached Thebes he was seen to be so fine a little bull that he was taken straight to Amun's priests, although Anpu protested. Merchants jostled them both, and pushed them both, until they found themselves in a courtyard of Amun's Temple. The chief merchant—who somehow had his arms round Anpu's shoulders—and Anpu himself were rewarded by the High Priest with a small amulet apiece, and the promise of merit before the god. Then Bata was led away.

"He shall be sacred to Pharaoh, the Horus of Gold and Mighty Bull," promised the High Priest, "for a finer specimen than this spotted bull you call your brother has never come my way." He gazed at Anpu thoughtfully, tapped his own forehead, and told the merchant, "Look after him! Whatever strange thoughts the gods have sent him, *he* has brought *us* a most worthy gift."

"Come, my poor friend Anpu," said the merchant in high fettle, "and speak no more of brother bulls. Now we're both in favour with the strongest priesthood in the land—which is worth a summer's harvest in itself. My trade will prosper—and you shall have a third of all I gain."

Anpu went with him unwillingly, yet convinced that he could do no more to help Bata, who was now in the god's own hands.

Pharaoh himself soon visited the Temple, accompanied by his Great Royal Wife, and the High Priest delightedly showed them the perfect bull: "O Sovereign, my lord! He shall live ever in the Temple precincts—a symbol of the Beloved of Amun."

"See how calmly he stands," said Pharaoh, stroking the silky hide. "There is no wrath in him, he's all merit from horn to hoof. He is a worthy symbol of ourselves." And he laughed at Sitamun's timidity. "Stroke him, my Lotus. He is tame as a young calf."

Sitamun stretched out her small palm for the bull to nuzzle. As he did so, he breathed for her ears alone, "I am Bata. Cruel one, how could you forget me? Yet I forgive you everything—for the gods made you, and see, great Amun brings me to you once again."

Sitamun looked wildly at the High Priest, clutched her throat, and fell unconscious to the ground. Her lapis necklace broke, and the beads rolled away in all directions.

"My Majesty never guessed the Great Royal Wife could be so nervous," remarked Pharaoh, as two scared priests of Amun waved ostrich feathers beneath her nose.

That evening the Lord of the Two Lands visited his wife, for she lay unwell upon a couch. It was reported that she wouldn't eat.

"O Sovereign, my lord!" she cried out as he approached—
and her bosom heaved up and down with the strength of her
anxiety—"Forgive thy servant, who cannot rise to greet
thee! It was not I who shamed thee in the Temple—the God
himself struck me unconscious to the ground! I saw a light,
and heard the voice of Amun saying: 'Let not Pharaoh
mis-read the signs I send him. Shall this bull live within my
Temple as his symbol? No—the beast is sacred to myself,
Amun. His blood shall be spilled without delay before the
Temple.' Now therefore, my lord, I pray thee, let the
priests do this thing at dawn tomorrow, so evil may be
averted from my Sovereign and calamity from the Two
Lands."

She fell back, half-swooning; her ladies closed in around
her, uttering shrill cries; and Pharaoh went away, meditating
on the message he would send to Amun's priests.

Next morning, before Re had risen from the Underworld,
Bata was led garlanded outside the Temple. There the
priests made him kneel while they invoked the god. Bata
saw a knife raised in the High Priest's hands, and cursed
himself for having been so eager and so stupid; now *this*
death had been brought upon him by his wife! Yet, as he
gazed unhappily towards the Temple's interior and far-off
sanctuary of Amun, he saw a strange vision: Anubis, prick-
eared Opener of the Way, walked forward, saying, "But
the Way is not yet open for you, Bata. Fear not the knife, for
this is of the gods."

Then Re rose above the horizon, the knife descended,
and Bata's throat was cut. The priests used cords to drag the
body back into the precincts. Bata's blood had been carefully
conserved, as an offering—but two large drops of it fell into
the dust outside the Temple, and there they fertilised two
seeds of a persea tree.

Years passed. Two young persea trees grew up and flourished; the soul of Bata lived in them, moving from one to the next just as it chose. It wasn't lonely there; indeed, it had a wonderful view of all State processions. Each time his wife was carried beneath him in her litter Bata looked down, and wondered sadly if he should speak. It seemed to him that Sitamun often looked unhappy. Yet something told him still to hold his tongue.

And Sitamun had reason for unhappiness. Is it because I betrayed Bata that the gods send me no children? she wondered; once again she visited Amun's Temple to beseech his aid. Eventually a day came when Bata could contain himself no longer, for he loved her dearly in spite of all her faults. As she left the Temple the righthand persea tree leaned over her, and a voice sighed from its branches, "I am Bata! I am his Ka that lives now in these two trees! Cruel Sitamun—why do you pass me by, unspeaking?"

Then Pharaoh's wife's mouth opened wide, wide in horror, and so did her eyes. She clasped her hands together tightly, sweat poured down her cheeks, and she fell back insensible upon her cushions. The litter-bearers carried her towards the Palace at a run.

When Pharaoh came to see her, he said, "Quickly—my treasure of Osiris! Tell me! For my Majesty is sure a god has spoken to you once again. Is it not so?"

"O Sovereign, my lord, it is so!" She nodded her head dolefully, and her soft hands pressed themselves together. "And it is a strange message that I bear! The High Priest of Amun has served his god most faithfully, and is to be rewarded with a gift of fine furniture to be made by Pharaoh's craftsmen . . . a cabinet of persea wood, inlaid with ivory, ebony and gold! The wood is to be taken from the two young persea trees outside the Temple."

"It is indeed a curious command." Pharaoh looked at her somewhat narrowly—he was beginning to wonder what there was between the High Priest and his wife. Then he became agitated, in case Amun read his thoughts and was annoyed; he added smoothly, "But let it be so, O dove who reached me from the wilderness!"

When the Sovereign had left her Sitamun looked about her most uneasily, and her hands rumpled the hangings of her bed. She was thinking, Bata is still alive—perhaps this is why I'm childless to my lord! Wife to two men at once . . . *This* time, the carpenter's tools shall make an end of him. I will go myself to watch, and then—if no voice speaks from the cabinet—I shall know that surely I am free.

Pharaoh's craftsmen were surprised and flattered by the presence of the Great Royal Wife. As their work progressed she would stroke the separate pieces and murmur, "It's strange how wood has a sense of life about it . . . if it had tongues, what things it might not tell! Come, my poor persea trees—are you speechless?"

A young carpenter, who was carving a piece of wood into an ankh, symbol of life, glanced up at her, and his hand slipped upon the wood. Splinters flew in all directions; the piece was spoiled. Sitamun opened her mouth wide to reprove him. The largest splinter flew straight into it, and down her throat, before she could so much as cough.

The carpenter prostrated himself in horror. The Great Royal Wife covered her face angrily with her fine linen scarf, and withdrew. In her Palace apartments she summoned her ladies, swallowed sesame oil, and lay down that night hoping all was well. But the Ka of Bata lay deep inside her, rejoicing in its closeness to her it had so dearly loved. It was dark and warm there, and very comfortable, and it could hear the beating of her heart. Later it slipped down into her womb, and there remained in great happiness and peace until nine months had passed, when it was born again. The first cry it gave sounded to its mother's ears just like, "Ba-ta, Bata, Baaaa-ta!"

Pharaoh was enchanted with his son; he couldn't understand why Sitamun seemed to entertain mixed feelings for her baby. Sometimes she would cuddle him as though she would never let him go, and at others she would snatch him from the hands of the royal nurse to shake him, crying, "Wicked one! How dare you! There's no outfacing such a one as you—you are bolder than a bull, more double than two persea trees!" The baby would crow delightedly, and bump his head against her breast; he was where he'd always wished to be.

Then the Great Royal Wife would put him on her knee, and say, "This is the way the Royal Heir rides, trit-trot, trit-trot—" and she would jump him up and down fast and faster, rather hard, until they would suddenly start laughing both together. *Then* she would press him to her breast. How happy Bata was—for the first time he was in full control. As for what the gods thought, no one knows for certain, although there were rumours that Thoth and Nut were most amused by the dark god Set's discomfiture.

King Solomon's Throne

King Solomon was a lover of wisdom, as everyone knows. He had received from his father David the pearl "seven times purer than the sun"—that pearl of salvation which God had placed in the belly of our forefather Adam, so that it might pass through the line of great King David till it became the essence of the Virgin Mary, mother of the Christ.

But King Solomon was a sound lover of women too. For in his heart God had placed this knowledge that his seed would be blessed, and so the King wanted many children. Even Pharaoh's daughter became his wife—but for all that, King Solomon still sighed after each beautiful woman that he saw: he loved foreign women well. His wisdom was huge, and his loving as vast—if not vaster. Often wisdom and loving together shared that fine King's heart; though they were sometimes a little out of step.

Now, Solomon's fame had spread very far with the traders, and Masters of Caravans. These merchants had brought him all precious things for the building of the Temple at Jerusalem, and for his palace; then they had travelled home to their own peoples, and spoken with awe of the King's piety and sweetness, his wisdom and his love. Among the Masters was one Tâmrîn, who did much business for the Queen of the South. Some people say she was the Queen of Ethiopia, and others that she came from Sheba in south-west Arabia, but, wherever she came from, her native wisdom was still in a state of unenlightenment: she worshipped the sun; yet some questions, as she worshipped, puzzled her very much indeed.

This merchant Tâmrîn had brought to Jerusalem red gold from Arabia, as well as rare wood and many excellent jewels. And when he came into the King's presence he was overcome by the King's personality, and marvelled at his wisdom—for Solomon was loved by everyone who saw him, and his judgments were just. He spoke graciously to those who served him, and dealt very gently with them, for he had an understanding heart, and all men learned of him. Tâmrîn was amazed to find here a King who was no oppressor: whose words were as the water of life to his people, and who was a father to orphans. He saw that God had given to Solomon grace, and honour, and glory and riches, and that there could be no king like him in any other land. So when Tâmrîn returned to his own country he told the Queen of Sheba all he had heard and all he had seen, and she was struck with amazement, and immediately her desire was towards the sight of King Solomon, and to set out at once in the direction of his city, Jerusalem.

When the precious gifts she had brought him were carried into the King's presence he rejoiced exceedingly in them, and paid her great honour—for fairer than any of her gifts was Queen Mâkĕdâ's face, and no sooner had Solomon set eyes on it than he felt himself stirred, and he straightway desired to have a son by her. Throughout many days, while he discoursed eloquently on those questions that puzzled her, and her admiration grew for his wisdom, and she marvelled at his splendour and his grace, King Solomon, in some portion of his intricately-fashioned mind, was turning over this problematical question of a possible son.

At last they turned to the consideration of strange and magical things: "Will my lord speak now in the understanding of his heart about the speech of beasts and birds?" asked the Queen meekly; and slightly withdrew her right hand, which was somehow at that moment in the King's.

Then King Solomon spoke of the speech of beasts and birds.

"Will my lord explain now to his humble sister how he

147

came by such knowledge?" asked the Queen serenely; moving very slightly on the jewelled throne till the King's thigh was no longer pressed to hers.

So King Solomon spoke about himself; and as he did so his hand strayed as though absentmindedly, and touched the dark tendrils of hair curling about the base of the Queen's neck.

"Oh!" she cried out, "there is a fly upon my neck!" And she slapped at the spot reprovingly, and murmured, "Will my lord speak now of the encroaching ways of insects during the hot weather?"

"Mâkĕdâ!" said the King reproachfully, "I have spent many, many days discoursing with thee, and answering thy questions: is the wisdom of my understanding, and the glory that God bestows on me, as nothing in thine eyes? That was no insect—which thou knowest! Alas, the King's wisdom is nothing in this matter."

"But it is surely true," said the Queen very sweetly, "that the King's wisdom informs him in everything? For the God of Israel made him so—and therefore, my lord knowest it was an insect that alighted on my neck. I look upon thee, and I see that thy wisdom is unfathomable, and thine understanding inexhaustible—it is as the sun to the darkness, and a fruit tree in a garden, and the Morning Star among the host of heaven—" so she spoke on for some time, while the King grew very restless on the throne beside her, and gnawed his bearded lip. In the end he retorted somewhat tartly, "Wisdom is surely thine as well, and springs from thy whole person! Though as for King Solomon, he possesses it in the manner that the God of Israel—on the King's entreaties—measured it." And he added explosively, "What use is King Solomon, if he does not exercise love upon this earth?"

The Queen gave him a look from her long, beautiful eyes, and murmured soothingly, "Is it not enough that the King should love his God? Tell me now—O my lord!—whom should I worship? The sun is very great—and my fathers worshipped him. Yet it seems to thy sister that the King has a God who is greater than her own."

Then King Solomon ceased his momentary sulking, and waxed most eloquent upon the subject of his God; and eventually he converted the fair Queen of Sheba, and they met with each other often, that they might speak of these great matters to their hearts' desire; and the King managed to put from his thoughts the Queen of Sheba's beauty—till it was almost time for her to go. Then again he pondered on it longingly. Why did God send this most splendid beauty to my kingdom, and from so far away, if He does not mean to send me seed by her? As though by inspiration he recalled what God had said to Abraham: "I will make thy seed like the stars of heaven, and like the sand of the sea." Is this not why (he thought) I so love women? That my children may rule over God's enemies, and destroy the idolators. And besides (he thought wistfully) she is so *very* beautiful. . . .

But in no way could he prevail against the Queen of Sheba's determination to return virgin to her people. "For if it were otherwise, would I not be shamed?" she said. "Now swear to me, King Solomon, by the God of Israel, that thou wilt not take me against my will." And King Solomon swore. Yet he pleaded, "If so be that thou should'st come to my chamber by thine own choice, then let my oath be forgotten?" And the Queen of Sheba smiled at him indulgently, as at a child, and agreed: for the moment she had forgotten about that fine King's wisdom.

Well—King Soloman withdrew to his apartments, and put his wisdom quietly to work. He considered all he knew of the beautiful Mâkĕdâ, and all she liked, and was. He remembered her great fondness for basking in the sun— that she came from a hot land, and was unaccustomed to the cold; and that, if they had been seated together in the shade some little while, she would shiver and say, "O my lord, I beseech thee that we may continue these our discussions in the sun." When he remembered this, King Solomon smiled his smile that won all men's hearts, and went up on to the rooftop of his palace, and whistled to the birds. He whistled and whistled very loud and clear till they came flying—the doves of Jerusalem.

So King Solomon commanded, "Fly now in all directions! Go out over sea and land, till you come to the coldest place on earth; and then bring back word to me." And immediately the doves rose in a white cloud, hovered a while, then flew away North, South, East and West.

During their absence the King went once more to visit Queen Mâkĕdâ. He seemed shaken with a great sighing, as he said, "I am in sorrow for thy refusal! Grant me one small request, before thou leavest me."

"O wise King Solomon," said the Queen, looking at him lovingly, for she held him in true affection, "if it be not that sort of request thou hast already made too often, then will I grant it: speak."

"I am building a fine Castle," said the King thoughtfully, "and ask only that the Queen of Sheba spend one night in it before departing from my presence."

The Queen was much surprised. The King's palace at Jerusalem—for which Tâmrîn the merchant had supplied so many goods—was only just complete, and she had never seen anything more regal in her life. Still, she answered, "Another royal abode? My lord, I had not heard of it! Yet will I grant thy request. Let us set out for it today, and hurry there; for then must I return to my own kingdom—so long without its Queen."

"Stay but a short while yet," implored the King, "for in truth this particular Castle is unfinished, but—" he added, holding up a hand to prevent an outburst of reproaches which he could see gathering on the Queen's lips, "it will be finished soon. Soon, *soon*," he added passionately, to her surprise. "In the matter of a moon or so I, Solomon the King, will take thee there." He broke off their meeting somewhat abruptly, leaving Mâkĕdâ the Queen frowning after him, and went up on to the palace rooftop to scan the wide skies North, South, East and West. Towards sundown, the flocks of doves he had sent out that morning could be seen returning home.

They fluttered to the ground about his feet, and to his hands and shoulders. In turn they made report. One said it was very cold in this place, another that it was even colder in that place, and a third appeared all ruffled up because she was *still* cold after the long flight home. Yet Solomon wasn't quite convinced that she had found the right place for his Castle to be built. He looked about him at the thronging doves—each one of whom he knew by some slight difference from the others—and inquired, "Where is the little dove with the brown and silver mottled wing—she who always fed from my hands with special trust and love?" And the birds answered, "O lord King Solomon, that little dove is not yet returned. Perchance some sad misfortune has overtaken her in her long flight . . ."

Wise King Solomon shook his head. He dismissed the doves of Jerusalem, and went down into his palace, and waited for the dawn.

It came; yet with it came no missing dove. Then, towards midday, when the air was very still, there was a sudden waft of hot breeze from the desert, and with it arrived a tired white form with one mottled wing, fluttering to the King's feet as he took his ease in the rose-scented gardens of the palace.

"Well, my small friend," said the King, who spoke the language of all birds and beasts (as is well known), "what news hast thou for me?"

"Let my lord King forgive his feathered servant this delay! Yet may he rejoice that it is truly found—that coldest place on earth!" And the dove shuddered to recall it. "I landed there at nightfall—and was straightway frozen to the ground! There I crouched till dawn, unable to move my wings—they were so stiff and hard that I feared never to fly again, never to see my wise King, nor Jerusalem his great city! I feared even that my heart itself would stop, and I might not live to tell the King the answer to his question."

"Well done indeed, my little dove!" exclaimed King Solomon gladly; and he called for grain, and gave her big handfuls of it. "Where is this dreadful place?"

"Far off in Persia, O beloved King. It is the summit of a high mountain, near the Caspian sea. As I flew low today, warming my wings to suppleness again, I heard a young man say that the range also contains the holy peak Mount Devadand, which the people hold in awe, so great is its connection with the world of light!"

"Why—thou art a learned, helpful little dove!" remarked King Solomon, much pleased; and he drew her to him, and warmed her kindly against his breast.

Then the King called to him his wise men and builders, and his merchants, and sent them deep into Persia, till they passed the great peak Devadand and turned north-west along the mountain range till they found the frozen summit that they looked for. Here they raised and furnished a castle more splendid than any seen in all that ancient world. Yet, truly, it was the King's own achievement, for without the aid of his strange powers, his wisdom and genius, the task could not have been accomplished in so little time.

Then King Solomon said to Mâkĕdâ, in high fettle, "Come, thou Ethiopian pomegranate" (or "thou Sheban quince") "let us go to visit my new Castle which thou wilt deign to consecrate with thy gracious presence for that promised night."

And the Queen of Sheba responded, "Gladly, King Solomon! Then will thy sister return to her own land—she will go increased in wisdom by the King's instruction, yet as virgin as on the day of her arrival."

It was so magnificent, that Castle, when the King's long train reached it from the slopes below. The sun hadn't set, but the icicles glittered everywhere with cold blue light that here and there flashed rainbows. The new stronghold was hung with them like fretwork—for only on small sheltered bits of ground had there been any thaw during the day.

As they reached the gates, Queen Mâkĕdâ shivered. "I am very, very cold!"

"Courage!" cried King Solomon, with his kindest smile. "Here is my cloak of furs." He placed it around her shoulders, yet she shivered still. He himself glowed with almost supernatural warmth, for among his many gifts was that of controlling the temperature of his own body by the power of thought.

"But there are no fires!" declared the poor Queen desperately once they were indoors. The cloak might have been made of linen, for all the warmth it gave. "I beg thee, O lord King Solomon, to have thy servants light a fire!"

"See! There are many lit already," replied the King, "though truly they seem to give out little heat, and so pale are the flames that they are barely visible. The cold is curiously intense! Are not these views glorious from this towering peak, my doe-eyed one, my gate of ivory?" And he led her to a window—but she hardly glanced from it, for she shivered so violently that her small feet vibrated on the floor, and she could think of nothing but the joy of reaching her own bedchamber as fast as possible and there huddling down beneath the coverings. Surely it would be warm?

"Thou art exhausted, my sister!" murmured the King solicitously. Nevertheless, he kept her there some while as he discoursed with entrancing wisdom on the ancient history of Persia, its geography, its flora, fauna, religion, and its arts. Although the words flowed beguilingly, the Queen could not pay them full attention. She retired almost abruptly, calling to her maidservants that they should seek for every fur that they could find and heap them on her bed. This done, she leaped into it, winding herself up in King Solomon's fur cloak, and thought compulsively of heat and fire and sun, and the warmth of her own land.

King Solomon, meanwhile, withdrew to his own

K

chamber. It was scented, and still. He commanded sandal-
wood to be scattered on the fire; then he sat before it, deep
in thought and smiling in his beard. At last he yawned
heavily and stretched, and called his menservants to remove
his garments and conduct him ceremoniously to bed. They
came running, marvelling to see that he never felt the cold
but even waved away a linen shift.

When he was alone, the King lay upon his back. He closed
one eye, while the other watched the door. His right hand
stroked his beard reflectively. He was thinking, Behold,
thou art fair, my love; behold, thou art fair; thou hast
doves' eyes! And: How much better is thy love than wine!
And it is probable he also thought, in his great wisdom,
Not—long—now . . .

It was *not* long before the hangings at his doorway were
pulled aside by a small, imperious, impatient hand, and the
Queen of Sheba stood there, shivering convulsively, and
glaring like a royal she-leopard. "Wouldst thou have me
freeze to death, King Solomon!" she cried, rubbing at the
tip of her nose which was purple as a grape from the vines
that little foxes spoil. "Is there nowhere in thy abominable
Castle that is warm?"

"Alas—only within the King's bed," coaxed King
Solomon dulcetly, sitting up; and even by the pale firelight
the royal naked torso appeared almost sunburned. "But some
hours after dawn the Castle itself will certainly be warm,
even up here." And he discoursed with moving eloquence
upon the Persian climate.

"Thou hast arranged it all on purpose!" cried the Queen,
stamping her right foot—an unsatisfying gesture, for she
could not feel it when it touched the floor. "Thy sister will
be as an icicle, long before dawn! How is it, O wise King
Solomon, thou impenitent, prophesying, Hebrew trickster,
thou art so warm in thy great warm bed?"

King Solomon merely stretched his arms above his head
and yawned, "Ahhhhhhh—." It was a sound of pure pleasure,

and there was not a goosepimple on the royal arms from wrist to shoulder. Then he added, "Make haste, my beloved, and be thou like to a roe or to a young hart upon the mountains of spices."

So the Queen of Sheba darted across the threshold of King Solomon's bedchamber and into the royal bed with no thought of anything but warmth. And Solomon gladly put his arms around her, murmuring, "Now is the King freed from his forced oath?" And thinking, "Doves' eyes, does' eyes, doves' eyes . . ." for he was already, in his all-embracing wisdom, mulling over a few passionate phrases for his Chief Musician to set to music for the harp. Then he embraced the Queen of Sheba—who did, after all, keep very warm that night; and there is little more that need be said.

Except that when day came King Solomon rose up full of happiness and wellbeing, and went out on to the chilly mountainside, where he touched the ground; and immediately his people were astonished to see a hot spring gush forth. There the Queen of Sheba bathed, while King Solomon watched her; there grew up around them a shielding garden, with jasmine and the *mahmudi* rose from which attar of roses is made. And King Solomon gave to the Queen of Sheba cakes with carraway seeds, and black and white mulberries, yellow plums, figs, nectarines, and sweet-smelling apricots in a plateful of violets. In his gratitude he gave her many things of value: cloaks of bearskin and leopard, wild fox and tiger; and a ring from his little finger, so that she might not forget him.

And he gave her a son, too, whom her people were later to call a shining man, since he grew so like his father Solomon in all his gracious looks and acts that they could barely be told apart. Because of that fruitful night which Queen Mâkĕdâ spent with King Solomon in his Persian Castle, the peak of that cold mountain where they slept is called the Takht-i-Sulaiman—the Throne of Solomon—until this day.

The Stolen Prince

There was once a Princess so lovely that she had many suitors, although her father was merely king of a little kingdom with a small army of a thousand men, and his country, which was by the sea, was only rich in olive trees and goats; he was no High King. You might have thought his daughter glad to leave there—but she was a dreamy Princess, who let one day pass after the next while she walked on the uplands, or through the dry fields where the snakes lay golden in the sun and wriggled hissing into their holes at her approach. She gathered flowers there: poppies such as Persephone had been plucking when Hades snatched her; or wild cyclamen; or the lilac and scarlet anemones that once sprang from Adonis' blood. And then she would walk home lightly, lightly—to find her father fretting in his small white palace because she hadn't been there to entertain her latest suitor, with his fine title, his wealth, and his bristly, discouraging beard.

"Ariadne," said the King one day in desperation, "for whom are you waiting? Did your dead mother give me a girl with no thought of Christian duty?" The poor Princess sighed. She wanted to please him; yet she thought: Is that all there is to life? Some plain prince with long lineage, a marble palace finer than this shabby one of ours—yet how I love it!—and a flock of dull, plain children?

"Father, you know I'm Christian; a devout daughter of the Orthodox Church! But this doesn't make me want these princes—they're so—so—" And she made a face.

The King looked at her narrowly. "Devout you may be, child—heaven grant it so!—but what do you think of when

156

you walk the uplands, and come home windswept with your hands full of wild flowers? They're dangerous places, the uplands—they were once the haunt of pagan gods." And he crossed himself; and then again.

His daughter was silent. She looked down at the anemone she was holding, and stroked its lilac petals, and then put it to her cheek.

"Father," she said at last. "Wouldn't you miss me? Who cooks for you as well as I do? Who makes such fine white goats' cheese, or stews your veal with wine and mushrooms and adds lemon thyme and rosemary and tiny peas just as you like them?"

"Hmmm-mm-mm . . ." Her father licked his kingly lips, then recovered himself, and said earnestly, "I beg you never to reveal these facts outside our palace! A Princess who cooks!" He looked over his shoulder as though a relation stood there, laughing.

"That's nothing to be ashamed of!" declared his daughter gaily. "Aren't we good hosts as a result? That last prince had three helpings."

"Glutton!"

"We-ell . . . and that's how he looked on me! As though *I* were a fourth helping. So I'll wait—I'll wait—" She sighed; and after a moment added briskly, "Now I won't keep you, father dear. For you've council matters, while I must make sweet things for the next Saint's day. Perhaps I'll seethe pears and figs in wine, and make—yes!—marchpane! Figures of marchpane, to delight the servants' children." She went off to the kitchens, carrying her flowers to be put in water. Their sappy stalk-smell was heady as sacrificial wine.

Barefooted country kitchenmaids scattered at her approach, though the head cook stayed to give her not only the country greeting of "Chairete!—Rejoice!" but the respect due to a superior in the culinary art.

"Fetch me the jars of blanched almonds and sugar, Clymene. Semolina, too. We'll need figs and pears; last year's cooking wine, and lemon, and—" The young Princess brooded, tapping her fingers on the scrubbed wooden table as Clymene flew here and there about the kitchen to fetch huge earthenware jars, amphoras of wine, and fruit and spices.

"You begin stewing, Clymene—while I make the marchpane," murmured the Princess. She put her long beautiful hands into the jar of almonds, and dreamily let the white peeled nuts slip between her fingers into the mortar. There was soon a fine smell of cooking fruit, and by evening the table's end was covered in marchpane figures ready to win the heart of any greedy child.

"Hph! Princess—" Clymene stood with arms akimbo. "Your Highness is sculptress as well as cook! You have some handsome people there! See the little man—oho, oho!"

"He is lifelike, is he not?" The Princess wistfully admired her own handiwork.

"More handsome than these great men who come to woo you, any day!"

"Would God I could make myself a husband!" said the Princess passionately, picking up the small figure and squeezing him to shapelessness between her palms. "I might have one then more to my liking . . ." And she turned and went quickly from the kitchen, while Clymene stared after her with open mouth.

That night, when the moon was shining very brightly— the moonspinners hadn't yet wound her off on to their spindles—the Princess, in her nightgown, flitted down through the palace to the empty, silent kitchens. Alone she staggered to and fro under the weight of the almond and sugar jars. She took the largest pestle and mortar, and ground and ground until several kilos of almonds were ready for her task. Then she took an equal part of sugar, and another of semolina; and with lemon juice and egg yolk and almond essence she worked and worked the mixture till it was pliable as clay. She gave a little gasp, crossed herself, and began to mould.

The Stolen Prince

Whether the pagan Muses stood behind her shoulder, or her Christian guardian angel, who can say? But she worked as though inspired. Praxiteles himself could not have had a student with a surer touch. Under Ariadne's skilful fingers emerged lifelike toes and feet and lithe muscular legs of marchpane. She worked upwards, from the table top; and when she reached the marchpane waist she lowered her creation to the floor, and went on moulding: up and up, torso, shoulder, neck, jaw; she left a great round piece of marchpane ready for the head while she accomplished arms and hands, and fingers. Then she took a deep breath, rubbed her palms in fine semolina to remove the sweat, and delicately, expertly, with a loving touch, moulded such features as the ancient goddesses themselves might have delighted in.

"Oh, my sweet Marchpane! Prince Marchpane!" crooned Princess Ariadne in awe when she had done. And wept a little, because of his perfection. But *he* stared blindly at her and didn't move: he was only made of paste. The Princess, in her white nightgown, trailed back to her bedroom and looked blindly at the moon. The moon stared blindly back.

Next day, when Clymene found the statue in her kitchen, she clapped her hands. "Didn't I say our Princess was a born sculptress?"

But Ariadne looked upon her handiwork, and sighed. Suddenly she swept Prince Marchpane into her arms and carried him through the palace till they reached the corridor and niche where St. Cecilia, her patron saint, stood carved and gilded in plaster on a plinth. She deposited Prince Marchpane before the saint and turned him so that his moulded marchpane eyes gazed at St. Cecilia's softer features. Then Ariadne prostrated herself on the floor, lying stiff as a rod, her head turned to one side, her eyes closed, her arms outstretched in the ancient posture of supplication. She began to pray.

She prayed and prayed and prayed to God. For that first week, as his daughter lay refusing food or drink, the King was scandalised, distraught. He closed the Saint's corridor to all the servants, while *he* lit small votive lamps, begging that his cherished child might regain her senses. Then, as the Princess continued to lie there with her eyes closed, praying —and she did so for forty days and forty nights as monotonously as the rain fell during the great Flood—he began to treat her extraordinary behaviour as though it were quite normal; and he would merely step across her body when he wished to pass.

At last, when Ariadne had become mere skin and bone, something happened. It was as though all the energy in her prayer had gathered itself together, and now hummed above her head like a swarm of bees—or was she hearing things, after her long fast? She opened her eyes. The humming stopped. She heard instead a distant sound which might have been sweet voices singing. It was morning, and the corridor was full of light. "Ah God, God, God, God!" cried out the Princess in piercing tones of bitter anguish; and, joining her hands before her face, prayed again in desperation. Then she ceased, and looked upward, and saw Prince Marchpane had turned to face her, and that his eyes were open and luminous with life, and his lips quivered as Adam's must have done when God first gave him breath.

Beautiful in his sweet-scented flesh which gave out a subtle smell of crushed almond, Prince Marchpane was a living, breathing man. What's more, he was a proper man in every way, since Ariadne was so good a sculptress. The palace servants were scandalised to catch a glimpse of naked Marchpane carrying their worn-out, feverish Princess to her own room. After that the nuptials were—as the King said in some annoyance—quite essential. God had raised up Prince Marchpane, a Patriarch baptised him, and the wedding was quietly solemnised. In spite of as much discretion as could be hoped for in the circumstances the news of what had happened spread and spread, and with it the tale of Prince Marchpane's remarkable, godlike, golden looks. Women gazed disparagingly at their bearded husbands and sighed for the beauty and luscious strangeness of Prince Marchpane and his subtle smell.

Word of him reached an older, darker kingdom, where Hermes' white crane was still held sacred. There, a lonely Queen looked daily in her glass, and sighed: her near-black almond-shaped eyes had never looked upon a worthy lover. This talk of Marchpane made her grind her small teeth as resolutely as Princess Ariadne had ground the nuts. "That crushed-almond man should have wedded our almond-eyed Queen," her courtiers said; and the Queen swept up in agitation, her green robe twisting about her like a serpent's tail.

"Build me a jewelled ship made of gold—and tell my goldsmith to fashion its long oars! Then make all ready for my sailing . . ." As soon as these orders were obeyed she set sail in greedy haste toward the isles of Greece.

There, the gold ship was seen rising over the horizon to speed across the waves and make its own gold pathway like a little sun. There were ohs! and ahs! and look theres! from people on each shoreline, as word spread of the strange sight. There had been no such sensation for many years—except the one of Ariadne's Prince.

The dark Queen had had herself inadequately disguised as a young sailor, her cloudy hair hidden under a stocking cap. She ran nimbly up the rigging and peered landward, where an interested crowd stood near a waterfront. She called out, "Master Mariner! Is this the kingdom where Prince Marchpane lives with his Princess?"

"Indeed, my Queen, the very one! There are the olive trees surrounding the shabby white palace where they live, as many have described. A poor sort of place!" He gave a rumbling, denigrating laugh.

The Queen's small pink tongue flickered in and out like a viper's. She licked her lips, as though already tasting something good. "Find me that paragon of all male beauty— then seize him, bind him, bring him here on board."

"Madam—it may start a war!" The seaman stared.

"Fool!" The Queen stamped her foot at him in mid air, absentmindedly, and nearly fell. "Have they seen us before? Do they know where we come from—or where we'll fly to? They will gape at a jewelled ship—but we shall trick them, and sail away. Do as I say—and quickly!"

The sailors didn't have to search. Marchpane was young and alert, and interested in everything. A golden ship, all jewelled, came seldom to that poor kingdom—if at all. He himself was standing near the shore when the foreign sailors rowed in, and went to meet them joyously, ready with a welcome. When they saw him, as vulnerable as any silly deer standing for dogs to pull it down, they let out a rough cheer, and boisterously rushed him. None of his countrymen realised what was happening. First, Prince Marchpane was surrounded; then he was swept toward the sailors' boat—but only his turned head could be seen, and not his struggles; and *then* he was borne off across the rippling waves. He shouted shorewards, and waved, but everyone merely thought, He wants a message taken to the Princess, to say he's gone on board . . . And when the boat didn't return with the evening tide, they said, "Naturally he dines with the Captain."

Ariadne was dining with her father. How long the time seemed in that quiet palace, without her Marchpane! Now and then the King spoke of the food, and in between whiles she heard the jug-jug-jugging of nightingales, whose throats throbbed with summer passion. Tall amber candles were lit, for the night was eerily dark and the moon in her last quarter. The three moonspinners had almost spun her down the sky on to their spindles.

The Princess grew more and more troubled by Marchpane's absence. She missed his tender glances, though she knew herself absurd to be upset because he'd gone to dine upon a stranger's ship! All the same, she rose before cheese had been placed beside her, hurried from the room, and down towards the sea.

The night flower scents were heady, but she paid them no

attention; her thoughts were on her husband. Her little feet ran fast as she pushed aside lemon verbena and juniper, and reached a path above the bay. She stared. There was no one on the shore below, for there was nothing now to look at but the usual caiques. The golden ship, and with it her precious Marchpane, had already gone! A round dancing patch of gold on the horizon, like a flung coin, was the last of the reflections where the dark Queen's galley fled.

In vain the King tried to soothe his daughter's sorrow. She showed no sign of Christian resignation, but tore her hair, and mumbled of the Furies, like a girl possessed. Then she demanded that the palace shoemaker should hammer out some iron shoes for her, so she might search and search throughout the world and never go illshod. Her father stood aghast when she commanded, "Three pairs! And I'll not come back, dear father—unless I've found him, or worn them out in vain." She sobbed, and tore her hair, and wailed aloud. There was no such carry-on since ripe Demeter mislaid Persephone.

"I said she shouldn't walk on those high places," muttered the worried parent, "you never know what strange gods may haunt them still ..." And he spent much time before St. Cecilia, begging her to restore his lovesick daughter to her wits. Yet one morning he woke to find that Ariadne, with her three glinting pairs of iron shoes, had tapped away down the highway to the sea, like a beggarwoman who has no special home.

She journeyed and journeyed—poor Princess Ariadne! She sailed by caique to all the islands. She tramped through Turkey, and begged her way through Persia and Afghanistan. She grew thin and brown and strained, and soon wore out one pair of iron shoes; but no one she met could tell her where Prince Marchpane was, or where the golden ship had gone. In time the Princess felt lightheaded—she had fed off roots and berries, and strange mushrooms. After eating the mushrooms she found herself far, far from this earth, inquiring for Marchpane from the Moon's own mother.

But the Moon, when she returned from circling the earth, grew sulky, for she was jealous of Ariadne's beauty—till the mother said sharply, "She only seeks her husband, sweet Prince Marchpane, who has been snatched away."

"I've never heard of him—nor seen him anywhere! Why don't you ask the Sun? *His* rays creep into more dark corners; so he may find this hiding husband easily!"

Princess Ariadne soon soothed her down; and next day, by way of peace-offering, was handed a ridged brown almond, and told to open up the shell only when she needed aid. Then the Moon and her mother watched her trudge off toward the Sun—but it was the same story there, as well: neither he nor *his* mother had seen the missing Marchpane. They gave her a special walnut, and advised her to seek out the dwelling of the mother of the Stars.

Long before she reached it poor Ariadne had already thrown away her second pair of worn-out iron shoes, and was almost worn out herself . . . She met the Star Children coming from the Day's white eye where they had lain well hidden.

No, they hadn't seen the Princess's husband. They were very, very sorry, but—

"I did! *I* did!" piped up the smallest Star, and turned a twinkling cartwheel so that several mariners below made errors on their charts. When he had danced a little, for sheer joy, he calmed enough to speak: "The White-Browed Queen holds him as her loved prisoner—her carved and fretted palace, high-standing on its mount near a black river, is his sad prison. I danced above the rooftops only last night, and watched him sighing in a courtyard. His eyes dripped tears, and the Queen herself kneeled beside him, coaxing him to eat. Here, lovely Princess—take this hazelnut! It may be you'll need it, if you try to rescue him!"

Then Ariadne thanked the Star Child, and ran full-tilt along the Milky Way in her last pair of iron shoes. There was a roaring in her ears, though the Furies, who had been dogging her unnoticed, covered their hideous faces and fell behind. She spun toward the earth as though a spider were letting her drop on a strong thread from its web. She woke, rubbing her eyes, to find herself in an unknown land. Nearby, a splendid palace towered, formidable in bone-whiteness and in size. Even as a Princess, Ariadne might have found it daunting; now she was a brown-faced, filthy beggarwoman, dressed in tatters. She gave a sobbing laugh and, grimacing, tore off her iron shoes—their soles were almost gone! She gazed at the palace. The sky above it was like thick bean soup, and the air about it heavy as though someone had absorbed the goodness before it could be breathed by human lungs.

Princess Ariadne's heart hammered in her chest. "I've come to the end of my endeavours! If dearest Marchpane isn't held within this place, I'll surely die." She bound the three precious nuts securely in a corner of her kerchief, and hobbled toward the palace, where she begged for work. Truly she was hungry! She could have eaten earth.

The Queen's servants weren't a generous pack; but her goosegirl had lately died of plague, and—since they were tired of falling over her unherded, hissing flock—they asked if Ariadne might take her place. *Then* she felt as though her heart sang in her thin chest—for she soon saw Prince Marchpane! He too was thin, though perfection still to look on; and the ribald servants jeered that this man snatched by the Queen to be unwilling consort could pine like any girl.

He pines! thought Ariadne gladly; and she drove her flock beneath the gallery where she had seen him; yet, though they were now so near each other, he was oblivious of it. What could she do?

Just then the wind tugged at her kerchief, which she'd bound about her hair. She put up her hands, felt the nuts securely tied where she had placed them and, remembering the Moon's instructions, drew out the almond. When she had jumped on it, and cracked the shell wide open—the geese came hustling round her in hope of grain—there flew out of it no kernel but a silver spinning wheel which grew rapidly to full size and spun on silver spools. . . .

Naturally, it wasn't long before the Queen heard that the serving girl owned such treasure, and she pouted enviously, and yearned for its possession. As she sat by reluctant Prince Marchpane, stroking his hand, and cooing her blandishments, she was secretly thinking of the goosegirl's spinning wheel. She told her servants, "That strange, tattered creature! Tell her a wheel like hers is far more suitable for me."

But Ariadne touched the wheel as though she prized it beyond life. She murmured, "Our loving Queen! Yet my wheel's most dear to me. Wait! If her Majesty lends me something *she* values greatly—just for one night—she shall have my wheel to be her very own."

The Queen laughed gaily when the servants told her what Ariadne said. "Does the girl want to go prinking in my emeralds or rubies among her smelly geese? Does she name what she wants—for that one night?"

The servants blushed a little, and murmured, "Prince Marchpane."

The Queen's almond-shaped eyes slanted even further as she laughed, and laughed again. "Does she, indeed? A forthcoming goosegirl! Well—she shall borrow my most valuable possession—" And she smiled a very subtle smile.

That night, once they had eaten together in her high hall, the White-Browed Queen murmured in Marchpane's ear, "My dear one—you've seemed sadder, lately? I would change your mood! See, here's a goblet of a wine you've never tried before. This will surely do you good . . ."

Prince Marchpane, smiling sorrowfully, accepted a glassful of the potent, resinous wine, which reminded him of the wines of Greece. No sooner had he drunk it than he reeled to his feet, then collapsed in heavy slumber on the tabletop. The Queen sat there and watched him; and smiled and smiled.

The Stolen Prince

When the servants had carried off the silver spinning wheel, and left Marchpane behind them lying on the floor of Ariadne's hut, she flung herself down thankfully beside her husband, and kissed his mouth. He lay still and pale, his eyes tight closed, his hands open imploringly, palm upward, as though they cried for help. She called his name, repeatedly. Again there was no movement, except deep, sighing breaths. Marchpane might have been unconscious.

Ariadne's thankfulness to see him changed to despair. She shook him, upbraided him; sang to him like the sirens—but Ulysses' crew could have been no more indifferent than he was. She whispered her long adventures in his ear, spoke of her search, her sorrow. She reminded him of how she made him. She cried about her blistered feet. "Speak to me, pity me, remember what you mean to me! My life—my candle in the dark!" But Prince Marchpane breathed and breathed, and never woke. He was oblivious alike to his wife's touch upon his cheek and her frantic tears.

At dawn came the palace servants, joking and sneering. They collected Marchpane, and bore him off to where the White-Browed Queen was waiting with another brew, to wake him up. "Refreshing sleep, my darling? Less sad today?" she cried; and ran off to try her spinning wheel.

"Will the Sun's gift have more power?" wondered Ariadne. She dried her tears, and then smashed the walnut angrily against the wall. Out flew a golden duck, which went quacking across the room followed by a dozen shining ducklings. All made of precious metal, yet alive, they waggled their tails and followed the Princess as she wandered ostentatiously through the palace courtyards with her geese.

"That girl again?" The Queen was already sick of spinning, and the silver wheel. "Pure gold ducks? They really might amuse me—a sensation with the ambassadors! Tell her I want them, and if she wants to borrow Marchpane one last time, let her have him. She had little joy of him before—

and as for him: *he* doesn't even know he went there. That poor girl thinks everybody in this world more naïve than herself."

Of course the night passed as before. The servants removed duck and ducklings while Prince Marchpane slept. (This time he snored.) Ariadne wept, implored, did all she could to rouse him. She even took a lighted taper and made a small burn on his hand. The hand recoiled; still Marchpane slept. At dawn the servants carted him away, heaving his inert body like a sack of grain, and treating the Queen's favourite with spite. "Ugh!" they said. "Queen's plaything —pretty toy . . ." and pinched him here and there. ("We'll say the beggarwoman did it.") But the Queen didn't bother about these marks on his sweet-smelling flesh, for she was bored. Gold ducklings she had, yet the mess they made was not so golden. Already she yearned for something new.

"Have those wretched ducklings penned! Then go and see if my goosegirl has something better to amuse me with— in exchange for one more night with my crushed-almond Prince."

Ariadne had already—and despairingly—opened the Star's gift of a hazelnut. "If nothing comes of this I'll not only lose my sweet Marchpane, my very life—but must herd those hissing goslings till I die!" When the nut split, out of it came a small tree shining even brighter than the ducklings. It was a tree from the spice islands, golden, and bearing nutmegs made of gemstones. She was sitting outside her hut, turning the tree round and about in her brown hands, when the Queen's servants came to offer the third unfair bargain.

In the next hut to Ariadne's lived an old, bent, inquisitive man: a tailor, so poor he often sewed all night to earn his bread. His life was sad, his only pleasure to eavesdrop by the thin wall. Those two nights when Ariadne had leaned over the unconscious Marchpane, and bewailed her situation, had been the most entertaining that tailor ever spent. On the

third day he turned her fantastic story over in his mind: it pleased him to think he might meddle in some action before he died. Besides, he was making clothes for Prince Marchpane, and had come to like him for his generosity and kindness.

Towards noon the old tailor toddled to the palace; and—once he was alone with Prince Marchpane, and measuring him here and there—asked, with winks and noddings, where he slept; and if he'd slept well, the last two nights.

"Heavier than I ever slept before!" said the surprised Prince. "And naturally I sleep here in the palace. Do you make riddles, tailor—what do you imply?" And he looked rather sternly on the tailor, who grinned and chuckled, then told him, in a whisper, all he'd overheard.

"My wife!" said Prince Marchpane, in a daze. "My own true wife?"

He took agitated turns about the room. His situation was peculiar: he had only been breathing for about a year, and therefore his experience of women, though exotic, wasn't wide. What won't they do, he thought bemusedly, in their love or greed? It seemed to him the Queen had gone too far; and he dearly loved his own devoted wife. When he thought about the iron shoes, he cried. And he longed to return to that happy, homely, shabby palace, with its olive trees and goats, and its delicious, simple food. He strode up and down, up and down, while the old bent tailor—pleased to think he could checkmate so powerful a Queen—watched him with delight.

Towards evening Prince Marchpane went to the stables, where the fine black-maned horse Arion, given him by the besotted Queen, stood in a stall. The handsome beast pawed the ground eagerly when his master came, and Marchpane fed him carrots, and an apple, but hurriedly removed his palm when the horse began to mumble it as though the skin still held a taste of sugar. Arion stood docile while Marchpane saddled him and tied a bag of money to the saddle, and stroked the warm, soft muzzle, murmuring, "Rest quiet until tonight . . ."

The White-Browed Queen had grown so greedy since she had Prince Marchpane, and a silver spinning wheel, and a gold set of ducklings, that she could barely wait for the next excitement. In fact the thrill of each new acquisition lasted very little time, and she was all the more impatient for another. During that day she was thinking obsessively about the golden spice tree hung with nutmegs made of gems. She thought, I'll plant it in my arbour . . . No!—in a porcelain pot outside my bedroom. And she wondered if it would bear further nutmegs, and if they'd taste well in food, or if her cook should keep some ordinary ones as well.

At dinner, she hurried Marchpane through his meal: "You're very slow tonight! Surely you don't want another slice of partridge breast? A pear, as well as grapes, is most unwise . . ." Her small feet, in their scarlet shoes, fidgeted unbearably beneath the table; and the diamond crescent moon she wore in her cloudy hair trembled with her agitation.

Prince Marchpane said, "It's the heavy air about this place which makes me sleepy, I believe." He yawned and yawned as though he couldn't keep awake—yet the Queen took no chances: she picked up the frosted glass of wine that she had ready, and gave it to him in a way she thought beguiling, though it was very firm. (When she was older, she would be a dominant old hag indeed.)

Prince Marchpane stroked the goblet as though he loved it. "Wine the colour of the moon . . . Exquisite stuff! Ah!— what was that?"

"What was what?"

"I thought a mouse ran across the room and slipped beneath your skirts, my beauty, but—"

The Queen was screaming. She leaped up, flapping her napkin round her as though the air were full of mice. The

L

footmen came running to peer beneath the table, while the Queen urged them on and shook out her skirts. During the commotion Marchpane emptied his wine into a bowl of flowers; then he yawned most noisily, and fell back as though sleeping in his chair. While the Queen's servants carried him to Ariadne's hut, and removed the priceless gemstone tree, Prince Marchpane was enjoying some dramatic snores.

"Oh darling Marchpane, my Marchpane love!" mourned Princess Ariadne when the servants left. "How I adore you! How sore my feet grew as I searched for you! How I kneaded you, and moulded you, and ground you when I sculpted you! And I made you only for a cunning Queen who cheats us both . . ."

At this, Prince Marchpane opened his eyes and sat up, and put his arms around her—and what they said to each other the gods alone know; but it took some time. Then, towards midnight, when the bone-coloured palace was grimly etched against black air, and the stars were almost hidden by writhing mists that rose from the sluggish nearby river, Prince Marchpane and Princess Ariadne stole to the stables. Arion came clopping quietly from his stall, enticed by Marchpane's sugar-smelling hand. In silence they mounted him; Ariadne was perched before Marchpane on the saddlebow. How that horse flew! Pegasus himself could not have carried them from this enchanted palace at such a speed and no one from the Queen's dominions ever caught them up again.

The White-Browed Queen woke next morning, and stared at her precious spice tree. The corners of her mouth were drooping. It would be better—she thought—if the tree bore plums or peaches; something more succulent. Nothing's ever quite right—what will that mindless beggar girl produce today? When her maids rushed into the room, scared and weeping, she could at first barely understand their babble; but when she did realise her loss she beat her little fists upon the coverlet, bit her pillow, and howled as loud as any dog. What were ducks and spinning wheels to delightful Marchpane, whom she would never see again?

But then she had a quite amazing notion: she, too, would mould the husband of her dreams. She shot out of bed, crying, "Hurry, hurry!" and sent for fine almonds, sugar, semolina, eggs, lemon, and almond essence, and began to work. Progress was slow, since she was no such sculptress as the Princess; yet, recalling the perfection of her captive, she did accomplish something in the end. She placed the statue where she worshipped—heaven knows where *that* was—and threw herself down to start her invocations: what had the Princess said?

"Such a filthy mess I'm in," she began. "Such servants' joyless work! To Hades with anyone who says otherwise. Now must I stiffen up upon this floor?" So she lay there by day and night growling out profanities, and on the fortieth day spat on the statue's feet and yelled, "All this simply to get myself a rotten man!"

Which is what she got, for *her* marchpane went bad in the sickly heat and humid vapours of that country. The sculpted man smelt so nasty that his noisome, maggot-ridden form was buried hurriedly outside the grounds, while the servants called a doctor to their Queen. She was almost overcome by fumes, and by the misfortunes she had brought on her own head. "*Thén katalavéno!*" she kept weeping sadly in missing Marchpane's own tongue. "*Thén katalavéno*—I don't understand . . ."

But Princess Ariadne—whose father had died while she was away—and Prince Marchpane became King and Queen in their own palace. They spent happy evenings walking the silver uplands. They carried home armfuls of honeysuckle, wild clematis, iris, and cyclamen. They made love in the lemon groves, and listened to the nightingales—and if Apollo showed himself to them they didn't mention it, for they were wise as they were good, and had already fought one battle with the gods.

And King Marchpane became an expert wine-maker, and kept bees, and read Homer in the evenings, sitting in the kitchen where his wife prepared the veal or cooked the Paschal lamb just as he liked it; but there's a rumour that he never, never let her make a marchpane man again.

Trandafir

The forest was very still, that evening. It was summer-time—a long, hot, humid Continental summer, when flowers opened at morning to great heat, and night dews were heavy and refreshing. "A fine summer! Yes, indeed, a summer to remember," the peasants told one another thankfully. The corn was tall, plump-grained. The sunflowers were a fine crop, too—their plate-sized blooms of harsh mustard-gold, dark-centred, turned toward the sun's light on coarse, thick, green stems. After the day's work girls and men would wander two by two up forest paths, in search of shade and love.

Mihail Dobrescu took his girl into his arms beside a rosetree. She was shy, and kept talking while he tried to kiss her. "Oh," he said at last, "why won't you look at me—why won't you kiss me properly, Irina? Your eyes are all for that fine rosetree, not for me at all!"

She smiled at him; her long eyes slanted. "It's a very handsome rose, at least!"

"Yes—the largest and most handsome that I've ever seen," responded Dobrescu, throwing himself down within its shade. "But it's always been finer than any other, and the blooms it produces are perfection. They're like you!" And he tried to pull her to his side, but she resisted.

"Irina!" he said, impatiently reproachful.

"I'm still looking at this tree, Mihail! It's a queen of roses—you know, it must have been flowers like these that St. Elizabeth of Hungary found in her apron."

"Miracles!" scoffed her lover. "Wonders! Marvels! How

175

women love them. But I—I am of the earth, earthy—And I want you here."

"So is this rose of the earth earthy," she teased him. "See what strong roots it has, spreading in all directions? No other flower grows nearby. It must have used all the earth's nourishment to produce such roses. I should like to take some home with me—how sick I am of sunflowers."

"Your father's sunflowers are his wealth! He has a fine crop—and will give you a fine dowry."

"Oh, that's why you want me?" She smiled provocatively, and sat down a little further off. She had plucked a half opened bud, and was fingering its petals. "If I'd the courage, I would pick that topmost, gigantic bud—but—somehow it would feel like theft!"

"Well," mocked Dobrescu, "perhaps it holds a Crown Prince; and he's far above you, my Irina. Now . . . come here—" This time he made a more successful grab. And for a long while there were only sighs, or silence.

Later, as they walked slowly downhill through groves of oak and beech, they kissed so much that she soon forgot the rosebush of the splendid flowers.

Dusk came to the forest: the Carpathians' foothills were mysterious with dimming light. People feared to walk alone at evening, for their country had been so rent with hostilities that no one knew when a band of Turkish warriors might not gallop up from the Wallachian plain to bring horror and rapine to the villages, and death or slavery to the young people. And sometimes bands of Hungarian or German knights would come swiftly through the trees, ready to kill first and ask questions afterward. The provinces had had so many overlords that people went warily, and those farmers who were brave enough to stay kept their eyes upon their crops, and prayed only to be left alone. Still many evenings were made horrible by sobs and screams, piteous wailing, or a sudden flare as some small farm went up in flames.

Dobrescu, walking with his promised girl back to her

home while tranquil light lent the land an illusive air of peace, thought grimly that each time they said goodnight could be the last. As they came through an oak grove he heard hooves thudding away somewhere on their right. The corn ahead was broken, riders had scornfully pushed destructive pathways through it. His arm tightened round Irina; his right hand touched his peasant's knife, without confidence but with bravado. How terrible the Turkish menace that always hung heavy on their land! And if the Turks went, who else would come instead?

Nightingales began their bubbling song, but no one lingered to listen out of doors. The forest, rising up the lower slopes of the Carpathians, was soon given over to night animals and birds. Higher up—much higher, on the mountain pastures—the shepherds wandered safely with their flocks, living the idyllic, stable life that was the one unchanging thing here in Romania. But in the woods there was only the occasional sound of footsteps as someone passed who daren't be seen by day.

The roses' petals were tight closed. Even the splendid tree admired by Irina had drawn its petals in so tightly that its surrounding fragrance had been drawn in too, like a small cloud of incense about the stem. That rosetree was old, with a long, proud history. She had gone from strength to strength, and produced blooms of greater and greater perfection. The single unopened bud now at her summit should prove her masterpiece in colour, shape and size.

A nearby firtree, which prided itself on jade-green needles and sleek, waxy, orange-brown cylindrical cones, was heard to murmur that soon the old rosetree *must* be passée. And a young oak, in which nightingales were pleased to sit, chimed in to say that withered age soon followed on maturity. The rosetree merely kept her petals shut, pretending not to hear. Yet she trembled when the nightingales sang, for she felt convinced that she was on the verge of something—something miraculous which felt like birth.

177

The night grew very dark. There was no moon. At last even the nightingales were quiet. The stillness was profound except for a wild, heartbroken cry from somewhere on the distant plain—a cry that was quickly silenced.

Dawn light came creeping with a fine, light haze, foretelling heat. Then the rosetree, strengthening her clutch upon the earth, and straining with all her roots, started to unfold her topmost bud. It felt heavy, quite different to the others. She strained, and pushed her sappy juices as high as they would go to help the bud expand. "Open, open," she kept saying within herself. "Open, my triumph! Show these lesser people what it is I still carry in my heart."

The bud straightened on its stem and, as the sun cleared the treetops, opened its petals suddenly, with such an effort that the outer leaves were left quite pale. Even so, it was the most perfect bloom ever produced—the best one that the forest could remember. Fir and oak were silenced. Waking birds twittered their awe and amazement. From the central cup of petals came rich, unsurpassed scent, and from the shelter of the tufted stamens came a hand which parted them—as a fisherman parts rushes—and a young man stepped out. For a moment he seemed dazed at his birth into the forest. Then he leaped to the ground and looked about him. And, while he grew quickly to full stature, it was apparent that he was—could only be—a Prince.

For a time he lingered, looking compassionately at the rosetree that had mothered him. He was her masterpiece and, if he went, how lonely he must leave her in the world. Yet there was work for him—or why else had she travailed in the night? He bent his head to breathe in her scent. He broke off her smallest bud, and put it in his green jacket. It was with remorse, though certain the world was calling him, that he left his birthplace and followed the forest path downhill. In the clear light of morning he crossed a sown patch of sunflowers, skirted a peasant's holding, and found himself on the very edge of the wide plain.

A dappled horse was tethered nearby, already saddled and

bridled. A sword was fastened to the pommel. Prince Trandafir put no questions to himself; he was too new-born. If it were someone else's horse—well, perhaps he thought everyone came out of rosetrees, and found horses where they wanted them. Anyway, he leaped into the saddle as though born to ride, pulled the horse's head round, and cantered off along the edge of the plain to look for some sign that would teach him where to go.

It so happened that during this fine summer the Turks had fought and made love and enslaved with all the enthusiasm of which man is capable when he gives his mind to it and his morals no attention. So the first small town that Prince Trandafir reached was ready to suppose him an unruly Turk, and to put him to the sword. Luckily, before anything too rash could happen, a young girl cried out that he couldn't be a cruel warrior, for he was the most beautiful person she had ever seen—his handsome, smiling mouth was like a rose itself; and if she didn't actually say that she was willing to be enslaved upon the spot, it was implicit in her tones. More and more women surrounded the dappled horse, and tried to catch young Trandafir's attention. The men sneered at first, and spoke of pretty boys who would run if they so much as saw an enemy. But when the stranger Prince laid about him with his sword, and they felt the flat of it upon their shoulders, they soon spoke differently and begged him—no matter where he came from or who he was—to stay with them and fight.

"It's a very odd world that I've arrived in," said Trandafir drowsily to himself that night before he went to sleep. "But not unpleasant—or not yet. All this fighting, though!" And he thought with nostalgia of his lost peace within the rose's heart . . .

About that time when the rose Prince came into the world, the Turkish Vizier was told by his Master that the Prophet's honour demanded further tribute. The Turkish hordes, with their janissaries and kettledrums, their fine Arab horses with tossing heads and splendid bridles, and their gay tents and enslaved women, made ready for deeper assault on the country's interior. No Romanian knight questioned how or why an additional Prince had appeared, to fight on their own side. They saw only that Trandafir was someone special, a natural leader, whose presence breathed out strength and charm and sweetness. Everything that other men did with so much effort seemed to come easily to their stranger Prince. They gave him a command of his own, and his men followed him most willingly. Those peasant farmers who had dared to remain working on their lands—though with fear of the Crescent ever in their minds—looked up as Trandafir's horsemen rode by, and cheered him, and were heartened. But some Transylvanian princes were very jealous.

"See him, our glorious stranger Prince! He's too good to be true . . . a hero from head to toe? He's a man like other men—"

"Yes—wait till he gets near the Turk's own women! Watch him forget his virtue then . . ."

Trandafir was soon very troubled. He saw the world was beautiful and harsh, and men both lovable and cruel. It saddened him to think that strife seemed the only way to save innocent peasants from torture and despair, and that agony must be inflicted on some men to preserve others from worse fates.

He lay in his tent, thinking the hard thoughts that men have always thought about the contradictions in the world. It was so fine to ride out across the plain, towards the distant Turkish banners! His blood sang a song of youthfulness and joy when he put his horse into a canter, and heard his men come streaming behind him, uttering loud war-cries, deliriously urging on their horses. The corn stretching far on either hand, the clouds streaming from East to West in the blue sky above, the thudding of hoofbeats: all these filled him with a sense of—*was* it joy? Or deliverance from doubt?

For then came the harsh side of the picture: the Turkish sabres slashing, soon scarlet in the sun; a fury of kettledrums beating away men's lives like giant hearts run mad. The screams. The blood. The smells. Terrified women stumbling from the tents, sometimes falling to the ground and lying still, sometimes caught up, still screaming, before the conquerors' saddlebows. Tents flaring with fire, to blossom like the rose—

The rose. The rose! thought Trandafir longingly as, after one savage raid, he rode homeward soberly. *She* was the reason why he couldn't give himself to life as unreservedly as other men. And while the rosetree had been carrying him he had heard only gentle words of lovers like Dobrescu and his girl. The rose had no dualities. Her weapons—thorns— were only for defence. Her sap ran in his veins, and fought with his fierce warrior streak that now sometimes drove him into battle for the sheer excitement of it—and—*and*—he realised in horror, an insidious lust for killing, the thrill of causing fear.

Where were the clouds blowing, that streamed so unceasingly across the sky? Wildly they formed and toppled and fell apart. They were like the ever-changing confusion of men's lives in this strange, lovely, corrupt world.

From this time on he felt a growing sadness.

But it was useless to long for peace in a country so divided, and so overrun. The Sultan's oppressive rule could only be resisted by a savagery equal to the janissaries'. And, after all, there was that fierce pleasure in the ride to battle, and welcome oblivion in drinking orgies afterwards. Yet, though in most things he now acted with his comrades, Trandafir still held himself aloof from the mean acts and bullyings that habitually took place. While other men shared out their spoils of war, the Turks' women, and mocked Trandafir for gentleness, he only turned away. Even so, the simmering battle-violence made him long to join them. Perhaps only the rose juice in his blood prevented him.

Then one day the Turks fell upon a village near the forest, and wiped it out, firing the homes and bearing off the women. Within the hour Trandafir and his men were in pursuit. Their horses galloped so fast that mud flew behind them, kicked into the air. Startled birds rose from the corn as though someone tossed them toward the sky.

Hard-breathing horses, lathered flanks; the Turkish outposts; the Turks themselves drawn up in full savage array before their camp, drums beating, Crescent banners flying.

That was the hardest clash of all! Men and horses fell tangled inextricably. Human and animal screaming inter-mingled from the first moments of fighting until victory—Romanian victory—led to a dying down of sounds, except the cries and sobbings of the wounded.

Prince Trandafir stared blindly around him at the scene. Silky corn rippled towards the horizon, but in the foreground lay the awful aftermath of war—dead and bleeding men, adding their scarlet to the poppies on the Wallachian plain. His own horse had a long sabre cut from withers to knee; its wild eyes rolled, its wide pink nostrils stretched and snorted.

Trandafir rode into an almost emptied camp. This time there was no need for hurried pulling out of reach: the Turkish horsemen—what remained of them—were in full flight across the plain. Trandafir rode past the bodies of his closest friends. His heart still black with murderous rage, he rode among the enemy tents. Others of his comrades had dismounted and, battle-scarred but with looks of set and hungry purpose, made their way towards the deserted women who were huddled together stiff with fear.

Some of them already knew of Trandafir. They held up their hands to him, and pleaded with him in their guttural foreign tongues. He paid them no attention. That morning he had ridden through the gutted Romanian village, and seen a sprawling, dismembered child. Now a woman was clawing at his bridle. Her tangled hair nearly hid her face. She was mouthing something at him, but seemed half dumb with shock.

He flung himself from his bleeding horse, seized her roughly by the arm, and forced her at sword point into the darkness of a nearby tent. Her body was slack and terrified in his arms, like the body of a captured hare. There was no room for peaceful longings in Trandafir's heart, only lust for cruelty—cruelty and conquest. He was barely conscious of the woman, who struggled weakly, then lay still. He knew only that, while his friends lay staring sightless at the sky, he was revenging them by rape and violence.

Later he pulled himself to his feet, and stared downward at the woman's face, barely visible in the gloom.

Her swollen and bruised lips parted painfully.

"Trandafir!

"Trandafir—I'm of *your* people . . . The Turks stole me this morning when they fired our village—They killed Mihail." She moved her head restlessly and moaned. "Turk —German—or Romanian!—" she laughed—"or even Trandafir!" Then her eyes closed; she began sobbing hopelessly, and was dumb again.

The Romanians rode slowly home in silence—a smaller band than those who had set out. Booty was strapped to their saddles, and camp women with their hands tied straggled in their rear. No male prisoners had been taken—the wounded had been despatched. The Crescent banners were still burning as the crescent moon rose into the sky.

Trandafir rode before his men. He was a hero in their eyes, and they fell behind to let him ride ahead as conqueror; but he was so ashamed and miserable that he would have liked to fall on his own sword. Back in the ranks of slowly plodding horses the girl was being carried by his men; but Trandafir couldn't bring himself to look at her again. Those bitter words, "Or even Trandafir!" rang continually in his mind. Her voice had been familiar. When had he heard her speak before?

The Romanian camp was by an oakgrove. That night he couldn't sleep. Sheer darkness seemed to have fallen on his spirit. Again and again he heard that bitter voice saying, "Turk—German—or Romanian! Or even Trandafir!" She was of his own people, and he was in despair. But—if she'd been a Turk? Or a Turk's slave of some other nationality? What difference could that have made to her pointless suffering—what difference in his cruel need to destroy?

Trandafir leaped to his feet, to pace up and down, up and down. This land was so beautiful—what was done in it, so horrible! He had wanted to serve men, to free them from such horror. Once he had involved himself in human life he was no more immune from darkness than other men. How he wished the rose had never borne him—Then, thinking of her, he knew at last where he had heard the woman's voice before.

Next day he learned of Irina's death. She had stolen a dagger in the night, and stabbed herself. The loss of Mihail, followed by Trandafir's cruelty, had unhinged her mind. Miserably he cut himself off from his fellows, who wondered at the change in him.

Autumn came, and then Winter. The Turks hadn't only been driven back, but held. The Transylvanian princes had won themselves precarious peace. When Spring came many more Romanians dared to descend from the high mountain pastures with families and flocks.

Then Trandafir laid down his sword. He gave away his horse and abandoned his command. All alone he walked up through the oak and beech woods till he reached the place of his own birth. It felt a long while since he had gone out to find what his human destiny held; and now he came back to seek a better one.

He looked about him. Oak and beech and fir were very still. It was a fine warm evening, and one of peace.

"Oaks—" murmured Trandafir, "I have come home to you. Where's the great rosetree, that beauty from which I came?"

"Dead, dead!" replied the oaktrees. "After your birth, my Prince, her task was done."

Trandafir felt as though a sword had pierced him. "Why did I stay away so long, when I could have served men so much better here? In the world they cause endless harm, whatever their intentions. Birds—can't you give me hope? Is there nothing left of that great living stem?"

But the woodpecker tapped out that he had never heard of it, nor seen it; the crow cawed that it was long forgotten; all the young birds of the wood, one by one, sang that it had disappeared while they were still unfledged.

Trandafir stood with his head bent, too sorrowful to go away. Just then a nightingale began his plaintive song. He sang a requiem for the rosetree that had once stood in splendour on that spot.

"O mystic rose of true nobility!" ended the nightingale. "Rose whose last, most perfect flower was a human Prince!"

"Little nightingale, here stands that Prince," sighed Trandafir bitterly. "The world is sick—and I've shared its joys, and in doing so have taken on that sickness till I was part of it myself. Human life is full of contradiction—but the rose's life is one that gives and never takes. How I long for that state of sweetness and peace! A life that only blesses, and when it ends leaves memories of fragrance."

The nightingale sang: "O Trandafir, let it be according to your will! Since you have chosen—and you choose wisely—it shall be my task to sing here till your soul has returned to its true nature, as a rose."

"Yes, it's my choice," said Trandafir gladly. "How should I hesitate? Sing then, O nightingale!" And very happily he threw himself down on the mossy ground that had nourished him.

All that night the bubbling song rang through the woods, gaining subtly in strength and beauty. Trandafir lay listening, and gradually the things of human life loosed their hold on him as he began to dream. The moss was more comfortable than any bed. His limbs were so at home there that they threw out shoots, then rooted themselves firmly in rich layers of leafmould. Rose juice nourished them, the life of sorrow and uncertain blessing was forgotten.

At dawn the nightingale ceased singing, and flew off; but near the place where he had sung was growing a new rosetree whose half-open buds sprang from the willing heart of Trandafir.

Rich Man's Gold

Deep in the northlands, where Winter grips like a clenched fist until Spring waters break and run and spread, rousing the country to abundant green, and encouraging young bright shoots on old dark pines, there lay the wide farmlands of Yuri Yevgorenko: had his wealth been strewn around his house you could have trodden upon gold for many miles. Yuri was a merchant too: "For farming," he said, "may fail, but factories prosper, men being as they are—with such an urge in their own souls to buy as I have in mine to sell." At night when he lay down to sleep he would twine his fingers in his stiff black beard, and instead of counting sheep would count coins, spinning, hopping their way ceaselessly towards his open palms. The gilding on his household's ikons only reminded him of his own wealth.

One night he lay smiling in his dreams when a voice spoke to him gently, compellingly, in a way to make him blink while still asleep. Next day his wife woke to find him wearing such a self-satisfied expression that even she was quite surprised.

"Anna Alexandrovna—guess who comes here today! Prepare yourself for a glorious surprise: he's even greater—richer—than our little father the Czar himself."

Yuri's wife stared and stared. He patted her on the head, chuckling. "There!—I'm not mad, though you've no wits as I've so often told you! But never mind . . . For it's the Lord God, with holy St. Nicholas, who'll honour us. Now you see how riches are rewarded—as I've often told you too. Mind you bring up our silly daughter to understand this truth."

187

"It would be greater riches still, to have a son," whispered poor Anna; beneath her breath, to spare herself the knout.

"Wife," said Yuri, and even his beard seemed to smile, "make such preparations as you've never made before." And she did. Rolls of velvet and embroidered linens were spread for miles in all directions; then, while Anna Alexandrovna was busy in his kitchens, Yuri went outside to plump himself down in a high carved chair, and wait for the Lord God to honour him as one rich merchant to another.

Evening approached. At last two forms appeared in the far distance, and lurched unsteadily toward the house. Yuri frowned, half rose in his chair, and then fell back, beating his hands upon its arms in rage. Two old beggars were defiling *his* velvets with their filthy feet! And they were singing, damn them!—a hymn, yet sung with such airs of ribald enjoyment, and such nudging of ribs, that Yuri went stiffer than his beard. As he was about to curse them they ceased singing, and one whined, "Yuri, Yuri, little prosperous father of the afflicted poor, give you peace— Peace to your house!" Then the other chimed in, "And rest too, little father. And give *us* rest, we beseech your Excellency, rest and lodging for the night." He made an unsteady imitation of a bow, till his white hair swept the velvet's pile.

Yuri rose and swore, danced and almost choked with rage: for hospitality is a holy duty, as everyone knows. Surely it was the devil's work he should be cursed with such a vulgar pair of scarecrows that very day? He gave one old man a kick, and snatched the other's staff to beat him with it. "Round to the back door, dirt! Or better still, the stables— and Satan your father stay with you! Look at this muck you've spread upon my carpets . . ." As the shamed beggars stumbled past, Yuri ensconced himself once more, and waited and waited and waited until darkness came.

When the rigid pines stood black against a midnight sky there came a flash of something bright and holy through that darkness, to hover at the stable window and speak outside it in an almost wordless prayer.

189

M

"Amen!" cried the shivering old beggars, rousing themselves from where they lay close to a sulky stove; they had wrapped their ragged cloaks around a half-starved serf girl, who cowered on the floor.

"Is it the Lord God and holy Nicholas who are within?" asked that nearly human voice.

"And what is wanted of the Lord God at such an hour?"

"A blessing, Lord! One for a woman in the next village, who labours with a son. She's poor, and in great misery, and fears the future for her many children."

The Lord God meditated, and then spoke, "Yes—she deserves a blessing, and shall have it. *This* boy shall save her; he shall grow to manhood and have Yuri's fortune for his own."

The little serf was prostrate on the ground with awe and worship. Although she felt the cloaks taken from her, she was never to feel cold or hunger pangs again. She watched the old beggars wrap themselves in their thin rags, and leave. They stole past Yuri, who was sleeping, and down the avenues of velvet he had laid in such great pride.

When Yuri woke at dawn he was almost frozen, and his beard rimed with frost. "Such stupidity, to have believed a dream!" he grumbled to himself. Then his eye fell on the little serf, who had brought him a dish of tea. *Her* eyes were beaming with delight. "Ah, Yuri Yevgorenko, little father, that was no dream! Last night the Lord God and St. Nicholas slept in your stables." While she told him what had happened her voice lilted as though she sang a Magnificat in the onion-domed church nearby.

Yuri gnawed uneasily at his bearded lip: he had been much deceived! But he was too good a merchant to spend time pitying himself. He saw the Lord God as an expert dealer who had done him in a bargain. "Come," he muttered, "we'll get the better of him yet!" He had horses harnessed to his troika, and drove to his poor neighbour's home.

"Peace to this house!" he cried, in the melodious bass voice that had cozened many people into parting with their most precious things. And he begged the poor woman to sell him her new baby, ". . . you've been much blessed with children, Grushka, and you know my unhappy Anna yearns for sons to inherit when I die."

The mother was desperate: she loved children, and knew it would break her heart to part with this fresh, milky-smelling baby; yet, looking round, she thought he might well die of her grim poverty. She did as Yuri asked, though tears flooded down her cheeks as the small bundle was borne away. "Be good to him, Yuri Yevgorenko," she pleaded. The rich merchant-farmer nodded, smiled, and held the baby to him—like a bear about to have a meal.

He didn't go straight home. Instead, he ordered his driver to find a path into the thickest woods. Where the snow-drifts came almost halfway up the trees he threw the babe into the deepest drift of all. "Hah!" he told himself, looking back triumphantly as they drove away, "there lies *one* who won't inherit all my wealth."

After they had gone a warm wind smelling of the South began to hum and murmur through the trees. The snow melted quickly around the baby, and he soon lay gurgling in the heat. A crocus thrust up to tickle underneath his toes, and anemones made a thick shield against the frost. Even his mother's body hadn't been so comfortable a resting place. He went to sleep.

That evening Yuri sang about the house in his fine mellow bass as he thought how everything he touched turned to his good. Tonight he was expecting guests: two merchants, both his debtors. "One's poor, wife, and the other rich; but since they're coming here to pay what's due, we'll feed them both the same: after a substantial meal and much good vodka men part easily with gold! Light the samovar, and see the tea is of the best."

His guests were made uneasy by his graciousness, but soon Yuri grew uneasy too. Why should one or other of the merchants excuse himself every few minutes to go outside? Either they can't control themselves, he thought, or they're hiding something priceless in their carriage. Yes, that's it. They don't want *me* to see—yet they're afraid of thieves. Nothing else could explain it, except two chills . . .

After that he coaxed them, and wooed them, fed them and wined them, trying to discover what the secret was. At last the rich one, who feared stubbornness would annoy this influential man, spoke up reluctantly: "Yuri, we came far from our way tonight. A wolf pack was howling near the usual road, and terrified our horses. As we came down a forest track we heard a small cry from among the trees. We stopped—Behold, a miracle of sweet St. Nicholas himself! A newborn baby lying on the ground, all round him snow and ice—but where he lay the earth was warm with spring, and bloomed with flowers. Except for this we would have guessed some peasant had abandoned him, but now we knew the child was holy. My friend and I—though you see us embarrassed by our acquisition!—have decided to adopt this babe. We have him in our carriage, swaddled in my sable coat."

Yuri got up to hide his agitation, crossed himself three times, and went to the samovar. His beard trembled with his indignation. Ah, Lord God! he thought, you cunning one! Am I to leave this child between the hands of those who, underneath their suave attentions, must be my enemies? He turned back to the guests, raised his arms as though to take the whole world in a generous embrace, and cried, "Dear friends of all my life! How my heart overflows with gratitude! The Lord knows I find it hard to hold back tears of joy. You know my Anna weeps her lack of sons— and now you bring this holy gift to her, to our sad house. I thank you from my soul."

"Yuri, Yuri, not so fast!"

"You're utterly mistaken . . ."

They were both in love with the child, and wouldn't give him up. Neither side would budge—or not till Yuri, his face flaming above a beard that bristled like an angry badger, shouted, "So be it! My enemies declare themselves—a good thing too! Now pay me what you owe, and leave my house! Why, if you'd shown the slightest compassion for my wife, I'd have forgiven all your debts, filled up your pockets with bright gold, hung my own sables round your necks . . . Alas, alas, it's only selfishness that fills this world!" He put his head between his hands, and wept.

Then the two merchants exchanged a covert look, and hurriedly gave up the child.

Many years went by, and Yuri's little foster child grew tall and strong. Nicholas, they called him, and Anna Alexandrovna loved him dearly, and came to feel he was her son. The neighbours knew how she adored him. Yuri couldn't harm him openly, though his heart was rent by evil; obsessed with hatred, he brooded on how he might arrange some fatal accident. But the boy Nicholas was nimble, clever, and adroit at everything—and managed to avoid a falling tree, and to stay on a bolting horse. He had grown in wisdom, too, and it was plain that he was fitted to command. Suddenly Yuri could bear the sight of him no more.

"Come here, Nicholas, beloved boy!—I must talk with you," he said. "You understand what your inheritance will be? Well, we want you to have every rouble—yes, *every* rouble, for your own: no, don't thank me! You know how blessed we are in having such a son—! But I've stupidly lost count of what I own, and unfortunately the best accountants are all dragons. In the tenth land—the country that lies beyond countries three times three—lives a sage heathen dragon. His fiery, pagan wisdom will soon penetrate this mystery of my belongings. Since I'm too old for such adventures, you, child, shall go and look for him. And by the way, don't believe silly stories you may hear: stand up to him, speak to him frankly, and he won't gobble you—it's only tremblers who annoy these dragons."

The stories were bad indeed, and Yuri knew them all. But Nicholas trusted his foster father, had few misgivings, and started diligently on the long, tiresome journey. At last he reached something he had never seen before that made his dark eyes open wide: the sea. It was vast, green and deep, and surged and heaved as though the heathen dragon lived beneath its waves. On the shore an old ferryman leaned against a small boat's side. It was his fearful task to row in that rough water year in, year out, while his hands wore to their bones. The flesh had been ripped from them like ribbons, and blood streamed endlessly upon the pebbles at his feet.

"My little uncle!" Nicholas held out a coin. "Will this take me across the sea? I seek the heathen dragon's home."

A smile flickered over the ferryman's sad features. "No one pays me with roubles! Child, you're surely my most welcome passenger for many years, if you'll give my message to that wicked dragon: tell him I've plied this task faithfully and well for thirty years. I take no payment—and see how my hands are nothing now but bone and blood! Tell him I claim retirement, and ask who'll come to take my place."

"Most willingly," said Nicholas, shuddering, and averting his eyes from those bleeding hands.

The boat soon flew up and down on the high waves, and the ferryman's blood left a slimy trail behind them in the water. As the bows rose on a tremendous crest they could see the farther shore, and a wide road winding off into the distance. They saw too a strange pillar which gleamed like gold, almost joining earth and sky. When Nicholas reached it, after parting from his sad new friend, he found it *was* gold: all made of golden coins. He heard a sighing as they shifted one against another, and the sighing soon made words: "God has brought you here, sweet boy! But do you seek a monstrous, cruel dragon—the heathen master of this land?"

Nicholas quailed inwardly, yet answered stoutly: "Yes, I do, though I hope he'll prove less cruel than you think."

"Then, sweet boy, do something for my sake. It's a dull, lonely business, standing day and night not knowing who one's owner is! Ask that able, cruel dragon: who owns a gold pillar by the highway to the sea?"

"Most willingly," replied Nicholas in his courteous way.

At long, long last he came to a deep hollow, scattered with bones and boulders, with low buildings at its centre. He knew it for the dragon's home, since on the path there lay a greeny-yellow scale or two. Nicholas's knees began to shake, and once he crossed the threshold they shook so much that they gave altogether, sturdy though they were. He found himself kneeling, murmuring a prayer. When he opened his eyes again he saw no dragon, and no flamey breath. An old woman stood there, her head kerchief-swathed like any grandmother's. Her rheumy eyes popped with amazement.

"Boy, boy, I couldn't believe my nose! It *said* it smelt a Russian in our house." She crossed herself, backwards. "And my lips—*they've* said for days that Russian flesh was coming; they swore that they could taste it. Now, if you want my son, he's flown on scaly wings to prey on Russian cities, where they call him Kostchei the Terrible—isn't that nice? The Czar has a sick son—mmm!—and every day my lovely pet hovers outside his window. That's where you'll find him."

Nicholas's knees quaked still, but he managed to stand upright and sound firm. "No, grandmother, I must stay here. For Yuri Yevgorenko, my fond foster father, has sent me to find out what he owns."

The old woman pulled a face which made her look twice as old as she was already—quite a feat. "Child, you're too innocent! Only a wicked foster father would send you here to be devoured. I love my strange, arrogant son, but he's implacable, as everybody knows. Something in me warms to you, as well, and feels you would be wasted in a grill.

Roll yourself under that bed against the wall—*I'll* put your question to my son, myself."

Nicholas was happy to obey, and felt almost safe beneath the bed; he raised his voice and implored her to help the old ferryman and mournful golden pillar know their fate. She prodded him with her feather duster, as a signal to keep quiet. "Hush! Keep small and hidden and don't breathe! I hear my honey love's approach."

He hastily drew down the coverlet over the bed's side as the ground began to shake. The room was flooded with an evil, fungoid smell. The old woman muttered sadly, "Oh dear, he's in a temper! His breath *is* bad . . . that always shows. The Czar's son must be better, and my cherished lambkin famished. Even those selfish peasants have learned to keep out of sight!"

The dragon slouched into the room. His flames were more subdued than usual, for they were unfed; and he dragged one wing, sore where new scales sprouted to replace some old ones. As his tail slid across the threshold he looked around and snorted.

"Ah, you've been cooking, little Mother? Good, good indeed, my stomach grumbles with its emptiness. That pesky small Romanov's better, so hurry: bring the pot you've stirred upon the fire, for I smell it's full of fine ripe Russian flesh. Wherever did you get it? There's nothing like one's mother's cookery, say what you will."

The old woman quickly said a prayer backwards before an ikon that was upsidedown. "O scaly joy, you're quite mistaken! You've flown so fast and far above those dirty cities that a Russian smell is stopping up your nostrils. Still, there's vodka for you, son, my treasure. Will you take a drop?"

"More than that!" The dragon rolled over on his back like an ungainly dog, and rattled his claws exhaustedly in the air. "Hurry, little Mother, the fire in my belly's almost out."

The old woman brought a big goblet of vodka from her cupboard, and secretly added some special drops. The effect

196

on the starved dragon was most sudden: he grew very drunk,
laughed in a silly way, winked, hiccuped, and seemed about
to sing. His mother hushed him, tickling him under his jaw.
"Come, little merry one, I've riddles for you . . ."

"Ashk 'way!" The dragon lolled his head. "C'n alwaysh
ansher riddlesh on empty shtomachsh, hic."

"Well, these aren't exactly riddles, but you know your
mother's curiosity! Tell me: who'll replace that poor sad
ferryman, who's worked so hard for thirty years?"

The dragon smirked and winked. She cajoled and tickled
him some more, till he told her whose fate it was to be.

"Ah!" she said, staring fearfully towards the bed, for she
seemed to see some movement underneath it. "Indeed!
And is that so? And as for Yuri Yevgorenko—has he a great
deal of money? Is it true that only my intelligent, dear son
could count how much that merchant has?"

"Now th'other side, 'swell," said the dragon, turning his
right cheek; so she tickled him there too, and reproved him:
"You haven't answered me, my Kostchei; Dragon Dragono-
vitch, my scaly joy!"

"That Yuri's richer'n *anyone*. Yuri knowsh what Yuri'sh
got. Yuri'sh gold c'n cover earthshurface twenty—hic!—
milesh round Yuri's house—" The dragon closed his eyes
and seemed about to sleep. Then the old woman rubbed his
right ear so hard that he woke again, saying "Ow!"

"Just one more question, dear one! Whose is the pretty
pillar of gold coins that reaches from earth to heaven on the
highway leading to the sea?"

The dragon tried to concentrate: he *knew* it was unwise to
answer questions, but his mother's presence always under-
mined him when he felt unwell, or tight. His eyes flew
together in a squint of concentration, but he failed to clear
his head, and let fall a name. Then, very angry with his
mother and himself, he staggered out of doors, where he
flopped around muzzily, and found it hard to leave the
ground now he was unsteady on his wings.

When he had flown clumsily away, his mother cried,

"Boy! You can come out now—" and as Nicholas emerged she looked him over thoughtfully, and nodded. "So, little longears, eavesdropper, my friend! No need to ask you what you heard, your eyes are wide as saucers . . . Off with you quickly—a second time I couldn't save you from his wrathful hunger!"

As Nicholas came near the golden pillar he heard it clinking and rattling already with excitement. It was crying out from top to bottom in a million little voices: "Well? Whose am I? Whose are we? Did you ask?" And in dazed tones he replied, "Indeed I did! And—and you belong to me . . . yes, you're the property of a poor foster child of—" his voice now trembled on the name, "Yuri Yevgorenko."

From top to bottom the pillar gave out a million small whoops of excitement, till it unsettled itself, and the coins came spinning down in golden spirals, a fiery whirlwind. It collapsed like a giant Russian snowman melted by the sun, and the ground itself looked as though the sun had fallen there, it was so heaped and scarred with gold. Nicholas knew these riches couldn't come with him just yet, but he bent and burrowed his fingers deep into the glinting metal, to show and feel his ownership. Then he went his way.

Soon he reached the deep, green, heaving sea, where the ferryman was waiting. His hands were bloodier than ever, and the bones showed whiter through the scarlet, as he posed his question between lips that winced in pain: "Whose destiny to row instead of me, my child?"

Nicholas looked at him long and steadily, but sadly too. The shock of learning Yuri's true feelings had gone deep. He felt hurt and disillusioned. His foster father was truly evil—yet, all the same, it was a tragic destiny that waited here. Sombrely he said, "My little uncle, it is Yuri Yevgorenko who replaces you."

Rich Man's Gold

After weary travelling he reached home again. The evening star shone brightly up above; and the house shone brightly too, for night after night Yuri had celebrated his foster son's meeting with the dragon and certain death. When Nicholas walked in, full of life, Anna Alexandrovna's lips trembled into pathetic smiles of joy, though Yuri's went rigid as he suppressed some fearful oaths. His face was purple as a pot of damson jam. Veins stood out on those big square hands of his which, that night, gave all his men and women house serfs a harsh beating; yet next day he managed to appear with beaming smiles spread thick upon his face like butter to disguise a heavy pancake.

"Excellent work, my boy! And such stouteartedness must be rewarded! Now I'm just off on a short journey— trade—Wonderful chance for you to learn about these matters— Enjoy yourself at the same time! Come along, we start at once."

Nicholas gave Yuri a hard, searching look, but was on his guard now: what harm could come to him? And he *did* enjoy that trip: big country fairs where peasants brought their cows and geese and gingerbread to sell; small-village markets where merchants set out goods, and bargained without raising of eyes or taking off of tall fur caps. Best of all, at country dances he met ravishingly pretty girls with whom to dance polonaises and mazurkas. However, all the time he kept one very watchful eye on Yuri Yevgorenko— who seemed only fatherly and kind, happy to see his foster child's success. Nicholas almost began to doubt the dragon's mother's words.

Then, one morning, he walked down early to the banks of the great Volga, where Yuri was arranging to send home all his new purchases.

"Ah, Nicholas—at the right time, my boy! I've few transactions left to make, and they're uninteresting for someone young. You earned your pleasure trip—now, back home with you by ship, and keep an eye on my belongings. Wait! I'd quite forgotten—here's a word I've written for our dear

Anna Alexandrovna and your foster sister. See they get it safely!" He kissed Nicholas on both his cheeks and strolled away.

Until noon Yuri's chosen ship sailed down that broad river under a clear northern sky, till at midday the crew made fast by a small quay to cook their meal. The smell of bubbling fat was strong, and Nicholas decided to escape it by jumping ashore to take a walk along the river bank. Soon he saw a flock of fine fat sheep, white and beautifully woolly, guarded by an ancient man. Shepherd he might be, but his gaze was so regal and commanding that when he called out, "Boy . . . ! Here, and show me what you've got there hidden in your pocket," Nicholas obediently handed over Yuri's letter, though his strange docility surprised him.

The old man seemed to read quite well. Immediately he scanned the letter's contents, spelled out words beneath his breath, and muttered, "Just as I thought!" Then he tore it into shreds, and scattered these to the four winds which blew them here and there among the woolly sheep. "Now," he said, "here's another letter, child, which I myself have written ready for you. It too is for your foster mother—take it; may you be blessed by God!"

When Nicholas reached home on that second occasion he found Anna Alexandrovna with his foster sister Nadia in the living room. They had hung the wooden walls with fir branches and ribbons. There was a festival feeling in the air, and the well-stoked stove gave out a welcome heat. Nadia's long fair hair was loose, for she'd been brushing out her pigtails, and her face flushed with pleasure when she saw him. Nicholas suddenly saw that she put all his country mazurka girls to shame. His thoughts were on Nadia, and he forgot the letter he had handed Anna as he entered, till she gave a loud exclamation of surprise and joy.

"Children! Your dear father is so unexpected! What a man for making quick decisions."

Nicholas looked at her, bemused. Wasn't it the shepherd's letter that she held, and not Yuri's at all? He looked closer, and saw to his amazement that it was clearly written in his foster father's hand.

"What does he say, my Mother?" asked Nadia curiously.

"Well—oh, how to tell— No, never mind— Quite flustered—" She had to sit down, and then at last after many exclamations, and getting up and sitting down again, she told them, "You're to be married! At once! Before he gets here! There—it seems he has his reasons, though what they are— Never mind, I'm to see to— Kiss me, yes, that's right, Nadia—roasts, beer, a priest of course—" and she hurried from the room still uttering incoherencies of joy and stupefaction.

"Shall you mind, Nadia?" asked Nicholas, trembling slightly.

"Not—not *too* much," said Nadia, looking sideways and trembling too.

So the onion-domed church rang out all its bells on the next day. The priest chanted, and swung his censer. There were imposing gold crosses and ikons, crowns held over the young couple, and evergreens hung up for happiness. Afterwards, Anna Alexandrovna led them home triumphantly to her best bed, decked out in the most bridal manner. Nicholas got in one side, and Nadia the other. They met in the middle. There was a sound like cooing doves. Anna Alexandrovna drew curtains carefully around the bed.

A little later, outside the house, there was a different sound—of jingling troika bells. Yuri entered, stamping his leather boots to shake off the snow.

"Well, my dear wife! I suppose you've sent young hot-head to my soap factory, as I desired? Last night the vats would have stood lidless—there would have been such a bubbling and a seething as would have boiled any stupid fellow to his death, if he'd not known his way about, then slipped. Of course young Nicholas is new to it, but he doesn't make mistakes!" Yuri's rumbling laugh sounded as though it came from some deep pit far blacker than his beard.

Anna paled. "See—see what I've done with him, sweet husband! Your—your letter's here—"

Yuri glanced at it, and gave a roar like an exploding vat. "Incomparable fool! These aren't *my* words—that boy's a forger! Where's my daughter now?"

"Upst-stairs!"

A bear pursued by swarming bees couldn't have been angrier than Yuri. The young couple heard his coming, ceased their loving, and got out of bed. Nadia was hit first, then Nicholas was grabbed and shaken up and down like a cross child's wooden toy. "Hah—beggarwoman's brat! Steal my daughter, would you—and so steal my wealth?"

In the end Nicholas had to hit him below the belt. "Now stop it, little angry father. Listen—when you can—! *I* shall bring Nadia much wealth, for overseas our God has given me a pillar of pure gold richer than all you own."

"Wh-aht?" gulped Yuri. Still clutching at himself he leaned across and patted Nicholas's cheek as though he loved him. "Tell me more—"

Together they reached the sea a few days later. With a train of troikas they had driven fast, to a jingling of bells that seemed to shout in Yuri's ears, "More gold, gold, gold!" The ferryman laughed joyfully to see them coming, and rowed with quick strokes as though no longer feeling pain. When Yuri saw all that money on the ground his eyes filled with tears of ecstasy. He kneeled to croon over it, ran it through his fingers, patted it; and even prayed in his excitement, though in what direction, heaven knows.

It took them three days to ferry Nicholas's wealth across the sea. He paid the ferryman a handsome sum, and watched him pocket it and go laughing up the shore. Then Nicholas turned, to tell the merchant it was time to go. Yuri had climbed back into the boat to search diligently for one more coin. He even sought beneath the oars—which immediately stuck fast to his hands.

When Nicholas at last got his fat horses moving they broke into a canter. He shuddered to his soul, feeling pain even for his foster father, as a constant sound like wolves howling in a lonely wood echoed after them. His horses carried him swiftly towards Nadia, a double inheritance, and joy for both his families and for himself; but Yuri spent the rest of his days in endless ferrying of travellers who paid him nothing, and for every speck of gold that he had gathered his hands bled drops of blood.

The Small Red Ox

Einar turned on to his back, winced, and twisted again till he was lying so that as few bruises as possible were in contact with the ground. He could barely move his right arm, and in panic wondered if his shoulder were badly damaged. These repeated beatings were bad enough, and the hunger—but to live crippled would weigh things so heavily against him that he might as well give up. The fingers of his left hand moved up his right arm till they reached his shoulder. He held his breath—and pressed: agony! But nothing grated, and exploring fingertips found nothing more sinister than bruised and swollen flesh. He lay quiet then, consumed with hatred.

The hatred was almost worst of all. In a way it gave him strength—yet instinctively he felt it to be false strength: to hate and hate till you were nothing but hatred in a battered skin could lead only to sour survival, never to escape. If you were free inside, *they* couldn't touch you—and so *they* hadn't won. But tonight the hatred was as agonising as this other pain, and he had reached a pitch when to think compulsively of it was pleasure.

Turn over on the other side. Wince. Try to relax, try not to think of food. Think of that woman who married your father, tricking him with soft, sweet words. Hate her. Hope for her death. Einar remembered how he had once lain shamelessly eavesdropping in the loft. He had peered through a floor crack, and seen her with her arms round his father's neck—while her eyes had roved the room covetously, taking in the good solid comforts of the farm. He heard again her lying, lisping voice. How much she wanted a son! How fine a son Einar would prove to her, if others never came! She'd barely mentioned the three daughters of her first marriage. And who would? thought Einar venomously. Perhaps his besotted father had expected three lisping golden girls, twittering like birds, always working and always merry. By Odin, couldn't he have shown a little sense? Asked to see the girls—asked if *their* father had provided for them? Their father! What sort of father had that strong, seductive woman given them?

Troll's wife! Einar moved angrily—and moaned with pain. Yes: some troll from the lava fields got those three beauties on her in a dark night—or even a troll might have considered twice (no—three times)! They had pretty names, those girls: Katla, Hildur and Alvor; but he thought of them mostly as One-Eye, Two-Eye and Three-Eye. Small wonder that the woman hadn't brought them down to the farm till she was safe wed . . .

Einar clenched his right hand, and dug his nails deep into the palm: the pain offset his other pains. If human sacrifice were still offered Odin he would have offered up Katla with pleasure: sweet One-Eye, who had worked on his shoulder while the others held him, then twisted it again. Her hair was mouse-coloured, and she always smelt of sweat. There was something wrong with her left eye, which was often closed right up till only a red rim showed under short, sparse lashes. And it ran, gummily. At the memory of that pink eyelid and constant gummy drip Einar's stomach heaved. He turned his thoughts hastily to Two-Eye—Hildur: a big strong girl, muscular as a man, yet given to sweet lispings like her mother; cruel.

How he would have liked to revenge himself on Katla and Hildur if he had the chance! (Frigga—how his body ached!) Break them on the wheel, put them to the fire—He would have danced while they burned, sung as they screamed. It was Hildur—he was sure—who had poisoned his father. He remembered going quietly to the kitchen on that dark day of snow and biting wind, and seeing her drop some strange-

205

N

looking root into a pot boiling on the hearth. She was murmuring some sort of rune, and when she'd dropped in the last stalk she had laughed a soft, triumphant laugh that he was never to forget. Then she'd turned, and seen him . . .

He had ducked to escape the viciously thrown log, and had rushed out, bewildered, into the dancing snow-flurry. It was the first time that open violence had been used against him—that day his father died.

Suddenly he lay rigid. A slight sound overhead . . . a very slight one, but his ears, sharp for danger signals, heard and interpreted this one correctly. He held his breath. If *they* were to come now, and start in again, then nothing, not even thoughts of the brave Saga heroes, could have prevented his breaking down and sobbing like a baby. His eyes stared at the wooden partition of the ox's stall, but in his mind he saw what happened overhead. (*They* had once made a crack there, so they could spy on him.)

One-Eye, Two-Eye, or—Yes, there was certainly an eye there now, a gloating, gloating eye, watching to see if punishment had been effective.

He closed *his* eyes and breathed noisily, now and then giving a low groan as though still aware of anguish while he slept. After some while there were faint sounds of withdrawal overhead—then nothing more. His relief was so great that he lay weeping till he fell asleep.

It was pitch dark when he woke to an awareness that someone had been standing near him. His muscles tautened— then relaxed. It was all right. His stepmother must have been in with Kolbeinn's fodder, for he could smell the ox's sweet breath as he chewed. Kolbeinn always breathed heavily while eating, and even in the winter his breath smelt of clover. It was a very comforting smell, as Kolbeinn chewed and chewed; it was good.

Then Einar tensed again. The eye was there above, watching him! This time he somehow knew whose eye it was, which sent an extra shiver down his spine. Alvor was above him in the loft.

The Small Red Ox

Even in his thoughts Einar had hardly ever dared to torture Alvor. Indeed, he always tried to keep them away from her. Of course it was nonsense to think that anyone could *watch* his mind—but he'd often wondered uneasily if she could . . .

Had his father ever guessed at Alvor's secret? Pretty, pretty Alvor, who looked so truly a golden girl. Charm—oh yes, she had charm! And so *much* golden hair which she wore braided round her head above a thick gold fringe which hid—*Ugh*! Nausea rose in him. *Ugh*—that first time when Alvor, innocently looking at him, smiling, had parted the thick fringe with her hands to let him see the small slit hole in her forehead. At first he had stared uncomfortably, pitying a pretty girl's disaster. What a disfiguring type of scar . . .

It wasn't a scar. Between the puckered edges of that—that *hole* something moved . . . glistened. It was luminous and moved from side to side as though seeking something. A black spot in the centre moved too—the pupil: beneath the fringe of soft gold hair Alvor had a third eye. After that day she had only to touch her forehead, and smile at Einar, for him to leave the room hurriedly, fighting down his nausea. A monster, a troll's daughter . . . probably a witch.

Above him, steps withdrew. Alvor had risen from the floor to go humming down the stairs. As she entered the kitchen she broke off humming to say, "He's awake. Who'll take him food? Whose turn to throw pigswill in his face?"

"Pigswill's too good for him. Let him starve, the brat! To say the farm was his!"

"Why—that's true," said the mother, lazily stirring the big stewpot. "Or is—until he dies."

"Hildur could make a special brew!" snickered Katla.

"Quiet, eager one! There are three of you who'll need a husband. Have you thought of that? Why else is Einar still alive?"

"I'll have him, then." Katla rocked to and fro with laughter. "He's my size, that little husband!"

207

"Aren't I the eldest?" Hildur rose in wrath. "Why should Katla have the farm?"

"Yes—you're the eldest, but—"

"And I'm the youngest! *Yet*—" said a very gentle voice. They all turned to stare at Alvor, who stood in the middle of the room and smiled at them, and held her fringe apart with two white hands. The eye winked, and glistened moistly, and the hard black pupil stared.

"Oh—so you want him, Alvor—"

"Pretty Alvor!" said the mother, looking warily from the corner of *her* eye.

"Yes!" Alvor smiled merrily, and stroked down her fringe. "How I frighten him!" She danced a step or two gracefully, nodding her head. The eye gleamed between tossing hair. "There's so little scope, here. But at least our child could scare him sicker still—Give me the soupbones, Mother. I'll take them to him, myself."

The food was twice as disgusting, after it had been in Alvor's hands. Einar couldn't swallow it. He was now shivering with fever, and almost lightheaded. He began to dream—and to speak: "I want to go away—right, right away, Kolbeinn! Alvor wants to marry me. I need food. Oh Kolbeinn, in your soft red coat and white splash on your forehead, how I love you—you're the only thing left in this accursed place to love. I love your soft muzzle, and your gentle munching. I love your large kind eyes, and their beauty, and your funny stiff white lashes. I'm so hungry—I want to die, but not of hunger. Kolbeinn, help me!"

Kolbeinn's munching grew very loud, till it sounded in Einar's ear, like speech. "Unscrew my right horn, little Einar."

Einar lay there in the straw asleep; yet he felt himself rise and enter Kolbeinn's stall. His hand slid along the ox's neck to touch the base of his right horn. Kolbeinn had fine long horns: pure white at their curving tips, ivory-yellow and mottled grey towards their base. When the right horn was twisted, it really came undone! Yet Einar hardly felt surprised. He turned it upsidedown and out of it, on to his palm, flowed good things—fruits, and meat; and finally it yielded up a draught of milk which tasted as though some-one had put honey in it. Then Einar replaced Kolbeinn's horn, and kissed him on the muzzle.

What an odd dream, he thought when he awoke. A line of wintry sunshine gleamed above the outer door. His aches and pains had almost vanished. He felt stronger, and stretched himself, saying, "Oh, if only I weren't so hungry—But I'm *not*!" He was utterly amazed. Why—his stomach felt quite plump with food ... and surely that round thing lying by his hand was some luscious fruit? (He'd never seen a peach before.) Einar grasped it, and stroked the furry velvet skin. Then he ate, savouring the juice. And then he said, "*Kol*beinn?"—his eyes round with awe.

Kolbeinn looked back at him over the partition, to make a gentle sound like "Moommmmmmmm—"

"Kolbeinn ..." said Einar contentedly. "I do love you, Kolbeinn."

"He's getting fatter!"

"*He* hurt *me*, yesterday," complained Katla.

His stepmother said, "These last weeks, that boy's been finding food somewhere—it worries me."

"Don't worry, Mother!" responded Katla fiercely, "I'll soon find out about this sudden strength." And she went hastily up the dark old farmhouse steps, to lie full length in the loft and look down into Einar's sleeping quarters. But Kolbeinn spoke a warning in his strange muted-bellow tones.

"My little Einar, look up! When the eyes look down on you, stare back, stare long, and think of me."

As Einar obeyed, the baleful eye at the long crack gradually closed its lid, and Katla, sprawling on her face in the loft's darkness, slept.

"Now, Einar—dear friend who was always kind to me when we were working—unscrew my horn and eat your fill."

Hildur was very cross with Katla when she found her sleeping, and next day said, "Mother—let Katla cook while I lie watching to see how Einar tricks us. He steals our food—or someone else's!" And, as Katla had, she lay watching in the dark. But Einar guessed her presence, and stared back, stared long, and thought of Kolbeinn. So in her turn Hildur fell heavily asleep, while underneath her Kolbeinn's horn provided a delicious meal of partridge, pineapple, and mead.

Alvor was contemptuous of her two sisters for their failure. "Our stepbrother has learned a thing or two—but will he put *me* to sleep by gazing upward?" And she laughed, and looked around her haughtily, and next day went tripping up the stairs herself.

The moment Einar sat down on the straw his bones shuddered within him: Alvor was up above! He gazed over fearfully at Kolbeinn, and the little ox's kind dark eyes looked back as though to comfort him. Then Einar lay spreadeagled, looked upward, and met Alvor's eyes staring through the crack. *But* he looked back, and looked straight, and thought of Kolbeinn. Still Alvor's eyes stared. Then Einar looked back, and looked straight, and thought harder still of Kolbeinn. An amazed but sleepy expression crossed Alvor's face; she raised it slightly, to part her fringe—but, before she could, she fell asleep just as her sisters had.

Einar was delighted with this victory. He ran into Kolbeinn's stall, threw his arms around his neck, and kissed him. "Oh, small red ox, my friend, how I do love you!"—and he grasped the horn, ready to unscrew it.

Kolbeinn moved uneasily, and tried to drag away; yet he could move no further without crushing Einar against the wall. He stood pawing at the ground and looking from the corners of his eyes as Einar unscrewed the horn. The food was sparse that night: two roasted eggs, some milk, and that was all.

"I hope it's not drying up!" said Einar, as he replaced the horn. He petted the unquiet Kolbeinn's muzzle, then returned to his own side of the partition, yawned, and slept. Above them Alvor still slept as well, but even in her sleep she had rolled over till her forehead was above the crack. The fringe had fallen apart and, all the time that Einar had been eating, the wet, white, glistening eye with its hard black pupil had been looking down.

Next day, towards nightfall, there was such wailing in the farm! Einar found his stepmother lying in a heap, and the three girls huddled round her. "She's sick, sick!" moaned Katla, clutching at him. "And calls all the time for you!"

Einar came closer, and tried to fight down his fierce joy. If she would die, that woman—! He felt shamed when she looked up at him to blubber, "Ah, Einar, Einar—how I've wronged you, son—" Then she fell silent, shifting on the bed as though to ease some pain; and afterwards cried, "Forgive—Will you forgive me, Einar, for your father's sake?"

This was almost too much for Einar; yet he fought down anger, and managed a grudging, "Very well—"

His stepmother tossed about some more. Her voice was weak and sad as she murmured, "Prove it, prove it—or I'll not die in peace. Do one small thing for me?"

Einar drew back warily. "If I *should* do it—then I will."

His stepmother sat up. She seemed stronger than before. Her white teeth glinted. They looked ready for a good sharp crunch. "If *you* won't do it for me, Einar, Alvor will! Kill me the red ox Kolbeinn, that I may eat flesh, and grow well."

Cruel, evil woman! Einar almost shouted it aloud. So they *knew*—somehow they knew. Alvor was smiling her sweet, placid smile. The thick, fair fringe covered the horror in her forehead. He guessed bitterly what must have happened, and blamed his own stupidity, for hadn't Kolbeinn tried to warn him? The ring of faces watched him with avid cruelty. If he disobeyed, Alvor would take a knife, and . . . He must be more cunning than them all.

He said gruffly, "Perhaps my father would have sacrificed the ox—But I'm an unskilled butcher—and it's no fit work for Alvor"—(Ugh—isn't it!) "so when morning comes I'll go for farmer Hjarda. He's skilled, and won't spoil the flesh for you, Stepmother."

As he left the room, he heard their laughter.

It was already quite dark where Kolbeinn stood munching in his stall and turned to look at Einar with large sad eyes. Could he already know? Einar went to him, and ran his hand along the warm red hide and thick neck until he touched the hair rising like a curly wavecrest at the base of Kolbeinn's horns.

"Ox, my friend! How brainless I was—" He kissed the white splash on Kolbeinn's forehead. "Now they seek to kill you—and through me!"

Kolbeinn blew noisily. His shiny pink lips moved against one another in a ruminative way. Einar felt his heart was broken. He had willed to live, to be a strong man; one day to defeat the four beastly women here on his father's farm. But if they first killed Kolbeinn, nothing would matter any more . . .

Outside, the bitter night was thick with snow-flurries. Icedrifts were everywhere, even the waterfalls were frozen. The land stretched on and on, terrible in every aspect at this season. No man could survive without food, friends, or shelter. Even the strongest ox—Yes, his stepmother knew how she had cornered them.

"Kolbeinn," he whispered in the pricked furry ear, "she has beaten me—that hag, troll-woman! Odin's curse on her! She would have your flesh tomorrow. Yet I'd sooner die than be *your* death. Come—we're going . . ." (Would those Saga heroes, the Sons of Droplaug, have faltered? They would have gone into the storm, laughing!) "Come, Kolbeinn," he whispered once again.

The little ox backed obediently from his stall, while Einar struggled to force open the stout wood door against resistance from the blizzard. Had evil foes risen up against him? Such storms were sometimes caused by giants beating at water with huge oaktrees—and witches could cause this sort of murky darkness—

At last, with one violent shove, Einar succeeded. The door crashed back against the outer wall. Luckily the wind's howling drowned every other noise. The sky was invisible, mere blackness which released swirling icy sparks that danced straight into Einar's vision, making him dizzy. He could see nothing except this mad, swirling, black-and-whiteness. He fought for breath, and groped behind him towards Kolbeinn. The ox's muzzle breathed warmth into his hand.

But it was terrifying out here! Einar seized the curved right horn, and clutched it near the base.

"Oh Kolbeinn, it's your magic horn! Can't you help us?"

Neat hooves already stood deep in snow. Einar put his arms around his friend's neck, and closed his eyes. As well die here, as somewhere else. Kolbeinn's neck was so comforting, so strong and warm. His clover breath smelt of Spring.

How warm—how warm! thought Einar. How surprisingly, beautifully, warm . . . He drifted off to sleep.

And woke to the sound of Kolbeinn's munching. The sleek red neck was bent as he munched sweet new grass—
Grass!

Einar looked about him in amazement. The dreadful landscape, the cruel snow and ice, the snug old farm which had been built deep into the hillside with only doors and

213

windows and odd bits of wall left visible, had vanished. He and Kolbeinn were in a wood. Birds were singing. Light poured down on them between swaying birchtops. A small stream ran nearby. There was grass for Kolbeinn, berries for Einar: big, luscious berries, twice as sweet as any he had eaten. And a wild bees' nest yielded up its honey.

He rolled over and over on the grass, ecstatically; then put his face down to the spring and drank deep, deep.

"Kolbeinn!—" he almost sang it, getting up again— "my magic, magic friend! Why didn't we leave long ago? Kolbeinn—?" But Kolbeinn merely shook his head as though flies bothered him, and snorted gently, and then lowered it to place his horns so that Einar felt himself invited to sit between them. The little ox, carrying his burden, set off purposefully into the wood. A wood—in Iceland!

The trees grew closer together, till they almost shut out the sun. The babbling of the stream gave place to silence. Soon the Springlike wood had turned to forest. How odd that twigs should gleam so brightly where the sun was so excluded . . . Bright, bright, the colour of a sunset, a copper tinge to every bough.

Kolbeinn stopped suddenly, almost shooting Einar over his head. A forest of tangled twigs barred their way.

"What should we do now?" pondered Einar.

Kolbeinn snorted. He just stood.

Einar had already begun to understand that some decisions must be his. It had been his readiness to sacrifice his life for Kolbeinn that had led to this adventure. Now he could feel the red hide quivering beneath him—was the little ox afraid? Afraid of what? That he, Einar, would make some mistake?

"Ah, dear friend Kolbeinn, if I must make our decisions, I won't fail you. Frigga be my guide—" He dismounted, took his strong knife from his belt, and attacked the barrier of twigs: they were shiny and hard, and the knife slipped on them. They were made of copper!

Just then he heard a fearful sound, a deep, roaring bellow.

There was a crashing ahead of them, and the twigs clanged together like small swords—it was as though an army fought.

"Kolbeinn!" exclaimed Einar, forgetting all about the Sons of Droplaug. "Oh, Kolbeinn, run! That sounds like some gigantic bull!"

A bull it was. A vast black satiny bull, three times as high as Kolbeinn, twice as broad. His eyes gleamed first red and then green as he came charging through the trees, and the copper buckled away from him as though it were only parchment.

Einar himself ran: he and Kolbeinn had just crossed a glade, and he ran the whole length of it till shame halted him and he slowly returned, holding his knife before him. The little ox had backed some distance, and now stood pawing at the ground before the onrush of the big black shape.

The bull halted, and pawed too.

Kolbeinn pawed once more, delicately.

The bull snorted.

Kolbeinn snorted, delicately.

The bull lowered his head.

Kolbeinn lowered his.

When horns met horns it was with a tremendous clashing sound of bone on bone. The black shoulders heaved and pushed, the short stout red neck pushed back. Forehead to forehead, horn interlocked with horn, ox and bull swayed to and fro in combat. And then—and then there was a truly awful cracking sound. Kolbeinn went down clumsily on his knees. During a dreadful moment Einar thought him dead— but Kolbeinn, pressing forward, had merely lost his support. The black bull's neck, forced sideways at a cruel angle, had been broken. He sagged, and crumpled into a satiny black heap. One horn had cracked too, from base to tip.

Kolbeinn turned his head to Einar. His big eyes gleamed. A shower of coppery twigs fell, as though a sudden wind had brought them down. The trees parted, and the way was clear again. . . .

Night came. Einar longed for sleep, yet the little ox went plodding on restlessly, swinging his head from side to side. Now and then he paused to listen, as though for danger. So strange a feeling of enchantment pervaded this night world that Einar found himself wondering if Alvor, thwarted of her cruel designs, had some hand in it. The thought was horrible—the thought of Alvor's third eye, peering through the night forest, was more horrid still. That huge black bull! Was Alvor a *hamrammr*—a shape-shifter?

It grew suddenly cold. Einar half expected snow to fall, but the moon rode clear in an almost cloud-free sky. Moonlight blanched branches and twigs, which clustered almost as thickly as the copper ones. Einar, who had removed his belt and used it to secure a bundle of copper twigs, thought these were even prettier. *Was* it the moonlight—or were they really silver? Just as before, boy and ox found themselves halted by an impenetrable lacing of bright metal. Again Kolbeinn shivered.

"Ox, my friend, what is it?"

But Kolbeinn only shivered.

The—the *thing* came unexpectedly from the left: a *draugr*, corpse of a dead warrior, hideously bloated, and discoloured by frostbite. In the Sagas *draugrs* were often guardians of treasure. This one's weird greyish colouring merged so well with moonlight and shadow that he was almost on them both before they saw him. Kolbeinn made a high screaming sound, and shifted sideways till brought up helpless by a hedge of twigs. Einar leaped to the ground. He knew his knife was useless against such an apparition— immense, its dead eyes rolling in its monstrous head. Only an arm's length separated it now from Einar.

There was no help from Kolbeinn this time. There was no hope anywhere—

By the Thunderer! thought Einar furiously—and his sudden rage cast out his fear. To be trapped like this! And after Kolbeinn's epic victory! No: he himself must—and would—do *something*—

The Small Red Ox

As the dead man raised an arm to strike, Einar hurled the bundle of copper twigs straight at his belly. There was a flash of copper light. Einar shielded his eyes automatically from a brilliant yellow glare, while he thought: This—this is the end—this horror will kill us as easily as though we were two hares, while I can't even see—

Nothing happened. He lowered his arm. Stared. And stared.

Where the corpse had come sneaking through the forest, the ground ran molten silver. Silver twigs showered from the trees. Skywards, towards the moon's placid roundness, something dark and winged was flapping hurriedly away, fire streaming from a savage rent in its soft underbelly. Even while he watched the dragon-flight became unsteady; wings began failing, as their tips streamed fire. A long way off the monster crashed to earth, and even here the forest trembled at the impact.

Who had animated that dead man? There were *hamhleypur* who could assume the guise of dragons—

Einar threw his arms round Kolbeinn's neck, and buried his face, trembling, against the warm red hide.

After this second victory it seemed always pleasant in the forest. There were mushrooms and berries for Einar, and when he grew tired of these he would unscrew Kolbeinn's horn and help himself to hare or rabbit. The ox's coat had a russet sheen, and his horns an oily glisten. Gradually Einar grew brown and tall. How long ago had they set out? This seemed a timeless place. Eventually they left off wandering, to settle by a stream. With the aid of fire and stone Einar—who had carefully hoarded some silver twigs—managed to shape himself a reasonable sword. Afterwards, he made ornamental casings of silver for Kolbeinn's horns. "Together we make a handsome pair! Ah—no hero from the Sagas ever had a better friend than you, my Kolbeinn! You're my *haminja*—my good fortune and good spirit guiding me."

But one day Einar woke uneasily. He sprang up, clasping his new sword. Was it sunlight on the twigs and branches round them—or had they turned to gold? What third monstrous enemy—

On the stream's other side he stood: a giant *berserkr*. He laughed at Einar, taunting him. His shield and helm shone and winked light in the sun's rays. His brawny arms wielded a massive sword. The tusks protruding from his mouth were like the fangs of some weird animal.

Einar felt cold. Here, surely, was the end to all adventure! What could mere silver do to such a man? *Was* he a *berserkr*— or part troll? When he threw back his head and snarled, the hair parted on his forehead: beneath the helm's rim winked a single eye.

Kolbeinn was nuzzling urgently at Einar's palm. He turned, and patted the red neck. "Yes—it's a true farewell this time, my friend! And an heroic parting. Perhaps we'll meet yet—in some *Valhall*."

Kolbeinn's eyes brimmed light. They were moist, as though with tears. Once more his muzzle thrust at Einar's palm. He backed away.

The *berserkr* strode into the stream and splashed across it. Einar stood on the high bank, and waited. He felt curiously confident. At least he was to die a hero's death.

The fight was hard. The *berserkr's* first task was to scale the bank, for then his shield and great sword would give him immediate advantage. Einar, in his superior position, just managed to hold him back. Clash! Swish! Clanggg! So went the battle.

When at last Einar began to falter there was a sudden rumbling of hoofbeats. Kolbeinn had charged! Slipping and sliding he went over the bank's edge, down on to the warrior. As the massive sword cut into his breastbone he uttered a high, almost human scream; even so, it was less terrible than the *berserkr's*, for the silver-cased right horn had penetrated his forehead eye.

The Small Red Ox

Man's blood and beast's blood mingled together in oily streams on the water's surface, and was gradually washed away. The silence was almost worse than the screaming. The dead *berserkr* still clutched the handle of his sword, its tip was deep in Kolbeinn's chest. Einar had leaped down the bank to kneel beside the little ox. Kolbeinn just moved his muzzle very weakly to place it on his friend's hand; and so he died.

For three days Einar wept so heavily that he could neither eat nor drink. Somehow he managed to haul Kolbeinn's body up the bank; and there he made a funeral pyre of branches, and placed the small red ox upon it.

"Goodbye, dear friend. I thought it was my time to go! You—you should have had a viking's funeral . . ."

He could hardly bear to look at Kolbeinn's poor dead eyes, once so full of liquid light, and feeling; but he steeled himself to take the graceful, curved right horn.

"I shall always drink from it—and when I use it I'll remember you, my Kolbeinn, my lifesaver!" Then Einar lit the pyre, and turned away.

He crossed the stream and trudged on wearily into the forest, through the grove of golden trees that the *berserkr* had been guarding. Einar hadn't yet the heart to enrich himself, and—numb with sorrow—wandered during many, many days. Sometimes he stroked the horn and talked to it, as though Kolbeinn were still there.

But the worst of sorrows lessens, or at least grows more endurable. And at last Einar began to take an interest in life again. He must plan a future, although he would never try to find his father's farm. On that day, when he faced things as a grown man must, he found the magic horn had not forgotten him. Just as Kolbeinn had, it always helped him. It brought him luck in every way, so that he acquired property, and true renown. And one day, when he was fondling it and telling it how badly he still missed Kolbeinn, and how lonely he felt, it brought him a girl as golden and pretty as Alvor had been, but whose forehead was innocent of a third eye.

They hung the magic horn above their bed—Einar suspended it there by a fine red cord. Later on he would often take it down to show it to his children, while he told them once again the story of the small red ox.

Sea Magic

Colm was cutting peat. He worked in a lackadaisical way, for his ears, heart and mind were occupied with other things, outer and inner: the flight of birds, drawn against pearly clouds which drifted so high they were like a distant arch of feathers almost obscuring a pale disk of sun; the beat of Atlantic breakers as they fought eternally to eat the island; the beat of his own heart when he thought—as he too often did—of Selva, spinning the rough, rank-smelling wool of little, scraggy, highland sheep into thread so strong and springy that even her cross grandmother forgot an old woman's jealousy of a lovely girl, and forgot too to scold her.

He sat back on his haunches, the shaped bone knife swinging from his right hand. A rich smell of earth rose from the deep-scored line. It was a good place for cutting, where few people came. He grinned to himself. They were frightened! Let their loss be his gain. He looked about him at the wide green spaces, and the big grey boulders that the islanders believed were once toys for giants' children when the giants inhabited the islands. There were *duns* up here, too: bright green mounds with entrances to fairy kingdoms. You couldn't trust a fairy, or so the island people said. They could assume any shape they pleased. They were courteous, and would ask you home for meat and drink. Take their offerings—and you were doomed to forgetfulness! Colm didn't believe these stories—or he would have cut his peats elsewhere.

In the shadow of the giants' toys were many nettles: sovereign plants against all magic spells. When giants and

221

fairies had fought each other—so people *said*—the giants wore shirts of nettles as a sure defence. Colm put out a hand to pluck one, but its sharp reaction made him drop it hurriedly. He smiled to himself. Anyway, he thought, nothing in earth, sky, or sea, could make me forget my Selva.

A light wind was blowing from the sea. He stood up. The surface of a nearby troutstream, bubbling and burbling over golden stones, was rippled suddenly with wind-flaws. A shadow crouched on a flattish boulder, and watched him. He whistled at it, as an otter whistles its mate, and a blunt muzzle moved and wrinkled as the otter whistled back. Then there was a rushing movement, and a long sleek thick tail whisked with joy as the beast humped itself past him, almost crossing his feet, and dived into the stream with an elegance and speed that seemed to make it one with the rushing water. A head rose for a moment. Two bright eyes considered him. A second time the otter dived, and disappeared rolling and twisting, part of the driving stream.

Colm smiled again. Other men might be soft in their minds—the things they believed, and told you to believe!—but he: he was soft in the heart, certainly. He freed otters from the hunters' snares, and remained silent when he found an eagle's nest. Once he had even helped a salmon to escape. He had found it netted and desperate by a waterfall, and fighting with extraordinary courage for its freedom. So Colm's fellows thought him daft as he thought them. Worse: someone who lost them scanty island food! He laughed aloud. Well—at least Selva was on his side; she'd sooner go hungry than eat a friend. As for those dour clansmen with their constant talk of hunting, stalking, and full bellies! Let them come here and catch a fairy and eat *that*, and get shut inside the bright green *duns* for many years.

Of course, there were other reasons why they were afraid. That huge, dark, slaty pile of stone which rose so grimly at the island's tip, and looked so near from this wide, open space, was said to be the giants' ancient stronghold.

Sea Magic

Some people swore it was still inhabited and that the last gruesome giant rambled out at night time, with his hideous wife, to seek lambs and young children—or even adults—as their food, and gather nettles. When the thick sea mists crept inland, bringing a false dusk with them, the islanders called in their sheep, their cattle, and their children. If a beast were missing, or a child had strayed, there would rise up a terrible wailing, as people besought the Shining Ones to descend and lay the blame where it belonged. As if it weren't easy enough for child or beast to wander, fall from a cliff, and be claimed by the battering sea!

Colm arranged the folds of his garment in such a way that his pile of peat could be carried as though supported in a sling. "Come and get me, giant, I'm here for the plucking! Come carry me home. It's a rough track down, and tiring. Selva's grandmother—would she pray to the Shining Ones for me? Not she—she'd sooner a harsh dark huntsman from the village for a grandson-in-law."

Then he felt pangs of contrition. Giants and fairies he might scorn, but he'd meant no disrespect to the Shining Ones, naming them so lightly in his heart. Forgive me, he thought humbly. Don't turn the glory of your faces, and your caring, from me and Selva. And he put back some of his carefully-cut peat as an offering for grace. Although he'd been orphaned when barely seven, it seemed he could still hear his father's words echoing down the years: "And whatever may come to you, Colm, my boy, never forget the gods! Never forget the respect due to them, nor neglect their love and service . . . Other men I've seen neglect their duties, piling it all on the Chief Priests to do for them; and terrible harm I've seen come of it, and retribution. . . ."

As a very little boy Colm had been taken once to the other island. He had seen the ring of stones, and the altar, and an avenue of stones leading across the land. He had hidden his face against his father's side in the darkness before midsummer day, and waited tense with dread and fearful joy for the dawn's first breaking when *the* Shining One

223

would descend from heaven and walk over the hills and up
the alley to the greatest stone of all. No one spoke of it—
they just stood, and hid their faces, and avoided their priest
who had touched the secret of the universe. Terror and joy
were indistinguishable when they mixed in godliness. Under
each of the major stones, it was said, lay the body of a strong
young man whose sacrificed heart had helped to sanctify the
Way.

Colm straightened up, balanced his peat again, and began
his trek homeward. Far to his left the sea stretched endlessly,
turbulently in motion from land to horizon. Somewhere
beneath it lived that other god honoured by his fisherman
father: Manannan mac Llyr, the King of the Sea. Sometimes
the manes of his wild white horses could be seen, as they
pawed their way upward from the seabed and tried to drag
his war-chariot clear in his attack upon the land—though
often they grazed peacefully enough, with easily flowing
manes and tails, as though their strong master had signed
eternal peace. Colm had seen the green flicker of the seaweed
glancing off their flanks, had heard them neighing and
whinnying through his dreams. This was natural, for his
own father lived now with Manannan, carousing in spirit
with the Sea God while his human bones helped whiten and
strengthen the underwater Palace walls.

"Come, Giant!" cried Colm toward the island tip. "Come
carry me home!"

By the time he reached the shallow valley, the sun had
completely disappeared. The feathery clouds, now all
joined together, shut it out behind a strange bird-wing
formation. Dull streamers of sulphuric-looking mist had
wreathed and twined their way inland from the slaty stone
pile at the island's tip, blotting out everything lying in its
path. And a terrible wailing and crying came out of the dark
hole that was the entrance to Selva's grandmother's hut.

"Gone!" she cried, and for the first time clutched Colm
to her as though he were her son, and twined her withered
arms around his neck. "Gone, gone, gone!" She sobbed and

moaned. There was a reeking mistiness still in the hut. Selva's spindle lay broken on the floor, and beside it a crushed nettle leaf.

He put her from him, his heart thumping unevenly with horror and disbelief. "Gone? Gone where—how? Who—"

"A hand!" she burbled, clutching him again; and this time he didn't try to free himself. "Huge—vast! On the end of an arm so long—" She screamed as though it were all happening again before her eyes. "A mist in the entrance, crawling towards her, and from it coming this hand—and plucking her out easy as a bean from its pod—Oh, the horror of it!" She wept against him, and he held her, smoothing her scanty hair, till he heard her mumbling, "And she the best spinner in all the island, and what shall I do now for bread?"

He stood on the upland, in the brilliant morning light, and those things he had never believed in continued to happen. He was wondering how to get himself inside that terrible place of a giant's stronghold, and if it *was* mist that hung over it still, or smoke from some immense cooking pot, cooking, cooking something . . . delicious . . . for a giant's meal. It was three days now since Selva had vanished, and all attempts to get close to the stronghold had failed. There had been volcanic rumbling sounds, and a shower of large black boulders flung through the air towards him as though hurled by an enormous hand. Once already he had dodged too late: his grazed and swollen left ankle hurt with the dull agony of chipped bone.

He slumped down despondently, and put his head in his hands. Selva—*Selva*! When he looked up again he wasn't alone. On a nearby boulder perched the largest bird he had ever seen; her bright, keen eyes were watching him. Golden-tawny she was, like the sun, and pride and power were in every line of her, and her beak and pinions could have carried off a calf. He gasped. He had seen many of her kind in the island, sailing the winds like little gods of the air, or stooping to kill with queenly ferocity. He had even held their eaglets, and successfully mended a wing of one, last summer. But this creature! She was like the spirit of all golden eagles rolled into one and dressed with brazen feathers. The shifting of her claws on the boulder was like a rattle of bones.

"Colm, I will help you fly there."

Did he really hear such words? Or was he responding to his instinctive knowledge of birds and beasts? He hobbled towards her to climb on to her back, and was raised by her strong wings as she took off with an up-and-down beat, catching the rising air as they swung skyward far above the island. Now he could look straight down to the sea's fronded floor where dolphins and seahorses guarded the courts of Manannan. He glimpsed a city, and shuddered. Could that be fabled Tir-nan-Og, country of eternal youth? To see it was the worst of omens, a true warning of death.

He tightened his hold about the feathered neck, and saw the sun reel sideways above him as the great bird wheeled lower to landwards and glided over the black-towered stones. She turned, swooped, turned again, and then came level with the highest stones, where she hovered, waiting for him to slip from her back on to the uneven wall.

He found himself looking down into a huge dark room where his poor Selva sat kneedeep in nettles, weaving fast as she could weave from their fibrous stems and leaves. Her eyes were red with weeping—her arms and hands red from nettle stings. He was so overjoyed to find her alive that he thought no more about the eagle, already speeding back into the sky like a ray of light leading to the sun.

Before Colm could call to Selva he saw a thread of mist creep through the doorway, followed by a giant hand which tossed another bundle of green nettles towards the weeping girl.

"Take and spin, take and spin, girl! Spin hard and fast and true! Three rooms of nettles shall make my shirts again, and

when you've done you shall go nicely in a pot of nettle
stew. If you break the thread, or cease your spinning, you
shall stew the quicker. Are you spinning, girl?" And a rope
of nettles was thrown through the doorway to catch her
stingingly around the neck.

"I'm spinning! I *am* spinning—" wept Selva, not daring
to pause and pull the nettles off, though the pain had made
her nearly snap the thread. The dark room was filled with
the rank, juicy smell of cut nettlestems.

Then the mist and arm withdrew together. Almost at
once the giant could be heard crashing away over the rocks
outside. Immediately Colm let himself down the gleaming,
slaty walls, handhold to handhold, and waded through the
nettles, regardless of their stinging, till he had Selva firmly
in his arms. She was filled with wild joy, and disbelief—and
her tears and spinning ceased. They stood clasped together
in a close embrace.

A shadow fell across the doorway. Colm raised his head.
Selva's hands fluttered helplessly towards the dropped
thread. They had both forgotten that the giant had a wife.

"Girl, girl—have you spun out your life already?" she
mumbled through her great lips; and she moved *her* hands
to snatch up Selva for the pot—then lowered them again.
She had caught sight of Colm. Straightaway tears of
passionate excitement started to her tremendous, hideous
eyes. "Little fellow—oh, how handsome!" she mouthed.
"How nobly formed—so unlike my husband! How I could
love you, if we weren't ill-matched in size. Delicate thing!"
And she breathed so hard from robust emotion that the
windiness of it knocked him to the floor. Yet, as he fell, he
kept his wits, and cried out loudly, "Both for the pot—or
neither!"

They could almost hear the wheel of her thoughts turn
creakily in the strong old head so far above them. Selva
shuddered, and moved close to Colm, who sat up and held
her hand. Both felt they could endure being boiled or stung
to death, so long as each died with the other.

Then the giantess bent to pluck Colm off the floor, and set him high upon the wall. She looked at him with cow-eyes of love—the size of her irises almost made him faint—and prevented his coming down again. "Off with you, little fellow! I'd live with you gladly, if you weren't mere beetle stuff. Still and all, I'll not have you a crunchy morsel for my husband's teeth."

"I'll not go without my girl!" declared Colm.

The giantess thought it over. Then she gave poor Selva a sly and jealous glance. "You may save your girl, little fellow, and that's a promise, if you'll find me what I want. Come back before the last green nettle's spun here—and come with a rope of fine pearls large enough to suit my ample neck!" She flicked one finger beneath Colm's buttocks, and he went soaring over the wall to land in a stream the other side; while within the giants' stony lair the terrible green spinning began again.

The water cooled his nettlestings, although it couldn't quench the fire of his sorrow. He swam downstream, till he came to where it joined the sea. He knew there was no hope for Selva—he might just as well drown himself. Where would a poor island boy find such pearls? As he despaired, he felt something nudge against his knees. A sleek head, a whiskered muzzle! Round eyes stared up at him, a strong body with a sleek wet pelt drew him towards the waves. He rode the friendly otter as though it were a dolphin, for they went far beyond any distance he could have swum, until they reached a shelf of rock just beneath the surface of the sea. If he and the otter spoke to each other, Colm never knew; or how they communicated in some other way; but certainly the beast taught him that they must seek together for pearls like marbles in the Palace of Manannan, King of the Sea.

On the deep-lying shelf of rock they waited; while Colm saw nothing but seaweed, and fish, and a dim dazzle of green. Then—

"Now! With this coming wave!" And, as they dived, the

water not only parted but seemed to alter strangely, to shiver into forms and colours, walls and plants, walks and winding pathways. For some while they swam, by habit, though they could have walked. Sometimes they heard hoofbeats above their heads, and these came from the foam horses of Manannan, grazing delicately higher in the sea. Green lilies swayed beside them, and the houses they swam past were of marble, beautifully veined with pink. As Colm's eyes grew accustomed to this new world he saw gold striping the pavements, and rock-crystal carved into roses bunched with crimson and sepia seaweed. The light was heavenly-green. Eels undulated past them, with a fiery blue rippling glare. Occasionally, something black and slippery and monstrous would slide away, and enter some hole into the bottom of the sea.

They reached the Palace walls. If Colm had known it, the first thing he saw here was his father's bones, whitening the Palace windowsill. By this time he and the otter were both walking. The otter carried a rich coat of brown fur over one arm, carelessly; and he had the features of a bold, brave, rather truculent young man. Colm was overawed, for he guessed himself to be in the presence of a true Prince of the Sea.

So they came to the throne room of Manannan mac Llyr. The King was at home now, for his wild warfare with the land had temporarily ceased. His daughters sat about him: gleaming, exquisite girls. Their hair was like bright water in the path of a setting sun, and they had seals' eyes with deep kindness in them—which increased as they listened to the weird tale that the otter-Prince had brought. And when he had told of Colm's savage dilemma, and mentioned how the island boy had once saved him from a trap, the eldest princess threw her arms around her brother's neck. She felt her heart pierced with undersea joy, and—something she had never felt before—earthly sorrow, too. She called her attendants and ordered them to bring her own particular cup. It was made of shell and coral, seamed and mounted in gold. She mixed Colm a drink with her own hands, then offered it smilingly.

"In my father's house, earth stranger, you shall find what you need! Who else has pearls fit for a giantess but the King of the Sea? There are pearls without number in Manannan's treasury. All oysterbeds send their finest tribute here, it's only for him that an oyster willingly sacrifices its own life! Tomorrow you shall make your choice, Colm of the islands, but today you shall eat and drink, and dance with me."

Colm hesitated. Hadn't he always been warned to distrust what fairies give? Yet this woman was no fairy, she was daughter to a god. If he refused her hospitality, could he demand the pearls she'd promised him? The King himself smiled, the otter-Prince, and the other golden girls. He couldn't meet trust with suspicion. He took the cup gravely from her, and drank. Then he said wonderingly, "But I've searched for you all my life!"

And she answered, "Yes . . ."

And he said, "It's—strange; but I don't remember how I came here! Or why."

She said, "You came to seek me, surely?"

"I remember nothing—nothing!"

"Memory isn't important, Colm—only the future! Trust me, and I'll do the remembering for us both." She smiled seductively at him, and held out a hand, which he took in his.

"Where is my memory, though?" He wrinkled his brows.

"You gave it me as a gift, when I promised to marry you." She looked down at their joined hands, and lowered her lids so that he couldn't see how her green eyes sparkled with triumphant joy. "In return, I promised you pearls the size of eggshells for your wedding gift."

"That was a strange thing for me to ask of you—and me a man!"

"Nevertheless, I'll keep my promise—at our wedding feast!"

Then music sounded, with the compelling rhythm of the sea itself, and they all began to dance.

Meanwhile, in the slaty darkness of the castle on the island's tip, the spindle began to slip and jolt in Selva's hands. As though it had taken control, the thread moved fast and faster between her fingers. She cried out in terror, for at this rate the nettles would be spun long before her lover could return—even with one pearl. Already she could see a bare patch of ground beside her feet, as the thread spun fast and faster in the rhythm of a dance. She looked upward, and saw blue sky between the rocks that overhung the room.

She stood, still spinning as though she were possessed. She threw back her head again—and saw she could never reach that open space so far above; at least, not without help. The walls were black and slippery, and ran with moisture. Here and there were jutting bits of slate, but they were mostly near the ground, and she was no natural climber as Colm was. Still spinning frantically she went to stand on the lowest ledge, and found she could look out through a small square gap between the rocks.

Beyond, the little stream ran and tumbled joyfully, as though it delighted in the freedom that sent it rushing to the sea. She looked at it with envy, and cried out in sorrow, "Stream, stream, you'll surely take news of my cruel death to Colm!"

Close to the castle walls there was a sudden troubling of the surface. A great fish leaped clear, the sun shining on its scales. She could see its bright and cunning eye, a mesh of scars along its side. She recalled how Colm had told her that he once saved a salmon from the nets because of its royal struggles; and she thought she heard the fish speak, as it turned upstream to hold itself steady against the flowing current by undulating fins and tail.

"What message shall I take to Colm my saviour?"

"Not to forget me! Not to forget the need for haste!" cried Selva. "Tell him the nettles will soon be spun—yes, even three rooms of them, for they go so fast! I have a strange certainty that he no longer thinks of me."

"Yes, he has forgotten. He's bound by the magic of the Sea King's daughter. She gave him a draught of oblivion—and pearls she'll bring him as dowry for their bridal. Once they're wed, poor Selva, you are lost."

Selva wept desperately, leaning against the wall, the spindle dancing its joyful rhythm in her hands. "Kind salmon, tell him of my despair! Surely that will break the spell?"

"No words will break it." The salmon still held himself steady against the rushing stream.

On impulse, Selva pushed her right hand through the gap and held out a twist of nettle thread. The poison burned and stung her fingers, but she held it firm. "Sweet salmon, since Colm saved you from the nets, please take him this from me!" She dropped the thread into the stream. There was a swirl, a flash of silver. Fish and nettle thread had gone.

In the undersea Palace the feast was almost ready. Seahorses carried glasses of wedding wine upon their heads, and flickered to and fro between the guests. The moment approached when the Sea King's daughter and Colm would take their places at the table head. Then Manannan mac Llyr himself would touch their joined hands with his rock-crystal staff tipped by a conch shell, and they would be married. For their domain the King had offered them tenure of all the underwater land hereabouts where sweet Atlantis had once foundered; he himself would move to southern waters.

Colm couldn't look away from his sea girl's face—he could think of nothing and no one else, so entranced was he by her long green eyes and subtle smile. He bent to pat a tame seal, which nudged him hopefully for scraps of fish.

"Not yet, seal, my friend! The feast hasn't begun."

"But it will soon, dear Colm." The Princess took his hand, and led him to sit at the high table. Dolphins blew trumpets, as the Sea King strode forward with his staff. His cloak was held by oyster shells, his white hair and beard waved beneath a tall crown of coral and carnelian. As Colm stared timidly at the overwhelming god a blunt nose once more nudged his elbow.

"The feast hasn't begun," he repeated, tapping the blunt nose sharply with his hand. Between his arm and body there was a flash of silver as the great salmon swam to leave the piece of nettle thread before the bridegroom. It lay there twisted to the shape of a small dull-green ring.

Everyone stared. The Princess cried out in horror, "Colm! Don't touch it—don't!"

She was too late: Colm had already wonderingly put out a hand to pick it up. He said very slowly, "Why—isn't—this—" and he looked round him as though utterly bemused.

For one second the scene impressed itself upon his mind. He saw all its beauty, its colour; the god-King; the distraught face of his lovely Sea Princess. Then there was a sudden, strange, engulfing sound, as though the whole seabed had fallen in. The myriad colours round him all turned to one dim, watery, sea-green. Instead of carved ivory, and crystal roses, he saw a world of ruins. He turned gaping to his Princess, but she had changed as well: he saw a woman's body with long fish-like tail, a green face with seaweed hair, and two fin-like hands that rose to hide her weeping as she slipped from his side and swam away.

He was sitting on no Prince's throne-like chair, but on a ledge of rock. The courtiers had turned to cuttlefish, shrimps, crabs, mussels, and sea urchins. Colm stared about him in blankest amazement. What weird dead city was he in? For here and there were huge stone pillars, squarely hewn, leaning to right and left. Was *this* the capital city of Atlantis, long since drowned?

Colm started. Was *he* drowned—was he dead? He stared down at the ring of nettle thread wound about his finger. Selva—*Selva*! His lungs began to burst, lights shone before his eyes. Instinctively he raised his arms above his head, and rose, rose, rose to a smooth surface. The otter rose silently behind him, a sea-shadow, a humble, sleek companion.

It was low tide then, and the sea far out, or poor exhausted Colm might easily have drowned. Even so, it was a hard swim. At last he staggered on to pebbly sands, and lay there with lungs heaving. Why had he struggled to survive, he wondered bitterly, since he had failed? Selva would die—and did he want to live without her?

Then he grew conscious of lying on something very hard. He shifted uncomfortably, but it shifted too. He sat up, to plunge his hand beneath his soaking plaid. Round his waist was twisted and knotted a long piece of seaweed, which held secure a string of lustrous pearls as large as pigeons' eggs. For a moment he couldn't understand it; till he recalled how old traditions had it that the sea folk were proud, and always kept their vows. The otter, which had been crouching on the sand beside him, looked up with wistful brimming eyes, barked, and slipped back into the sea.

"Goodbye, Prince—and thank your sister!" cried out Colm, toward seemingly empty waters. "And goodbye, Atlantis, or fair Tir-nan-Og! *My* promised land is here."

That evening he stood with Selva on the green uplands, dotted with boulders, where the giants' children used to play. They held each other very close, in all the happiness warm human love can bring. There was no smoke any longer from the black tip of the island where the castle stood. Perhaps the stillness seemed ominous to Selva, for she shivered, and burrowed her head against her lover's neck.

"Colm, Colm—when we've children, we must leave the island! Thanks to the high Shining Ones we were freed from evil. But who knows what could happen in the future?"

Colm's hands tightened suddenly on her waist.

"Selva! Look!"

Sea Magic

She raised her head. The sea, which had been pale and calm beneath the setting sun, was rent suddenly by commotion as though a whirlpool formed far out. Huge white wavetops rolled apart to reveal depths of deeper, swirling blue. A whale appeared, plunging and blowing heavily. Then the wild horses of Manannan's own war-chariot struggled clear and tore in towards the land, driven hard by his eldest daughter who, in her bitterness, had borrowed it and come to redeem her father's pearls. They glimpsed her long green hair, and the dolphins leaping and rolling to escort her in. The horses galloped with a fearful sound to match the Sea Princess's passion.

Colm and Selva could see nothing more, for suddenly a darkness fell. They groped their way homeward, hand in hand. By morning the island was gloriously green from end to end. Its black slaty tip, together with the castle and its sinister inhabitants, had all gone, washed away like lost Atlantis into the receptive sea.

The Graveyard Rose

❧

Five centuries have passed, and even now little has changed in that small village where Magdalena Untermeyer lived. The Gothic church still stands surrounded by its green churchyard—a pleasant place to lie at peace. Go there on an early summer's evening, when the limes have dropped their flowers, and the wild roses are coming into bloom, tangling on the graves. Think long enough, deep enough . . . until you could swear you're back in Magdalena's day, five hundred years ago.

The long grasses would have shivered in a light wind, and chants sounded from inside the church. There was a scattering of petals. Straw-coloured stamens centred the white-pink of a rose. Girls came to confession with airy skirts swirling, coiffed heads tossing. The village lads waited still, hungrily disconsolate, about the gate . . .

What did they wait for, once the girls had gone inside?

Another flash of colour up the path, movement. A face seen in the shadow of the trees . . . a smile.

The wild rose bowing as though to another . . .

Magdalena!

"She's so beautiful—" everybody said. "An only child—what a dowry!" "But *she* barely needs one. That hair—those eyes!" "That figure . . ." sighed the young men.

Magdalena smiled and smiled at her kind neighbours. She often smiled too at herself—in her own polished mirror—lost in dreams. The natural beauties of the world, and its terrors, passed her by unobserved.

There was one neighbour who didn't think so well of

Magdalena's chances. She sniffed. "She's been so spoiled by admiration that if the Holy Roman Emperor himself came begging for her hand she'd turn him down." And it seemed the jealous neighbour might be right: for Magdalena didn't learn. She refused this boy because he pined, that one because he was too merry. She rejected the alchemist's son, and the apothecary's; and the local farmers' sons because they smelled of straw. Even when she reached the age of twenty-three and the Landgraf's cousin came to woo her she deplored his redness and his shape; so that he reddened more in anger, and left—looking squarer in the jaw—and never came again.

Then Magdalena's father was annoyed. Formerly his haughty child had much amused him; he hadn't really wished to lose her. Now he began to long for a compliant daughter, and some grandchildren. He grew severe: "Magdalena, you're to marry the next man who asks you!"

"Nonsense!" cried Magdalena defiantly, biting her full red lips. She didn't fear her father, for she knew her power. "I'll have only one I love—one who's good enough!"

"Suppose he never comes?" cried her mother, secretly jealous. "Suppose you sit there like a booby goose, growing lines upon your face, while plainer girls fill cradle after cradle?"

"He will come!" said Magdalena shortly. Nevertheless she tapped her way upstairs in her high-heeled shoes, to search anxiously in her polished mirror for the first faint line.

Three years later she discovered it. By this time her parents were glum indeed. Her father was bent with rheumatism beneath his fur-lined robe, and longed even more for grandchildren to bounce upon his knees. Her mother's eyes glinted like an old hawk's. Magdalena needed all her self-possession when she went to Mass on Sundays, trailing her long skirts, the tippets on her sleeves dangling to the ground. Her eyebrows were arched, and her tall brow shaved at the forehead as was the nobles' fashion. Above it her frivolous headdress of veil and cone, or butterfly shape, took the wind with the pride and glory of a tall ship in full sail. She held her missal in one hand, and bowed her head to enter the church's dark interior—where she saw candles and cross and priest, and old-boned nuns who turned their faces to her and speculated upon when she'd join them. She saw intricate Gothic carvings of saints and animals, and Christ upon one hand and the Devil on the other. She saw a skull carved on a pillar's boss: its grin seemed to follow her passage up the nave. And from the corner of her eye she saw girls much younger than herself, with rings upon their fingers. They had children by them, and smiled and nudged each other as Magdalena passed. "There goes our dedicated, lovely spinster," one would whisper, "whose disdain has scattered all her suitors."

And a year later: "—whose suitors seem to have abandoned her for good!"

At last Magdalena's pride began to break. She felt that sunny days had gone for ever and it was always raining, since no young men's voices broke the silence. There was only her father complaining of his cramps, and her mother begging her to marry the cross-eyed chandler as his second wife before it was too late.

"Life's horrible!" wailed poor Magdalena. Was she mere disposable flesh and blood like other women? She ran upstairs weeping. "I'll never wed that ugly man! Life's finished for me, anyway. Now I'll only marry Death, would God he could come fast and take me for his own!"

She stared miserably into her mirror. A thin white hand descended on her shoulder, and she felt a gentle pressure. If she hadn't caught her breath, she would have screamed.

"Magdalena! Dearest girl—" murmured a low, vibrant voice.

Was it Death who had come into her chamber? She shook and shook. Who else would come upstairs unannounced?

But, when she dared to turn, the intruder seemed quite reassuringly human—as handsome a man as any she had

239

seen in all her years of killing other people's hearts. True, he was whitefaced; but his smile was gay. The coal-black of his velvet sleeves was dagged with fiery rose and orange. He wore jewels of diamond and jet, and looked as though he knew the world inside out from court to palace. All the same, she was still afraid. "You smile, sir—but your black velvet speaks of mourning! And how did you come here?"

He brushed the last part of her speech aside. "Who could be all darkness, when he comes to ask the hand of so spectacular a bride? Magdalena, your father shall give you to me!" He took her hand, and pressed it warmly though his was cold. "Smile, my beauty! I'm sure that I shall hold your interest as no man has yet done—" Then he fixed her with his strange dark eyes, and spun stories so extravagantly funny that she wept with laughter and forgot her fears—till he grew quiet and asked permission to doze a while: he'd much to do after he left. She let him fall asleep in her old chair of strong Black Forest wood, and watched him, frowning to herself. He was so handsome and so easy, and desired her; but still she couldn't be quite happy, knowing how she'd called on Death to save her. She crossed the room stealthily to find a stout ball of thread that she had spun herself, and tied one end around his ankle.

He woke at last, yawning: "Ahhhh! What dreams— Dearest child, I mustn't stay. Be assured I'll come for you within a week . . ." He touched cold lips to hers, and went clattering down the stairs, which rattled beneath his tread as though someone struck them with bones. Magdalena snatched up a long black cloak and followed him as swift and quiet as any shadow. It was dark, dark night—and the wind swaying the trees with a hollow groaning noise. She saw her visitor pacing ahead towards the church; then running, with long loping strides, while she ran too, holding her breath—and the thread. Quick and silent as a bat he was inside the porch. The door swung to behind him. Magdalena broke off the thread, fell on her knees, and peered through the keyhole. She suppressed a scream.

The Graveyard Rose

The church's dim familiar interior had changed: it glowed with rosy light. Misty, bony things had come out of the churchyard, and were warming their thin hands at a fire which flamed there in the nave. Neither Christ nor Devil was clear by this light, but the carved form of Death, the skull-head that had smiled at her, had grown and grown till it was life-size, and—living: unmistakably it was her bridegroom. Then she saw creatures from his kingdom carry in the newly dead toward the flames. Yes, Death's own comrades were coming two by two, bearing young men, old people, even babies, and casting them into—

Half-fainting, feeling a sick and sour horror, Magdalena dragged herself away on stumbling feet, back, back to her own home and upstairs, where she fell upon her bed to sob and sob in desperation.

"Never cry so, daughter!" said her hawk-eyed mother, concerned after a week. "We'll refuse the cornchandler, and you shall turn religious. It will save all our faces. Yet your father and I shall both regret our grandchildren." Still Magdalena wept, and wouldn't, or couldn't, tell her why.

That night the wind was blowing very hard, and she heard knock, knock, knock upon her window, as though the storm itself would enter.

"Yes?" cried Magdalena, fearfully raising up her golden head.

"Ah, my dearest, my devoted one, my bride," said a velvet voice she recognised, though now it had a low, dry tone to it, as if a hint of bone were hidden in the velvet. "Tell your true lover what you saw, the night you followed him of your free will?" He chuckled.

Still she wouldn't, or couldn't, speak. She shook so that the bed legs pounded on the floor, then at last cried out, "I saw nothing—nothing! Go away! Our Lord and Saviour send you far from me!"

"If you won't tell your loving bridegroom what you saw, then your father shall pay a forfeit, with his life," chuckled the hateful voice.

Magdalena pushed her face into her pillow like a child, and refused to hear or believe what Death had said. But next day when she went to wake her father she found him stiff and cold, his eyes turned up with an expression of shocked amazement in them; he looked like someone surprised by ambush. She wept inconsolably, till even her mother's tear-filled eyes softened when she saw Magdalena's face. "Child, we all die, for so God wills! Dry your eyes, and call the priest to see about your father's funeral."

At the week's end, when her father lay stiffly in his bed of earth, Magdalena went to her bedchamber and slowly, dazedly, took off her black gown. She climbed into bed shivering with cold and her depressed, unhappy thoughts. It was a very rainy night. The moon rose wan and almost invisible, above racing clouds that showed a pale, watery blue.

Something—someone—rose also, and hovered outside Magdalena's window to scratch loudly at the pane of horn.

"Beauty, love, my golden girl! Now tell me—what saw you, that night you followed your true bridegroom to the church's porch?"

Magdalena was so terrified that she could only lie and shake and weep. Even when Death cried out with something of a snap in his voice, "Your mother shall lie silent as your father, if you'll not speak!" her lips trembled too much for words. So Death went impatiently to her mother's window-pane, and clambered in with all the haste of an undiscriminating lover.

There was a feeling of hollow emptiness in the dead merchant's house. Geese cackled continually outside it, as though they spoke of what had happened. Haunted by shadows and the pining of her mother's little dog, Magdalena sat day after day staring into space, her hair unbrushed, her eyes wide and wild. Her father had been a loving guardian: how could she survive without him? She missed even her mother's harsh companionship. Now and then she half roused herself to wring her hands and say aloud, "If only

I'd taken for husband the first young man who asked me!"

Near the week's end the weather grew quite balmy. Scents of winter flowers hovered above the moist earth, and a large, round, perfect moon rose soon after dusk, looking yellow and edible as good Dutch cheese. Magdalena lit her tapers, and trailed upstairs to bed. Although the night was still it seemed as though the house was all alive. Shadows flitted suddenly from chair to wall, or down a passage; the little dog howled, and ran for cover. Magdalena thought she heard a murmuring, a sigh, a chuckle. She covered her ears with her thin hands, and lay down on the bed in her black mourning robe. She couldn't sleep.

Towards midnight, though there was no wind, her window blew wide open with a crash.

"My unattended bride—pretty, orphaned girl! So: what did she see, the night she followed her own chosen bridegroom to his revels?"

Magdalena felt her breath choke in her throat as though someone strangled her. She burrowed her fists against her breasts, as if seeking for inner help; there was none: she could recall no words of any prayer. Her silence goaded Death to anger.

"Pride has always been your downfall, Magdalena! You flouted your father, now you flout me too! Tell me what you saw! At once!"

Magdalena gasped and gasped. She couldn't speak.

Then Death's long, thin, white hands reached over the sill, and swayed towards her, as the scented summer roses had swayed in earlier years. At last Magdalena was speaking, almost babbling, crying out she would tell anything, anything— But it was too late. Death was in her bed. She felt his darkness invading, overwhelming her. Though she fought and struggled, and sweated, she couldn't fight him off. He held her in his arms all night, and by morning she was dead.

For three days the beauty lay upon her bier. The whole village came to look at her, and murmur, and shake their heads. Then she was buried. Someone else inherited the house, the fat geese, and the little dog. People turned their thoughts to living, and the trials of ordinary life.

Another three days passed. Magdalena's grave, which had been smooth and barren, put out a green shoot. Delicate leaves trembled from a stalk. A bud pushed up, and opened into a rose scarlet as poppies, or as blood. The rose nodded above the grave, and its scent was so alluring that everyone who passed the churchyard was drawn inside by it.

"As lovely as Magdalena was!" whispered the villagers, crossing themselves; and ceased to come too near.

A few days later, when the rose was wide open and scenting all the graveyard, young Prince August of Ritterstein passed that way. He was out riding with his servant, and whistled gaily as he rode. When he reached home again he threw down his wide hat and gauntlets on a side table, while his young sister came running to embrace him as she always did. This time he held her off.

"Carefully, Sophia! You'll spoil my lovely rose. Isn't she wonderful?" And he laid the blood-red rose from Magdalena's grave beside his hat, then stood back to admire it. The scent filled all the hall.

The Prince's servant shook his head. "*Meine gnädigste*, your brother's Highness won't be warned. He should have left that rose to die, one like that could only blossom from a dead maid's heart. She's calling to him from the grave, and he courts death itself—for she may come and claim his own heart now. Let him beware at midnight!" Again the servant sorrowfully shook his head.

But August threw back *his* head, and laughed. He had a stubborn chin, cleft in the middle, and bright blue eyes; and his laugh was as engaging as his looks. "Poor Franz! Indeed, I think the rose has life, for how she struggled with him on the grave! You would have thought it was some battle for her maidenhead."

The Graveyard Rose

"See, *gnädigste*? Her thorns scratched my palms until they bled—" Franz held out his hands—"*I* couldn't pluck her. In the end the Prince himself—"

"Why, you were careless, Franz." The Prince picked up the rose to run his fingers cherishingly up her stem. "For she has no thorns. She has as sweet and smooth a skin as any girl's."

The faithful servant looked down at his scratched palms, and at the rose, and shuddered; then he bowed, and went sadly away. Soon other servants bore in the evening meal.

But August didn't want to eat. He sat there fingering his crystal wine glass and staring across the room to where the rose lay on his hat. He kept thinking of his servant's strange words, and the flower's unusually sweet and pungent scent which in this warmth seemed to have increased, and breathed all about him where he sat. His sister was amused, then piqued, and then she laughed at him. "August has fallen in love with his graveyard rose!"

He didn't seem to mind Sophia's taunts. "She's more beautiful than any woman I have seen," he remarked dreamily. When his parents and sister left the room he stayed behind, his food and drink untouched. The servants eyed each other, but didn't dare to interrupt the Prince's reverie nor clear away. In the long room there was an alcove which contained a couch where he sat himself down and finally went to sleep. They left him, and the table, undisturbed.

How Prince August dreamed that night! He saw the rose growing on the grave; then the grave opened as though it were a bridal chest, and inside it he saw a lovely girl sleeping in Death's arms. She roused suddenly, and looked up at him with desperation in her eyes; but Death looked up too, and held her locked against his heart. The girl cried out to August, who went to rescue her, but woke. His throat was dry—dry as cemetery dust—and when he rose to look for his filled glass of wine he found it emptied, his roast meat eaten, and ripe figs bitten through as well.

245

"Our servants need retraining," he said crossly to himself as he went off to bed.

Next day Franz indignantly defended them: "Your young Highness is beneath a spell, didn't I say that this would happen? *No* one went in there while you were sleeping—I was outside the door, and I should know! It's my belief that what ate and drank your Highness's meat and wine was the graveyard spirit you harbour in your hat."

August laughed loudly, yet looked startled all the same, and soon grew very thoughtful; particularly when Franz cried out in terror, "That rose will come again at midnight, you'll see—*then* she'll not be satisfied with food and drink; no! What she'll come for then is nothing less than my poor Master's heart . . ."

That night the Prince pretended sickness, and refused to eat. He told the servants to leave out food and wine for him, in case he felt like supping late. Then he hid himself behind the couch.

The hours passed very slowly. The clock seemed to tick slower like a heart near death. A faint chill mist crept upwards from the floor. At midnight a cry was repeated from all the many towers of Schloss Ritterstein: "Twelve is the hour, and all's still and well!" No sooner had it died away than strange music sounded and brought with it waves of scent as the rose rustled upright on her stem. For a while she spun and twirled, as though someone were weaving music with her, like thread upon a spindle. Then she grew and grew while her form changed entirely, rippling into the shape of that girl in August's dream. She wore the white dress in which she had been buried, but there was colour in her cheeks—rose colour—and she ran to find the food like any hungry, healthy girl. Afterwards she wiped her face clean with water from a jug, then looked about her, sighed, and—just as August was thinking to step forward and present himself—ran back to the side table. The form rippled once more, the white dress turned red and green. Soon the perfect rose, giving out waves of scent, was lying on

August's hat as though it had never moved.

Next day the Prince sat by himself, deep in thought; he wouldn't speak to anyone. At last he decided to consult his uncle, who was always in the castle library.

"I said so." The old man threw up his hands in mingled excitement and dismay. "I *always* said so! I told my sister: 'If you don't stop that boy of yours from poking his nose into things that don't concern him, one day—you mark my words—he'll come back with Death's own bride.' But your mother never paid me the slightest attention, even when you were a child. Now what are we to do?"

"I don't know, Uncle, I'm asking you. Are you sure you really said all that?"

"Well, something very like it. But your mother is a woman, so— And another thing: let this teach you about the sex. Would you catch a man turning himself into a rose on someone else's hat? Particularly a *dead* man."

"That lovely girl is dead?" asked poor August, following one train of thought. "She looked so very much alive!"

"Death has taken her as his own bride, which puts her what we might call 'between'."

"Between what?"

"Between life and death, you young fool!" The old Count sighed, and nodded, and picked up a crumbling, ancient book. He fumbled through its pages, mumbling to himself, and then declared, "You've already taken the first trick, nephew, by plucking that scarlet rose which flowered from her heart. Death won't like that at all! Still—when she comes again, your part is this: offer her food and wine yourself, at midnight. Then—clasp her to you *all through the twelfth hour*. But be warned: Death is in love with this poor girl, and he himself will come to mislead you and try to take this trick." The old man shut the book and sighed, "I wish your mother had paid me more attention, dear August . . ."

That night Prince August made careful preparations. He

set the food and drink at some distance from each other, and hid himself in the shadow of a great winged chair.

After the watchmen had called the hour from the castle turrets, music and mist came together. The rose twirled and grew and changed into Magdalena. August stepped towards her boldly.

"Lady—will you eat and drink with me?"

Magdalena was so accustomed to feel loved—even in the grave—that she accepted the homage in his face unthinkingly. She smiled, nodded, and took the wine cup from his hands. Then she looked round for food but, before she could eat, the Prince came up behind her and held her in a grip as strong as Death's. "So we remain one hour!" he muttered between his teeth.

At that moment every candle in the room blew out. It was quite dark and silent. Magdalena was silent too, and her arms were cold, cold to his touch. She never spoke, nor moved. Towards the hour's end August felt as though a flower were wilting in his hands. Her breathing became shallow as she started to moan and stir and struggle slightly, while sounds rasped in her throat. She's dying! thought panic-stricken August, and slackened his grip—he wondered where to lay her down: he *must* find candles, and—and brandy. Just then he heard an eerie chuckle, close at hand. So Death had stolen her . . . A sense of repugnance almost overwhelmed him. He was about to let her body fall, when he recalled his uncle's words, "Death himself will come to mislead you . . ."

"Her death is an illusion!" he called out bravely. "And I shall hold her while she lives."

There was a rustling in the room as though bones creaked nearer. August felt sick with terror, but boldly held his ground. There was a stench of graveyard mould, and worse. Five bony fingertips touched him on the cheek. For a moment all was horrible.

Then: "One o'clock in the mornn-ning— All's still and we-ell!" came the watchmen's cry.

The room lightened. A ray of moonshine had shot between the curtains, and illumined Magdalena's face and the brown, withered rose upon the floor. August hardly dared to look, but his girl was sleeping and not dead. He bent to kiss her on the lips as her eyes opened and she smiled.

The next day they were married, though August's uncle and the servant Franz both shook their heads. Magdalena carried white roses to her wedding. If she faltered when she passed by a carved skull on a choir stall, no one noticed; except Death, who came to the ceremony unobserved.

Time passed, and Magdalena was so happy that she succeeded in putting all thoughts of her first bridegroom from her mind—although she did ask for skulls and other morbid emblems to be banished from the churches, and flowers and cherubim to be carved there instead. After nine months her happiness increased when August's son was born.

The babe was most endearing, the image of his father, with round blue eyes, and a small cleft in his chin. Magdalena doted on him, and unfashionably fed him herself; she often took him into bed to feed him there. One summer's midnight, when thundery rain poured down and sheet lightning flashed, she ordered her attendants to leave the windows open and let in some air. With it came a too-familiar voice: "Unfaithful Magdalena! Why do you destroy your true bridegroom's memory? At least you'll tell now what you discovered on that night you pledged yourself to me?"

With shaking fingers Magdalena hid the baby in his little shawl. She remembered Death's company, who had brought him children, and lied boldly, "What could *I* have seen on a night like that? Now believe me, Death, dear Death, I saw nothing but the looming church—and that you went inside."

"I *don't* believe you, treasured girl! How you would have warmed me if you'd told the truth—how I would have cherished you! Now what *you* cherish most must come to me instead." Death's shadow fell across the drowsy child, who woke, wailed, shivered—and fell into the coldest sleep of all.

Next day heartbroken Magdalena, mourning her dead baby, told August the truth of just how she had become involved with Death, and so brought harm to her old parents and her child.

"Now I'm accursed! And he'll never leave us two in peace! Oh, August, *liebste* August, what shall I do if he comes for you as well?"

But the young Prince scoffed—he was only concerned about his wife. Soon the Schloss echoed with marching feet as battalions of his soldiers took up their positions at doors and windows to guard the Princess. Although any tough colonel could have warned his master that not even regiments can fight off Death if he decides on harvest.

A week passed. Magdalena wept all day beside her baby's empty cradle. Two hussars stood guard at her window, which was high: so very high that it seemed halfway to heaven. Still—although the alert soldiers heard nothing—there came an eerie knocking on the pane.

"Listen, my heart's joy, Death's own possession! Will you speak out at last? What did you learn, that night you chose me for yourself? Why don't you acknowledge what you saw, as you peeped at me with your eager, deceptively guileless glance? Now speak! Or this time Prince August himself shall come to join me and his child!"

Then Magdalena did begin to speak—very fast and low: a rush of words, and honest ones too (the soldiers looked on horrified: had the poor bereaved girl lost her wits?). And finally she begged, in tears: "*Please* promise that you'll let my August stay? I've only found courage to reveal the truth because of him ... And please, please, sweet Death, say you'll never boast again that I belong to you?"

As she spoke Death was suddenly transformed. She saw him as he was at their first meeting: pale and handsome in his velvet, jet, and diamond—his least ugly guise. Yet still she shuddered in her soul, for she knew what—in the foolish arrogance of youth—she had bound herself to, half-consciously, half-unawares. He pressed a ring into her palm. She tried to give it back, but he sternly held it there. "Let this remind you of our pledge. And remember, Magdalena, there's a time for true, unguarded speech; and that your parents and your child might have been long and happily about their living in your world. Now *they* are all I have to remind me of a time when you and I were inseparable companions. Tell August he's been your fortunate redeemer! Live with him joyously, until— Well, *now* it shall be '*auf Wiedersehen*' to you both . . ." finished Death, with his cold chuckle. He kissed her hand, bowed slightly, and departed from Schloss Ritterstein for many seasons.

Then Magdalena and August, no longer afraid of Death, enjoyed great happiness, and lived eventually to be very, very old. They had children, too: many of them, to replace the pathetic babe they lost. But it's said that these children were as thoughtless as young Magdalena was, and one of them mislaid Death's pledge. Which is tragic—for its possessor has won freedom in this life, and in time a peaceful passage to his world.

The Castle of Ker Glas

"—the lance is all of diamond, the terrible crystal! Its splendour is so great, its flashing rainbows so unbearable to look upon, that whoso is its enemy, it blinds! Then let a man be at enmity with God and the lance will be against him! Yet there is healing, too, dear Angemar, and for that the cup which is of gold—"

The speaker broke off, for his companion had coughed warningly, and with his mailed fist indicated the tattered, hungry-looking boy who was tightening his horse's girths.

"You! Were you listening?"

The boy looked up, startled. He reminded both watchers of an animal poised for flight. He had known cruelty, and there was menace in the words. He fell on his knees, crying in his heart to Notre Dame for protection.

Angemar looked at Langennac, and Langennac at Angemar. Both were great knights, and followed the Code —which embraced only the nobility. It would be a small matter to run this peasant child through the throat with one sharp dagger thrust. . . . Still the two knights looked at one another, and then downward, puzzled. The boy was almost full grown yet had a child's expression—a child which hopes even while it fears. There was something about him, with his tousled hair and round eyes in a dark thin face, that made Langennac's hand unclench from his dagger's haft.

He said more gently, "And what did you hear?"

"Salve Regina!" muttered Peronik desperately. "My lord, my lord, I heard only of a diamond lance and a gold cup and—"

"Only!" said Angemar with an angry laugh, and a sideways look at his companion.

"And—?"

But the boy was now too terrified to speak. He could only shake his head, bow it, and wait for the descending point.

"Did you hear that whatsoever the lance touches, that it surely destroys—blinding first?"

"—and that the goblet heals—" the boy whispered tremblingly.

"Look up, child! Where are these objects to be found?"

Peronik quailed. "In—in the Castle of Ker Glas!" he gasped.

"And who keeps it?"

"It—it belongs to a—a magician! One Rogear."

"One Rogear," said Angemar's voice caressingly, with a note in it like honey on a sword point. "You see, he has it all pat. Spit him, my good Langennac."

"Not so fast." Langennac, who was the younger, leaned from his saddle and once more studied the upturned, troubled face. "Boy! You heard and understood all the great adventures that he who seeks the lance and cup must pass through before ever he sets eyes on Rogear's castle?"

"Ye-yes."

"Then you will know that such things aren't for you! Nor for any forest brigand, nor evil knight." The young man leaned back in his saddle, laughing. "He's no danger, Angemar! Boy—now understand me: you're not to speak of all you heard, to anyone. No good knight shall perish because you put a bad one on his trail! You hear?"

"My lord, by all the holy saints I swear—"

"Swear by one, and keep the oath! Remembering that even knights of unblemished fame have perished on the way to strange Ker Glas. Ride on, Angemar, my friend—"

The two destriers sprang forward into their bits. Tremendous muscled hindquarters swayed past Peronik's tiptilted nose. They were trained to kick out backward in battle, to deal fierce, battering death. He gasped as they moved by him, and afterwards wiped the sweat from his forehead with a dirty hand.

"Bah!" said Angemar, as their beasts thundered down the woodland ride, "You would have done better to spit him on your blade like a young squirrel—he had the same quick glance."

"You thought so? I thought him almost simple-witted. It's too fine a day for killing—and squirrels are quite pleasant things."

Peronik went into the dark, evil-smelling hovel where he lived now with his foster-mother. Sweat was still pouring off his face—and with some reason. Not only had he narrowly escaped death while tightening the horse's girths, but he had pledged himself to do a foolish thing: so foolish, it was as though an unknown part of himself had risen to suggest it. Else, how *could* he have made a desperate inner vow to Notre Dame that, if she saved his life, he would himself seek out the Castle? Now he was committed; and, he thought dolefully, his end might well be worse than if the knight had spitted him.

He crossed slowly to an old chest in the corner, and flung back the lid. There was a smell of must and rotting sackcloth. He groped, and pulled out a short sword, scabbard stained with rust. He groped again, to find a small round buckler such as footsoldiers used. Both had belonged to his foster-mother's husband, killed in the wars.

Now he must go, quickly, before she could return and scold him: she would be very angry if she found him with the sword. Though what use was it to her? He pattered out in search of his white, rough-coated pony, which was hobbled near at hand. Douceur was restless when he found her, tufted ears pricked—she still listened for the neigh of Angemar's proud stallion.

Peronik put on her string-mended bridle, freed her, and vaulted on her back. So, with his foster-father's buckler on his left arm, the rusty sword dangling at his waist, he set out to find the Castle of Ker Glas. For such foolishness he knew himself already dead—yet, suddenly, his terror left him, and he began to sing. . . .

He rode for some days, living off stream water, roots, and berries, and getting hungrier and hungrier. He didn't know where his adventure would begin, except that the first trial would come in the Forest of Illusion. If he could only free himself from its attraction he would find beyond it an orchard with a special appletree guarded by a dwarf who held a flaming sword. He must pass by this dwarf in safety (many knights had perished on his bright and dreadful blade!) to snatch an apple from the tree, and go on to seek a laughing flower. (Here Peronik laughed aloud: for who had even seen a flower *smile*?) Afterwards, there would be the great and monstrous Sea of Dragons, and *then*—

But why should he trouble about all that, when so many knights, brave and splendid young men, had lost themselves forever in that first strange forest which so far he hadn't even seen?

And, as he thought this, Peronik looked down to find himself dressed from head to foot in the most fashionable of Court clothes: green and scarlet, with long sleeves, and a coxcomb's hat with a liripipe worn at an angle on his head; while Douceur was transformed into a shining blood horse, with dagged hangings and a silver bridle. He carried a hawk upon his wrist, and at his side rode a lovely girl, who smiled appealingly when she called him Sir Pericles. In the distance white towers rose into the blue.

"How well you ride, Sir Pericles!"

"So I should," Peronik carelessly shifted his hawk a little, "since my father, the Captal, taught me when I was three."

"And you're so courageous! How many dreadful monsters have you slain already?"

"Monsters, Ghislaine? I have lost count of them. What's

one monster more or less, after you've been blooded with your first monster's tail? For me, that took place long, long ago. Look—we're in thick forest here."

"With you as my protector, why should it trouble me? And see! My father's courtiers come to greet you and lead us to his courts where he'll betroth us . . ."

"Can you sing?" she asked Peronik after a while; and he replied modestly, "Oh yes, better than anyone I know." He raised his voice and carolled a gay chanson. She controlled her face quickly—and her voice: "You are certainly surprising!"

That night they attended a banquet in the hall of a great château they had seen from far. He had scarcely been surprised when Ghislaine's father kneeled at his feet to give up his own sword, saying he would now be content to have Sir Pericles as Governor, for his wisdom, justice and piety were so renowned, and his goodness the envy of his enemies. (Why did Ghislaine keep laughing?) Peronik said with his famed courtesy, "Rise up, Seigneur, and we'll speak later . . ." He took a horn of wine, and drained it at a gulp— he could always outdrink other men.

Here were the knights now, pacing two by two to do him homage. Some of them kissed his feet, and one cried like a baby. "Come, Sir Knight," said Peronik sternly, "however moved you may find yourself on this occasion, tears are unfitted to your rank." And he touched the weeping knight sharply on the breast with Ghislaine's father's sword.

At that very moment his foster-mother's voice rang angrily around the immense hall, and drowned the minstrel's playing. Where was she? *Hidden*? Peronik started violently, and the company nearby began to fade, as her voice rose louder, angrier, until she almost shrieked, "That rascal, good-for-nothing, tattered, homeless thief! That brat of wicked ways whose wretched carcase I've walloped on my knees these many years! Gone off with my dear late husband's sword . . . Ah! there he stands! Innocent-seeming as a newborn babe, the very sword still in his grasp!"

R

The appalled Peronik stared about him, anguished by what this gay company would think, yet suddenly aware of guilt, and meanness. As his awareness grew, the hall and laughing company completely vanished. Tattered as usual, he was alone in a dark wood. The distant scolding of his foster-mother sounded farther and farther away. Panic-stricken and remorseful he fell upon his knees, while his ears burned with shame. In the dusk he could hear the gentle familiar movements of Douceur, as she cropped blades of grass with her soft muzzle. He crouched close beside her and, worn out and very hungry, went to sleep.

When he woke, the birds were already singing in the trees, but the fine trunks of birch and aspen, and the underbrush, were still mysterious blue-grey, for the true dawn was not yet come. Peronik was puzzled by a jagged flash of light that came again and again from one direction. He lay wondering about it, stiff and hungry. Then he thought of yesterday: he must have been sick, or in delirium! He dragged himself to his feet, yawning, and called Douceur.

She came whinnying toward him, and he leaned his face against the warm hide of her cheek. His mouth twisted wryly. "Ah, what a chilly, hungry adventure I've brought you on! What happened to us in that forest? Come, Douceur —we'll find water—" He led her through the underbrush.

The light flashed again as they stumbled out of the wood into a meadow. Peronik stood gaping. Even by this grey early light he could see that they were near an orchard, full of fruit, and that not far off stood one tree in a clearing by itself. The flashing light came from just in front of it, where a hunched, blackish figure stood, holding a long dark sword upright in his hand. Peronik blinked, and ignoble sweat crawled down his spine—for each time the sword moved a jagged flame ran up the blade and leaped into the air zigzag, as lightning leaves the clouds.

Then Peronik recalled Langennac's saying: "—and on the

258

wood's other side an orchard, and a dwarf who has killed many entering therein. Killed them before they could even touch an apple on his guarded tree!"

"So—" muttered Peronik, stroking Douceur who was trembling at sight of fire, "that was the Forest of Illusion we were tangled in all yesterday." He looked back at the wood, and marvelled at his strange and swift escape, and then felt sudden shame. For he disliked his foster-mother, and had stolen from her, and yet if her ugly voice hadn't roused him from his dreaming he might have lost himself in that strange forest all his life's days, as many knights had done.

But there was no time to brood on yesterday. That fearful, crouched figure by the tree had seen them and, coming forward, legs bent and massive shoulders braced as though prepared for battle, cried in loud rumbling tones, "Boy—step once within the circle of my sword and you are dead! Avoid it, and you may pass by me freely, without fear. Now, choose!"

Peronik was trembling like Douceur, but he tied her reins firmly to a branch before replying, "Sir—I *must* come and pluck an apple, if I'm for Ker Glas."

The dwarf gave a great baying laugh, like an immense hound's cry. "Ker Glas! Ker Glas! Fine knights and worthy ones have died before they reached that Castle's gates, and now a ragged boy with stumpy pony says he'll *pluck an apple* from my tree!" He raised the sword and whirled its point above his head so that it drew a flaming circle in the sky which seemed to spring upward toward outer space.

"If I *must* die," said Peronik in a small voice, "I would at least eat first—"

"There's a stream runs by the wood, and there are berries thick and sweet enough for your last meal," said the dwarf with a mixture of kindness and contempt; and he grounded his sword's point to the earth which, when touched, turned it dead and black.

So Peronik ate and drank, taking his time, and then he

watered Douceur, kissed her soft muzzle in farewell, and said his prayers. Afterwards he took up his small buckler and stumpy, blunted sword, and advanced into the orchard, feeling like a scared child at play with death.

"I have to fight you, dwarf! Perhaps you guard the tree because its fruit is dangerous for man—or far too priceless. If you're good or evil, none has said. Yet I must fight you for an apple—"

The dwarf merely stood there silently watchful, the sword's point with its enormous shooting flame aimed straight at Peronik's heart. The boy came forward bravely, yet certain it was all in vain. His sword and buckler were ridiculous! Suddenly, as though someone prompted him, words rang in his mind: words he had heard quoted long ago by the Sieur de Vernay's priest, "Wherefore take unto you the whole armour of God . . ." As though inspired he threw away his sword and buckler, drew himself very upright, and cried loudly, "I take to myself the shield of faith, which shall quench all the fiery darts . . ." The flame darted out and went right through him. He felt it as a stab of sorrow and a stab of joy at the same time. He closed his eyes, and expected to drop dead—but all he felt was an exquisite sense of tenderness, and freeing of his spirit. For one long moment he stood there enthralled, and then—not feeling that stab again—opened his eyes.

The hunched figure lay motionless upon the ground. The black sword, with its flaming point extinguished, lay beside him. The first sunrays of dawn shot over Peronik's shoulder, and lit the centre of the appletree. They seemed to linger on one apple larger and rounder than the rest. Peronik, scarcely able to believe he lived and breathed, leaned over the still form and plucked the apple from the tree. Then he picked up the sword.

Dusk was already folding distant, lonely-looking hills into its embrace when ringing laughter echoed through the valley. There was something so unnatural about laughter in such a place that Peronik looked round him nervously, and his fingers tightened in Douceur's mane. The laughter grew more and more hilarious as they descended a slope. The commonplace clip-clop of Douceur's hoofbeats was a comfort to Peronik's fearful mind. Laughter, he was thinking . . . Laughter's usually warm, and human—and—and beautiful. But this laughter! It had an eerie, unearthly quality that drew him on in a manner he found impossible to understand. Both attractive and terrifying was that laughter. When he and Douceur rounded a little copse, he could see why.

Ahead, the ground was flat. The sun's last rays slid along it, lighting up here a tuft of grass, and there a boulder. In their brightness they caught and held one single flower, swaying delicately on her long stem. "Her," Peronik thought at once, because this flower looked entirely feminine. As she swayed to and fro in a slight breeze it seemed that on her golden centre could be traced shadows like a woman's features. Her aureole of petals was golden too. In size, she was midway between a large daisy and a sunflower. As she swayed, she laughed.

Peronik could see nothing to laugh at in her companion. He too was golden, but as terrible as the sun in its destructive role. He paced round and round the flower, round and round on huge soft pads. His tail twitched angrily each time he neared her, and his mane shook angrily as though it were alive—no! It *was* alive: it wasn't fur, but many wriggling, darting-headed snakes. Each time the snaky mane came near her the flower swayed sharply on her stalk, and she laughed again—although her laughter held a high-pitched, nervous sound.

Douceur stopped. Her nostrils widened. She snorted, which brought the lion's head round in her direction. He was the incarnation of majesty, dreadful to look upon. The flower was silent as Peronik stared awestruck at the scene. He slid from Douceur's back, but could neither look away nor run.

The lion crouched suddenly, his eyes fixed not on Peronik but on the pony. She gave a sort of screaming neigh.

"*No!*" yelled Peronik, feeling himself released from the paralysis of fear. (Not Douceur—not his companion of many years, a pony as gentle as a lamb . . .!) He raised his arm which still held the dwarf's black sword. Something like a shock ran down it as the sword sprang into life with a flame that spurted heavenwards. Peronik thought he heard a far-off voice intoning, ". . . and the lion shall lie down with the lamb, they shall not hurt nor destroy in all my holy mountain. . . ."

The great beast didn't spring. His bunched muscles quivered violently but then he sank into repose, and bowed his golden head upon his paws. The snake mane lay flat around his head, its many watchful little eyes were bright yet friendly. The flower wore a shaken smile.

Peronik dared to go forward and stroke the muzzle, which was power, and plunge his hand into the mane where the snakes wound their wise heads round his wrist. Then, and then only, did he put down the black sword, and pluck the smiling flower.

After this it seemed as though the magic of her company made all endeavour fruitful. He wore her in his tunic, and by day she smiled, and by night closed her petals to sleep trustfully against her rescuer. When they reached the sea one evening she already drowsed, but when its surface humped and rose to reveal countless threshing reptiles—it was the Sea of Dragons—she roused herself, and at her first astonished smile the waters calmed, and all their horrors were subdued.

After Peronik had slept a night he tied Douceur's bridle to the tail of one young dragon, which had crawled ashore, and urged her after it into the water. For a little he feared she mightn't manage such a swimming feat; but she soon struck out bravely, and whatever inhabited the sea's bed never troubled them, not only for the sake of the shining flower who turned this way and that in his hand, but also because intuition had led him to harness a sea denizen to be his ally and lead them through those perilous deep waters till they came to land. And with this safe arrival they reached the pass that entered on the Vale of Joy, in which—so Langennac had told his fellow knight—even the most valiant might lose his way, to rest here in perpetual bliss and sweet, false sense of true achievement, sooner than pry beyond where all past gains might still be lost.

Peronik dragged on the reins, and his pony obediently slowed her pace. "Now listen," he solemnly told his three companions, the flower, the pony, and the sword, "if I once raise my eyes I'll be so happy with everything around me that we'll stay hereabouts for ever." So the flower understood that she must be his guide; and Douceur, that she must carry them without hesitation where the flower indicated. From that moment Peronik kept his eyes downcast as though he were a monk. All he saw was Douceur's veined cheek and neck, and the ground passing backward beneath her hooves. He felt the flower turning now this way, now that, and each time she turned he told Douceur, "Left, here!" or "Right!" Then he would add, "And now straight on . . ."

So they came through that most alluring place; and Peronik never knew exactly what he might have seen there—although he had heard girls' voices, and singing, and smelled rich flowery scents, and fought down a lazy longing to look up and be seduced into forgetfulness of what he sought.

At last, after much riding—all day, in fact—he felt the sword leap in his hand like a young salmon ready to jump a weir. At the same time all the rich scents and pretty laughter faded. He snuffed up reedy, weedy smells, which had a river tang about them. The air was clear and cold against his cheeks, and wild duck went flighting overhead. Then Peronik, weary and hungry from his long, fasting ride, dared to look up.

They had left the Vale of Joy behind (and for one moment Peronik regretted its untasted pleasures). Now before them lay the last, perhaps most troubling, challenge, on the way to strange Ker Glas.

The river was wide, placid, pink-tinged by setting sun. From the knights' conversation he knew it had one single ford. The flower had led him there unerringly, where waters flowed shallow over flat, half-hidden stones. Standing at the river's edge was a tall woman, dressed in black. The long points of her sleeves fell to her bare feet, and a black coif swathed her head and neck. Her beauty was one of high cheekbones and sharp-modelled chin; and though her figure was enticing there was that about her glance, so caressing yet so subtly dominant, to send a chill right through him, cold as death.

"Have you heart to ferry me across the ford?" she asked in a low, desirous voice. "Will you carry me over waters that have confined me to this shore, and find the Castle of Ker Glas and him I've long been seeking for my own?"

Peronik heard the danger in her voice, and his pulse beat sluggishly as though his blood had thickened and ran slow; but his answer was quite steady. "Lady—I do seek Ker Glas."

"Without me you'll accomplish nothing, little knight. Go your way alone, if I dismay you! Yet you'd do better with myself to guide the way."

"I know that I must take you with me," replied Peronik, though his mouth was dry.

She laughed. "Must! Why do all men fear such meetings? There are many worse than I who do go travelling!"

She had come closer, and even Douceur shied away.

"Poor pretty beast!" The lady placed her long hand on the pony's neck, and suddenly Douceur dropped her head in lassitude and sweat started on her coat. "What is your name, young knight?"

"It is Peronik."

"Well, Peronik, I do not know if you have heard or guessed *my* name—but will you help me up before you?"

He thrust the flower once more into his tunic—she had closed her petals tightly—and placed his sword under his left arm, and with his right hand helped the black-gowned woman up. Still her dark garments reached to the ground, and he wondered if she was in mourning. Perhaps what he should be feeling was pity, not revulsion. He put his right arm kindly round her waist, expecting to find her warm and pliant to the touch. She felt cold like stone.

They crossed the ford.

On the morning of their fourth day's travelling they saw before them the round central tower of Ker Glas rise up among trees, like a swan's neck above a nest. In all this time they had ridden mainly in silence, for the lady was no conversationalist, and indeed her mind seemed concentrated on one object, as a bloodhound's nose upon a scent.

"Will the entrance gates be guarded?" asked Peronik, breaking the long silence.

"Few win to strange Ker Glas—but against some there is no guard! The gates will open at my coming."

Peronik heaved a sigh. He looked forward to the moment when they should both dismount; it had taken all his courage to keep his arms around her waist during four whole days—and in that time the flower had never shown her face, but kept her petals closed as though she were asleep.

The woods about Ker Glas were very quiet, for as Douceur advanced with her dual burden the summer birds, which had been singing joyously, were silent. It was a place of magic beauty which yet held a sense of threat, as though the supernatural forces that dwelt there owned some terrible great sword. The sky was bluer, the leaves more golden-green, the tower whiter, than any Peronik had seen.

The Castle stood on a small island, surrounded by a moat. It had four towers on its outer wall. The drawbridge was down, as though guests were not feared. But in the wall the heavy wooden gates were closed.

"Let me down here!" said the lady eagerly. She almost ran toward the Castle.

Peronik followed across the moat more slowly, leading Douceur. He saw the lady raise her little fists, and hammer on the gates with an urgency and vigour that surprised him. He saw them pulled cautiously ajar, and a visored face and sharp swordpoint appear. Instead of parley he heard a great wailing cry, and the sword clattered to the ground, and there was the sound of mailed feet running. The gates swung inward, quite unguarded. The lady turned and beckoned, and then walked within.

Peronik still followed. He found her waiting for him in a court which had emptied hurriedly of human life—or nearly: on the far side lay the armoured guard. Peronik stared. The man couldn't have been wounded; did he faint?

"Now, Peronik, you've come to strange Ker Glas! Look round you—no other knight has yet set foot here. Many attempted it, but none dared take me up before him as you innocently did. What you seek for is hidden below ground— but first you and I have dealings with the Castle's master—" She placed the fingers of her left hand on his shoulder, and led him with her to a council room. Here they saw a dropped lance, and there a sword, for all the guard had fled.

Rogear sat alone, in state. He was an old man, with rosy face, white beard, and mild blue eyes that looked benign yet held sharp cunning in their depths. "Good day, Rogear!" She swept toward him in her black robes. "You guardian of the cup and lance, give you good day!"

Rogear heaved a tremendous sigh. "Madam, I didn't think that you would come! Strong magic has ever kept you out. But there's still magic here . . ." He pointed one finger, and all her robes blew suddenly about her as though in a high wind; yet she herself was still.

"Peace, my friend—not even you are strong enough! I've heard it said you always boasted that Ker Glas's impregnable, for none but fools would bring me here. Well," she touched Peronik again, "this is the fool!"

The blue, cunning eyes dwelled measuringly on Peronik. Again the finger pointed, like a snake's head, and this time at him. But the power that had protected him from the flaming sword protected him still: he felt nothing, it was as though he were hidden behind a wall of glass.

The old man raised both hands then, and let them fall in a gesture of despair. "Against such I have no power," he said tonelessly. "My guardianship is ended." He rose up, very tall and thin. "Child—have you brought me a gift as sweet viaticum?"

Peronik was startled. Then he remembered something. He thrust his hand into his pocket, and brought out the apple, rosy as the old man's cheeks. He offered it shyly, and Rogear snatched at it eagerly, and bit into the juicy flesh.

"It's very sweet," he muttered, as though surprised. Just then the lady reached across and placed her hand upon his mouth.

His face went grey, and sweat started from his forehead. His eyes stared as he collapsed, moaning, in his chair. The lady had taken his hand into her own, but though he tried to free it he could not, and eventually he let it lie there, and turned toward her quite trustingly like a little child. She took him in her arms to rock him almost as though he *were* her child; and presently he died. Then she finished up the fruit herself, and spat out the pips, and sat, black-garmented as any mourner, at his feet.

"Go now, true innocent!" she said, smiling for the first time at Peronik. "Seek what you came for, tamer of all things! You and I—we've been company for one another on the road, but we shall never meet again."

"Never?" breathed Peronik, backing towards a doorway. "Lady—I thought that you were Death!"

"No," she said. "I am not so great as Death—for he is sure. They call me Plague. Farewell . . ."

"Farewell!" echoed Peronik thankfully, and went as quickly as was decent from her presence.

He hadn't far to search, for music led him down corridors and stairway to a square chamber hidden deep beneath the foundations of Ker Glas. At first the latchless door stayed shut, but then Peronik's flower opened up her petals for the first time in four days, and looked about her, and at her smile the door opened of its own free will.

Peronik cried out. He couldn't help it, for to stand in the presence of the diamond lance was like being in the presence of the rainbow's living substance. His eyes hurt when they looked on it. So he put out a hesitant hand to touch the cup, and the warmth and healing tenderness that poured from it was like the essence of all summer and all love; his eyes were immediately healed.

Peronik fell on his knees and stayed there a long while. What am I, a mere brown peasant boy, doing with such holy things! Then Peronik gave thanks to God.

After a while he rose, thinking compassionately of the cup's careful guardian, poor dead Rogear. I'll dare to carry it upstairs, he thought, and it will heal him ... But no sooner had he timorously raised it than there was a splintering crash of thunder which seemed to turn the whole world upsidedown. Cup, lance, and Ker Glas disappeared.

Peronik found himself alone in sunlit forest. Once more he was dressed as some great lord or prince, but this time the clothes were real, and Douceur truly a white blood mare who looked at him with faithful eyes. So, overwhelmed with joy and humble gratitude, he mounted and rode to find the Court of the Great King, who proclaimed: "Only he who has looked on the lance, and held the cup, shall lead my forces where I will that they should go."

And after that, whenever Peronik rode out, it was with the Great King's forces at his own command.